I0540911

MALICIOUS INTENT

A LUCIUS FOGG NOVEL

DAN WICKLINE

DARK MUSE PRESS

This book is a work of the author's experience and opinion. Names, characters, places and incidents are either the product of the author's imagination or are used fictitiously. Any resemblance to actual persons, living or dead, or to actual events or locales is entirely coincidental.

MALICIOUS INTENT – A LUCIUS FOGG NOVEL

This book is licensed for your personal enjoyment only. This book may not be re-sold or given away to other people. If you would like to share this book with another person, please purchase an additional copy for each person you share it with. If you're reading this book and did not purchase it, or it was not purchased for your use only, then you should return it and purchase your own copy. Thank you for respecting the hard work of the author.

Copyright © 2013 Dan Wickline. All rights reserved, including the right to reproduce this book, or portions thereof, in any form. No part of this text may be reproduced, transmitted, downloaded, decompiled, reverse engineered, or stored in or introduced into any information storage and retrieval system, in any form or by any means, whether electronic or mechanical without the express written permission of the author. The scanning, uploading, and distribution of this book via the Internet or via any other means without the permission of the publisher is illegal and punishable by law. Please purchase only authorized electronic editions, and do not participate in or encourage electronic piracy of copyrighted materials.

Cover art by: Jason Crager

Edited by: Salomé Jones

Published by: Dark Muse Press

Visit the author website: www.danwickline.com

Version 2013.11.04

DEDICATION

To Debbie - for always encouraging me, supporting me and consoling me, for sharing so many adventures and misadventures, for being with me through the best and the worst times. I am who I am today because you were at my side and for still being my friend today.

Also from Dan Wickline

For more of Dan's work visit:
www.danwickline.com

ACKNOWLEDGMENTS

This novel would not be possible without the help and support of the following people: Debbie Wickline, Lisa Worby, Salomé Jones, Tyler Dranguet, Jocelyn Dupas, Tim Dedopulos, Jason Bruce, Emma Lou Grey, Natasha Von Lemke, Jason Crager and all of you who have followed Lucius and Jimmy since they first appeared on Twitter or picked up the novella oh so many years ago. Also a special thanks to my mother, Heather, who once said to me: "The comic stuff is nice and all, but how about writing a novel."

And to Tecarie Czarnecki, you are missed.

CHAPTER ONE

I jiggled the key in the lock of the old brass door handle. It seemed to be getting worse as the weeks went by. I had offered to replace it at least a dozen times, but Fogg rebuffed each proposed change with no explanation. He hadn't allowed any modifications to the brownstone since I'd been in his employ. He gave me a spell to use that would open the door, but I didn't like to use magic unless it was specifically for a case and as a last resort. Instead I'd taken to coming in through the kitchen to avoid the delay. This evening though, I had a guest with me and felt the front door was more appropriate.

"You're sure you still live here, Jimmy Doyle?" Emma asked, allowing just a hint of a giggle into her sultry voice.

"I did as of a few hours ago. But then Fogg suggested you stay with us instead of a hotel, so I'm not sure what's real anymore." I finally found the sweet spot and the key turned, allowing us access. "Here we go."

I opened the door and stepped aside to let her through. I'd been dating Emma Martin for about six months. She was a graveyard shift nurse over at County Hospital and with the way things usually went it was inevitable that we'd meet. Surprisingly, the hospital stay that finally brought us together wasn't mine. Her sister had been the victim in a case Fogg and I were working, a pitiful revenge plot that involved a demon. Luckily she lived, unlike the other victims. I questioned Emma in relation to the case. We both felt a spark that we pursued once things were cleared up.

The woman was gorgeous. Long black hair that fell like a waterfall over her shoulders. Creamy skin, rich brown eyes and curves that made whatever she wore cling in the most seductive ways. She lived in a little apartment not far from the hospital. That was usually where our dates ended. I had never brought her to Fogg's brownstone before. Partly because of all the crazy things that happen around there, but mostly because it felt like bringing her home to meet the parents. Had I any family, it would have been easier to introduce her to them than to my boss. I wouldn't have brought her by at all if it wasn't for her building being painted.

I'd told Fogg I would be away that evening but he insisted that would be impossible. He said Halloween night was too dangerous of a time for me not to be available. He suggested that Emma stay there. It took both my hands to pick my jaw up off the ground. Fogg hated having people visit. He never let anyone stay over. Before I could respond, he dashed out of the office saying he needed to tell Ariel to prepare a room.

"Are you sure about this, Jimmy?" Emma stood in the foyer looking uneasy.

"It's going to be fine. And if I know Ariel at all..." I took her hand and lead her into the dining room where two settings were waiting. "She'll have dinner ready for us."

The table was prepared with the nice china, the good silver and a pair of lit candles. Not how I normally got my meals. On the menu were sautéed carrots, baked potatoes and fresh rolls. All of it surrounding a perfectly prepared Beef Wellington. Emma saw the food and her eyes lit up.

"My mother made Beef Wellington for us on holidays, this exact meal. I haven't had it since she died." Emma smiled at me. "How did you know?"

"As much as I'd like to take credit, I can't. This was all Ariel."

"She's amazing." Emma took a seat.

"She certainly is." I was about to sit down next to her when the door bell rang. "That's never a good thing."

"It's probably just a trick-or-treater." Emma pointed at the window. "It's dark out now. This will probably be the first of many."

I headed back to the foyer where I found a tray of candied apples lined up perfectly on the table next to the door. A glance through the peep hole revealed only the top of a head which went along with the trick-or-treat theory. I opened the door to discover a tiny pale kid with fangs and another kid in a suit with a badge.

"Trick or treat?" the two boys shouted in unison.

"I'll go with treat. What are you supposed to be?"

"I'm a vampire and he's an FBI agent," the pale kid shouted. He didn't seem to have a lower level on his voice.

I made a note to tell Conrad Black, Fogg's pocket vampire, that the young were out there spreading the disease. I grabbed two candied apples and paused before putting them in the bags.

"You sure you want these? Vampires don't eat apples and FBI agents shouldn't eat sugar or they'll get too fat to chase bad guys."

"Yes, please!" the pair shouted in unison again.

I dropped the apples into their out-stretched bags and the boys turned and ran off towards the next brownstone. As I closed the door I thought to myself that maybe this was why Fogg wanted me home -- to handle the door. A job not exactly fraught with danger as he led me to believe. I went back to the dining room and took my seat. Emma had dished out food for both of us and was waiting for my return.

"Won't Mr. Fogg be joining us?" Emma asked.

"No. He doesn't eat."

"What do you mean he doesn't eat?" Emma showed the concern that any nurse would upon hearing that. "He has to eat something. Do you mean he just doesn't eat with you?"

"No, he doesn't eat at all." I took Emma's hand. "There are a great many things about Lucius Fogg that defy all logic and reason. I don't understand most of them, but you can't think of him like a normal person."

"That's crazy," she insisted.

"Any crazier than a demon possessing unknowing men and making them shoot innocent women?" I hated bringing up that, but I needed to get my point across before she spent the whole evening trying to understand things that couldn't be explained. Or in some cases wouldn't be explained.

The rest of the dinner went well. We spent most of the time talking about how good the meal was or how amazingly close it was to how Emma's mom had made it. By the end of the meal we were joking and laughing again.

When we finished, Emma grabbed the plates. "Which way to the kitchen?"

"It's better that you just leave them. Ariel will take care of it."

"I'll do no such thing. She made a wonderful meal for us. The least I can do is clear the table." Emma continued to pick up the plates.

"I did that once." I took the plates out of her hands and put them down. "By the time I got into the kitchen, Ariel was standing in front of me giving me a look that chilled my soul. I never tried it again."

"Is there anything normal about this place?" Emma looked at me.

"No," I answered honestly. "Fogg should be at his desk, might as well introduce you two."

I led her from the dining room to the office across the way. Fogg was sitting behind his desk as usual, books spread out everywhere. This always meant that he was researching something and wanted to be left alone. I hesitated saying anything, trying to decide if we should just quietly turn around. Fogg looked up before I made a choice.

"You must be Emma Martin." Fogg got up and walked around his desk, a warm and friendly look plastered on his face. "I'm Lucius Fogg. It's a pleasure to finally meet you."

Fogg was wearing his best suit. Pinstripe black three-piece that was custom fitted to his slender athletic build. A solid black tie pulled up tight against his white dress shirt. Every strand of his salt and pepper hair was perfectly in place. This wasn't the odd thing as he always looked immaculate, even on days with no appointments. The weird part was never in the years I had worked with him had I seen him get up to greet someone.

Emma put out her hand and Fogg kissed the back of it. "Jimmy talks about you all the time, Mr. Fogg. I feel like I know you already."

"Call me Lucius, please." Fogg was being extremely charming. "And if Jimmy has been telling you tales, then I am surprised you accepted my offer to stay here."

"He speaks highly of you, I swear."

"A sign of excellent manners, knowing when to tell a white lie." Fogg put his hand on my shoulder in a friendly gesture. "I trust your meal was satisfactory."

"It was amazing." Emma noticed the furry little creature lying on my desk. "Oh... you kept Mr. Whiskers?"

"It seemed like the right thing to do," Fogg answered.

Emma crossed over to pet the cat while I stood and stared at Fogg. I was trying to find some sign of demonic possession or mind control. This was not the Lucius Fogg I spent night after night working with. My detective instincts were screaming that something was up but I couldn't put my finger on what. Just then I noticed Ariel out of the corner of my eye. She was standing in the doorway.

"Emma, this is Ariel." Fogg gestured to the silent woman who had just appeared. "She will show you to your room."

"Thank you." Emma walked across, said hello. Ariel nodded and led her up stairs.

Once we were alone I turned to Fogg. "What is wrong with you?"

"What do you mean?" He sat back in his seat.

"You're being nice. You're never nice."

"It's obvious Miss Martin is important to you. I thought you'd appreciate the effort." Fogg began looking over his books again.

"I do. It's just..." I was at a complete loss for words. After a moment or two more of trying with no luck I decided to drop it.

I crossed over to my chair, ran my fingers over Mr. Whisker's soft black fur and looked at the stack of mail on my desk. I was about to sit down when I heard a loud crash from the other room. I raced back to the foyer. Fogg was right behind me. The first thing I saw was Ariel lying on her back at the bottom of the stairs. She was trying to get back to her feet. Then I glanced up to the top of the stairs where I saw Emma floating a foot above the floor. Her jet black hair was blowing in a non-existent wind. Her eyes were glowing like searchlights. I looked to Fogg. He seemed just as stunned as I was.

The silence was broken when Emma spoke. It was a hollow, unearthly voice. "Hello, Lucius. It's been years."

CHAPTER TWO

"Why is my girlfriend floating?" It seemed like a perfectly reasonable question for a somewhat irrational situation.

"I'm not exactly sure." Fogg took a step up the stairs towards Emma. "Who are you?"

I moved over to check on Ariel. She was able to get on her feet. She didn't look hurt, but I wasn't sure how I'd tell if she was. Ariel always seemed the exact same, happy, friendly and glowing with warmth. Even now, she was smiling at me. The fact she never spoke was really annoying right then.

"Are you Emma Martin?" Fogg asked.

Emma let out a maniacal cackle. "Have you ever seen Emma do this?"

She raised her right hand and a bolt of lightning shot out of her fingers. The flash of energy raced right past Fogg and struck me dead square in the chest. I was thrown off my feet and back into the door. Felt like I had been rammed by a charging bull. It took me a few seconds to catch my breath.

Fogg moved up a few more steps. "You have entered my house without permission. I demand you identify yourself immediately."

"Oh, but I had permission. You don't remember?" Emma's voice still sounded hollow, but it now had a sad tone to it. "I know it's been a long time. I'm not sure exactly how long. But you did invite me in and were quite happy to see me when I arrived."

Fogg paused. I wasn't sure if he was trying to make sense of what she was saying or if he was dealing with the realization of who she was. Either way, he figured it out and his whole stance changed. He went from opposing an enemy to a more open, unguarded stature.

"Natasha?"

"Yes, Lucius. It's me." Emma floated down a step or two.

"But how? You died sixty-five years ago." Fogg didn't move. "You can't be here."

"I thought you were supposed to be the world's greatest sorcerer." Emma... or Natasha rather, moved closer. "I've been here this whole time."

I got to my feet, not sure what to do. Ariel stood watching as well. I was concerned for Emma first, but I was also stunned by Fogg's reaction. He seemed to have the rug pulled out from under him. My hand ached for the revolver in my desk drawer, but I couldn't shoot anyway. I couldn't shoot Emma. I had to see how this was going to play out.

"Why don't we sit down and talk?" Fogg gestured towards his office. "You can tell me how you ended up in Miss Martin and what I can do to help."

Emma floated down the rest of the stairs and glided across the hall into Fogg's office. Her body never actually moved, just hovered as she went. I could feel a combination of anger and frustration building up inside of me. Whoever Natasha was, I wanted her out of my girlfriend immediately.

Fogg turned to Ariel and spoke quietly, "Go back to the kitchen and make some strawberries and chocolate. Use the special chocolate I've been saving."

Ariel nodded and headed off to do as she was instructed. I stepped in closer to avoid being overheard.

"What do you want me to do?" I asked eager to do something.

At that moment, the doorbell rang and a young voice shouting 'trick-or-treat' could be heard. Fogg nodded towards the door. I gave him a confused look.

"Please take care of the boy at the door."

"You're kidding?" I was completely dumbfounded. "You want me to give away a candied apple while all of this is going on."

"Yes. That is exactly what I want you to do." Fogg turned and headed for his office. "Come join us when you are done."

I turned around and grabbed one of the apples, snapping the stick in two. I stopped for a second and took a breath, then selected another apple with a gentler touch. I opened the door to find a boy of maybe nine years old standing in baggy pants, a gold sash, a vest and a turban. He was carrying a scimitar in one hand and a bucket in the other.

"I'm Sinbad and I'm here for treasure!" the boy shouted.

"That sword wouldn't happen to be real, would it?"

"No. It's plastic. Mom wouldn't let me have a real one." The boy's frown showed he had actually tried to convince his mom to give him a real sword.

"Shame. I may need something like that tonight." I tossed the apple into his bucket. "Have fun."

"Thanks, mister!" The kid ran off with his newly acquired booty.

I closed the door and headed into the office. Fogg was sitting behind his desk like always. Emma was sort of sitting in the red leather high-back chair across from him. I say 'sort of' because she was about six inches above the cushions. Whoever this Natasha was, she was really big on floating. I entered without saying a word and took a seat at my desk.

"You said you've been here all along. How is that possible?" Fogg asked.

"Isn't that obvious?" Her hollow voice couldn't disguise her sarcasm and anger. "The moment the spell was cast on this house, I was trapped here."

"You were dead." Fogg kept looking Emma in the eyes, but he was slowly closing the books on his desk that he had been reading earlier. "The spell shouldn't have affected you at all."

From what I could guess, the spell they were talking about was a spell that Fogg had put on the brownstone to keep himself alive. What the spell was or how it worked or even why it was necessary I didn't know. He never told me. What I did know was that inside the house time didn't pass. He also admitted to me that if he left the house, he would die instantly. Like one foot out and he'd drop dead. And since Natasha was supposed to have died the night he cast the spell, that meant Fogg hadn't left his home for sixty-five years.

"I had astral projected prior to being attacked." Emma was glaring at Fogg now. "I wouldn't have lasted long with my body being dead, but your spell has kept me in limbo this whole time. I have been trapped in that room for sixty-five years. It's like being in prison with no one to talk to. No one to touch. You might as well have condemned me to hell."

Ariel returned to the room with a plate of strawberries and melted chocolate to dip them in. She placed them on the desk and looked at Fogg. He nodded and she left the room.

"Oh, you remembered my favorite dessert." Emma picked up a strawberry, dipped it in the chocolate and was about to take a big bite then stopped and sniffed it. She put it back on the plate. "Added a little sleeping draft? A nice touch. I think I'll pass."

"You have to believe me, Natasha. I honestly had no idea you were trapped in there." Fogg's voice cracked as he spoke. "I would have found some way to help if I had known."

"Oh, but you did." She ran her hands up and down her torso. "You sent me this delicious new body to live in. I'm going to have so much fun in here."

"Don't get comfortable." My frustration was overflowing. "You won't be in there very long. I promise you that."

Fogg put his hand up towards me, telling me to calm down. "You have to forgive my assistant. The woman's body you're in means quite a lot to him. I'm sure with a little research we can find a more suitable vessel for you and return Miss Martin to..."

"Oh, I'm not giving up this body." She grabbed her own breasts and moaned erotically. "I can see all of Emma's memories and I like them. Jimmy here can be a very naughty little boy."

I picked up the gun from my drawer and pointed it at Emma. It was a stupid move, but my emotions were clouding my logic. "Get out of her, now!"

"Or what? You're going to shoot?" She let out a cackle. "All you'll end up doing is killing the woman you love. You do love me, don't you?"

"It's better than seeing her being used as a puppet!" I cocked the hammer back.

"Jimmy, please." Fogg stood and took a few steps towards me. "This won't solve anything."

I held fast, aiming at Emma's forehead. "I won't let her be used like this!"

"You have to trust me." Fogg stepped between Emma and me, blocking my shot. "Give me a chance to resolve this."

I lowered my gun and looked at Fogg. I hoped he had a plan of some kind. He usually did, but the look on his face didn't give me any confidence.

"Wise move. There's only one thing that will resolve this situation." Emma was back floating on her feet, both hands outstretched towards us. "The death of Lucius Fogg!"

She started hurling lightning bolts at us. Fogg ducked under one while I side-stepped the next. She could launch multiple shots quickly, but with very little accuracy. Still, if she threw enough of them eventually one would find its target. We couldn't stay in one place for too long.

Fogg grabbed my arm and pulled me towards the door. "Follow me!"

Lightning continued to strike all around us as we made our way down past the kitchen to the back hallway. Fogg led the way, ducking just in time as another bolt hit inches above where he'd been. I followed, but I worried that the confined space of the hallway would make it easier for her to hit us.

"Where are we going?"

"We need a place to regroup and plan." Fogg pointed to a door down the hall on the left. It looked like all the other doors and not particularly secure. The only difference was this one had a black handle instead of brass like the other nineteen doors.

"What's in that room?" I asked.

11

"Absolutely Nothing. Abre-a-Porta!" He reached the door and turned the handle.

"How is that going to help us? She'll be able to blast through that door in a heartbeat." I jumped as a bolt struck at my feet. My leap vaulted me into the open door.

"I know." He shut the door and locked it. "But it will do her no good. This is the Random Room."

CHAPTER THREE

"You'd be surprised at just how many questions I have in my head right now." I took a seat against the wall since there was nothing to sit on. "Sure, there are the big questions like 'Who is Natasha?' and 'Why does she want to kill you?' but there are also smaller ones like 'How does a guy with a cane suddenly move so well?' or 'What in the hell is a random room?' Is there any chance of getting at least some answers?"

Fogg walked back and forth in front of me. He was using his cane as normal. The strikes of the brass tip on the floor reminded me of the clicking sound a clock makes. Every three seconds another tap on the wood. Fogg didn't respond to my questions. I wasn't sure he even heard them. He was deep in thought and I knew I couldn't dig him out yet.

I glanced around the room. It was about twelve feet square with beige walls and wood floors. There was nothing special about it at all. I tried to think of reasons why it would be empty or called random. Then I noticed something odd. The door we had entered through was no longer there. I hadn't seen it vanish. I didn't hear Fogg say any spells or anything once we were inside. It was just gone. We were in a room with no way out.

Fogg paced for over fifteen minutes. I knew this because his cane tapped the floor over three hundred times. I'm not a fan of waiting. I hate it. But Fogg wasn't someone you could rush. He did everything in his own time. As much as I wanted to shake him until he told me what was going on, I knew I had to wait patiently. Lucky for me it wasn't much longer.

"I need you to get something for me," Fogg finally said.

"What do you need and where in the house is it?" I jumped to my feet ready to get to work.

"It's not in the house."

"You want me to leave you and Ariel alone with my possessed girlfriend?" I crossed my arms to emphasize my point. "I'm not going anywhere."

"There are only two of us," Fogg explained. "We're not sure where Ariel is and we can't remove Natasha from Miss Martin without this item. So one of us has to go get it and I can't leave."

"I have a different plan." I grabbed my notebook and pen from my jacket pocket. "Now tell me what it is and then show me how to get out of this room."

After he told me what he needed, Fogg finally decided to answer one of my questions.

"This is called the Random Room because it's always moving. When there are no occupants it floats between all the doors in the house, momentarily taking the place of an actual room and then moving on. It's never in one place for more than ten seconds unless the door is open."

"What if there are occupants?"

"Then it sits in space between dimensions until told where to reappear." Fogg gestured with his hands to help explain. "The room exists outside of reality, like it's sitting in an alley between two buildings. It's only accessible when pulled into a building."

"Why haven't I wandered in here before?" I couldn't believe I had missed it by chance all these years.

"It will only open with the incantation. You probably did find it and just thought the handle was stuck."

"Is that what's wrong with the front door?" I asked.

"No. That's just an old lock." He looked me square in the eyes. "And no, you can't replace it. Use the spell I gave you."

I gave him my best dirty look. "How about the way out of this room?"

"Simple." He pointed at the wall. "Just think about the room you want to be in, walk towards the wall and open the door."

I thought about mentioning that there was no door. But years of experience with Fogg has led me to just do what he tells me when it comes to magic. It's worked out for the best most of the time. And I just don't talk about the times it didn't. I stepped forward and by the time my hand reached the wall, there was a black doorknob waiting for it.

"Abre-a-Porta" I cautiously opened the door. Once I was certain no one was there, I walked through into Fogg's office by way of the side entrance.

I kept quiet, tucked into the corner of the room that you couldn't see from the hallway and waited. I had everything prepared. It was now just a matter of needing a little help.

The door bell rang and I could hear a muffled, "Trick-or- treat?"

Fogg insisted that above all else the kids were not to be ignored. I made my way across the office and out into the foyer. I had just reached the candied apples when I heard the hollow voice behind me.

"There you are, Jimmy. You haven't been hiding from me, have you?"

I turned back towards her and held up my finger. "Hold that thought for just a minute. I have a kid waiting for his treat."

I turned back around and opened the front door. On the stoop was a furry little boy growling at me.

"Don't you look savage. Are you a werewolf?"

"No, I'm a Bigfoot!" He brought up one of his feet to show me his greatly oversized shoes covered in fur. "I fight werewolves!"

"You have a great imagination, kid." I dropped his reward into his bag. "Have fun."

I closed the door and turned around to find Emma floating directly in front of me. She was hovering just high enough for us to look eye to eye.

"With that ability, you really don't need high-heels."

"Where is Fogg?" Her cold breath poured out of her mouth as she emphasized every word.

"Fogg? He's not with you?" I did my best to keep my anger in check.

"Don't toy with me. I can kill you where you stand."

"Why don't you?" I asked. "Why am I alive at all? You could have killed me when my back was turned. Why not just get it over with?"

"Because I know how much you care for this body." She took a deep breath and pushed her chest forward. "I'm having too much fun torturing you to end it so quickly."

"I thought all you wanted was to kill Fogg?"

"Oh, I do. And I will as soon as I find him." She placed her hand around my throat and released a tiny bit of the electricity. "I may not want to kill you, yet. But I can sure make you scream in pain. Now where is Fogg?"

The pain running through my neck was sharp and building with each second. "Since you asked so nicely, did you try the attic?"

"The attic?"

"Yeah, top floor of the brownstone. Fogg goes up there all the time to get away from psychotic women who are trying to kill him. You didn't think you were the first, did you?" I pointed up. "I'd definitely try the attic. There's a stair case to it at the end of the hall on the third floor."

"This better not be a trap!" She glared at me as she spoke.

"A trap for you or a trap for him? I mean, you didn't specify. If you're going to go up and there's only the one way in or out, then it's a trap for Fogg."

"Shut up!" She turned and headed for the stairs. "If he's not there, I'll have your head!"

"I didn't say he was there, I said you could *try* there!" I called up after her. "Not my fault if he's not there!"

"Shut up!" With that she vanished up the stairs.

I raced down the hallway again, this time turning into the kitchen. I was stunned to find it empty. I had hoped to see Ariel. I wasn't sure what Emma had done while we were in the Random Room, but as Ariel was the only other person in the building, I was concerned for her. I was about to go check the other room when I saw something small moving out of the corner of my eye. There on the shelf next to the marmalade and jams was a standard sized mason jar with the lid screwed down. Inside the jar, waving to get my attention was Ariel.

"I'll get you out of there." I grabbed the jar and twisted the lid.

Ariel was frantically waving at me, crossing her arms back and forth.

"You don't want me to open the jar?"

She waved her arms again. Then she made motion with her hands that I took to mean an explosion. I wasn't sure if that was right, but I couldn't think of anything good associated with the gesture so I screwed the lid back in place.

"You want me to leave you in there until Fogg can get you out?"
She nodded.
"Are you safe in there for now?"
She nodded again.
"Don't you need air?"
She shook her head.
"All right, I'll do as you ask. But I'm going to move you to some place safe. Some place she can't get to."

I didn't know how much more time I'd have so I ran back into the office and opened the big safe. This was the safe where Fogg kept all the magical items too powerful for anyone to just happen onto. I had the incantation and combination in my notebook for emergencies. I figured this counted. I made sure I was alone and got it open. Then I placed Ariel gently on the top shelf next to a simple chrome sphere the size of a baseball. I had no idea what that was about, but it looked safe enough for the moment.

"I'll be back for you as soon as I can." I gave her my best reassuring look.

She was tiny, stuck in a Mason jar, but Ariel gave me a smile that told me she had confidence in me. I closed the safe, spun the dial and then dashed for the staircase. I only hoped that Fogg was still alive.

CHAPTER FOUR

By the time I reached the ladder to the attic, I could hear a horrendous commotion above me. I climbed up until I could just see into the poorly lit space. The main source of light, not counting the energy bolts flying around the room, came from the opening I was currently in. I saw Emma standing in the middle of the attic, flinging lightning around randomly. Each strike would cause a fire wherever it hit. Then suddenly the fire would be gone. It took a few seconds for my eyes to adjust to the darkness, but I finally saw Fogg in the far back corner. After each of Emma's strikes, he'd do a quick and silent counter spell to put the flames out.

He was distracting her, buying me enough time to find Ariel and get her safe. That part was done. Now it was my job to help him trap Emma. The next step of the plan meant I had to get to him. I climbed into the attic and pulled the ladder up behind me, cutting off the light.

As I tried to cross the floor towards Fogg, I stepped on a loose board and instinctively dropped to a crouch as soon as the wood creaked. I heard something slam into the wall just above my head. I felt debris fly down at me driving a few splinters into my arm and shoulder. I did my best to ignore the pain. Natasha was smart. With the lights cut off, her blast would only pinpoint where she was, so she had changed to a non-luminescent concussion spell. I fished through my pocket for a quarter and tossed it across the room. A split second later I heard more wood blow apart at the other end of the attic. I began moving towards Fogg again.

"You decided to join us, Jimmy?" Emma's voice was still a mix of sultry seduction and hollow evil. "You know, once Fogg is dead, there's nothing that says we can't pick up where you and Emma left off last week."

She was goading me. Trying to get me to reply and give away my location. I wasn't that stupid. I reached Fogg. He knew I'd locate him before closing the attic door and stayed put until I reached him. It was part of the plan. I tapped on his arm twice, letting him know Ariel was safe. The next step sounded simple. There was a door at the far end of the attic. It opened to a small room where most of the plumbing pipes started. The room was no bigger than four feet square. It was exactly what we needed.

Fogg tapped me on the shoulder once and started out for the door. I dug through my pocket for another quarter. A quick flick of the wrist and Emma fired another concussion blast to an empty part of the attic. The noise allowed Fogg to move a bit faster. I waited, not making a sound. The next move was Fogg's.

"I'm not a fan of the silent treatment." Emma shot off five blasts randomly. "I'll blow this whole room apart if necessary."

I heard another stray noise, nowhere near the door. That told me Fogg was in place. She didn't fire this time.

"I'm tired of playing your games, Lucius. Elatee!" Emma cast a spell lighting the area around her. She put her hand against her chest. "I may be in control of this body, but Emma is still is here. She sees everything I see. She feels what I feel. So, Jimmy, if you don't come out right now... I'm going to make her scream."

"I thought you saw her memories?" I took a gamble, got to my feet and made myself a target. "Emma likes it when I make her scream."

She fired a concussion shot in the blink of an eye. I tried side-stepping, but still took the brunt of it in the shoulder. It knocked me off my feet into the wall. I was alive but I wouldn't be throwing a football for a few weeks. I hoped I bought enough time for Fogg.

"Abre-a-Porta." Fogg spoke softly and opened the door. The light poured in from the other room, making everything in the attic visible.

Natasha screamed, "No! You won't get away from me, Lucius!"

She flew across the attic, literally. The door was closing quickly. She fired off a blast, throwing it back open. She continued firing as she crossed into the room. The door slammed shut behind her and the attic went dark again.

I heard the sound of a chain being pulled and a light bulb burst to life. Fogg stood under the wall mounted lamp looking none the worse for wear.

"Well done, Jimmy." Fogg walked over to the attic ladder and lowered it. "Your timing was satisfactory."

"You owe me two bits. How long do you think she'll be stuck in there?" I followed after him as he headed down the ladder.

"The idea of a Random Room isn't unique. I'm sure she'll figure out where she is shortly." Fogg stepped down onto the second floor. "But I was able to change the incantation to work the door before she went in."

"It doesn't have to be 'Abre-a-Porta'?" I dropped down and pushed the ladder back up.

"Not at all." Fogg made his way down the flight of stairs towards his office. "That was just Galician for 'open the door'. The incantation just needs to be some variation of that."

"So what did you use this time?" I followed him.

"Welsh."

Just as we reached the first floor, the doorbell rang. Fogg didn't need to say a word this time.

"I know, I know." I headed over to the front door.

On the porch I found three children, two girls and a boy, dressed in identical costumes. They had on gray furry coats, drawn on whiskers, dark sunglasses and carried white canes. The taller of the two girls seemed to be the spokesperson for the trio.

"Trick-or-treat?" she said confidently.

"And what are you kids supposed to be?"

"Bored," the little boy said, which got him an elbow to the stomach from the tall girl.

The shorter girl finally spoke. "We're the three-blind mice."

"A very grim fairy tale, indeed." I grabbed three apples from the side table. "I have no cheese for you little rats. You'll have to make do with apples."

"Thank you, sir." They ran off in a single file with the tall girl in the lead and the boy trailing behind.

I closed the door and headed back into the office. Fogg was sitting behind his desk and had gone back to scouring through his books. I took a seat in the red leather chair opposite of him. I waited a moment for him to start talking, to tell me something. To tell me anything. He just kept reading.

"Who is Natasha?" I finally asked.

Fogg didn't respond again. He just kept flipping through pages. I stood up, took the book he was looking at out of his hand and slammed it down on the desk. He gave me a look of anger which I chose to ignore. I sat back down and tried again.

"Who is Natasha?"

"Does it really matter?" His question seemed genuine. "Does who she is change this situation at all?"

I leaned forward, closer to his desk. "Well, the only way I could answer that is if I knew who she was."

"Fine." Fogg leaned back in his chair. "Since you are obviously not going to drop it. Natasha was the wife of my rival, Kieran Drake."

He stopped there, not saying another word. I realized that getting the whole story was going to be like pulling teeth.

"Does this have to be a game of twenty questions or can you just tell me what happened?"

He looked away for a moment then back at me. It was hard to read him most of the time. At that moment it was impossible.

"Kieran was as skilled in magic and the occult as I was. Maybe more so. We both learned under the same teacher. He craved power and tried to dominate everyone around him. That brought us to odds. After a while, he became too much for Natasha to deal with. She decided to leave him. She came here, asking for my help. She was afraid he'd see her leaving as a betrayal and lash out against her. That's exactly what he did."

I watched the look on Fogg's face. After sitting in a room with him for years, I thought I had seen all sides of the man. But the look of sorrow and pain in his expression now was something I had never seen before.

He continued, "I responded too slowly. Kieran was my match but not necessarily my enemy, so I didn't expect the worst. He came in through the kitchen before I even thought of putting up defensive spells. By the time I heard the shouting and got up stairs, he had apparently killed her already. She was a talented sorceress, but nowhere near his level. I tried to stop him. We fought back and forth until he got in a clean shot. It nearly killed me. In truth it did kill me, a quick time-shift spell kept me from taking my last breath."

"What happened to Kieran?" I asked.

"He assumed I was dead and turned his focus away. I didn't hesitate." Fogg looked over towards the foyer. "He headed for the front door and I blasted him to ashes while his back was turned."

I had never heard the actual story of how the time-shift spell got cast and as much I was curious about Kieran, my bigger concern was his wife. "Was there ever anything more between you and Natasha? She didn't just come here out of the blue did she?"

"I sometimes underestimate your detective skills, Jimmy." Fogg turned and faced me. "There seemed to have been something there but we never had time to find out what. I've spent the last sixty-five years wondering about it."

Silence filled the room like a cloud cover on a stormy day. I couldn't think of a damn thing to say and Fogg no longer seemed chatty. He dove back into his books and I sat quietly, hoping that Emma and I would get the chance to figure out what it was between us.

The doorbell rang again followed by a scratchy and oddly familiar, "Trick-or-treat?"

CHAPTER FIVE

"What the hell?" I stood in the open door with my jaw on my chest.

"Heya, boss."

Standing there was my young friend Patches. He was an eleven year old kid off the streets who did some errands for me from time to time. I tried to get him into a foster home on two different occasions, but he kept running off. He got his name because everything he wore was hand-me-downs and covered in patches. Except now he was wearing a tie fastened to his dirty shirt and a suit jacket three times his size falling off his shoulders. To add to the strangeness, he was carrying a twenty-four by thirty-six inch frame held up in front of him and was speaking to me through it.

"Your note said to come in costume." He flashed a huge fake smile. "I'm the portrait of Dorian Gray."

"Nice cover, but we don't need it at the moment."

Patches shifted his grip on the picture frame. "Is everything okay in there?"

"It will be if you got the information I asked for." I put my hand out, trying to hurry the exchange along.

"Would I ever let you down, boss?" He handed me a slip of paper. "Ernie and Ryan are across the street, ready to help. You give them the heads up and they'll be running in with guns-a-blazing."

Having not wanted to leave Fogg alone with Natasha, I had come up with a plan. I'd write out a note asking the person reading it to call Howard's bar and ask for Ryan Aquino. It had instructions for Ryan that told him the information I needed and to have Patches deliver it in costume. I was certain that Ryan would call Ernie Psikla, my friend and police officer to get the information. Normally I wouldn't trust a kid in a Bigfoot costume to deliver the information, but Fogg added a somewhat powerful compulsion spell that would make anyone in a few feet of the note want to read it.

"Tell them thanks, but this situation is more in Fogg's world than ours." I handed him a candied apple. "You can all go home."

"Ryan knew you'd say that. He said we'll wait at the diner on the corner."

"Oh, did he?" I glanced across the street and saw the two men standing by the street light. "Was there anything else he said?"

"Yeah, I'll come trick-or-treat again in an hour to check on you guys." Patches gave me a devious look. "My second costume is even better."

"Hopefully this will be resolved before you need to put it on." I tugged at his tie. "Be careful with these neck nooses, once you put one on they're hard to get off."

"They won't get me!" He ran off towards Ernie and Ryan. I waved to them before closing the door.

I appreciated them having my back, but there was nothing they could do to help. I wasn't even sure how much I could do. I'd dealt with possessions before, but that was demonic based and we didn't actually save the affected person. As much as I wanted to just rip Natasha out of Emma, I couldn't. And Fogg couldn't either. He said he had a plan but didn't give me the details. Which usually meant I was going to hate it.

I approached his desk and handed him the slip of paper. He read it over and nodded. He then pulled out a piece of parchment and copied the information onto it. Once done, he folded the parchment to about an inch wide and rolled it up tightly. From a wooden box on his desk he pulled out a necklace. It had a small silver tube-like pendant. Fogg unscrewed the pendant from the necklace, slipped the paper into the hollow tube and reassembled the necklace. He then chanted some words that I believed to be Latin.

"Sit down, Jimmy." Fogg gestured towards the seat across from him.

I didn't move. "I'm fine. Tell me the plan."

He looked at me for a moment, as if he was hesitating. I really wasn't going to like this plan.

"All right." Fogg sat up straight in his chair. "I have looked for any alternative way to do this and there isn't one."

I picked up the necklace and examined it. "So tell me the bad news."

"Once a sorcerer takes possession of another body, as long as it's alive they control it." He made direct eye contact with me. "The only way to get them out is to make them want to leave."

"What would make her do that?"

"If the body was no longer functioning, she'd leave," Fogg suggested.

"Not functioning?" I was stunned. "You want to kill Emma to get Natasha out?"

"Of course not." Fogg got to his feet. "I have no desire to hurt Miss Martin. I have a serum, it can be injected or ingested, and it will put her into a profound state of unconsciousness."

"A coma?" I felt the bottom drop out of my stomach. "You want to force her into a coma?"

"Yes." Fogg had to know I'd react badly to this idea. "It will give Natasha no other option but to leave Miss Martin's body."

"And what's to prevent her from jumping into one of us or someone on the street?"

"She couldn't get out of the house before because of the time shift spell and she still can't unless she's in a body." He held up the necklace. "My personal defenses kept her from possessing me. The Celtic pendant you wear protected you. Once she is out of Miss Martin, we put the necklace on her to make sure Natasha can't return."

"What was the information for then?" I motioned to the note Patches had brought.

"Your friends found Natasha's maiden name for us. To affect a spirit in any way, you need a person's true name. With her full-name written out and in this pendant, she won't be able to re-enter once Miss Martin has regained consciousness."

I pointed towards the large safe. "What about Ariel, aren't you afraid of her getting possessed? And why haven't you let her out yet?"

"It's safer that Ariel remains where she is for now. Natasha's spirit couldn't enter her anyway."

"Someday will you tell me exactly what Ariel is?"

"If it becomes necessary, yes. For now it's irrelevant." Fogg's expression softened a bit. "I know this a lot to digest in a short amount of time, but the decision needs to be made and it should be by someone who cares about Miss Martin."

I sat on the edge of the desk and thought about what he was suggesting. I had spent three months in a coma after I got shot in the war. It's not something I'd wish on my worst enemy. Having to decide to put someone I loved in one, even for their own good – I didn't know if I could do that.

"Can you control it?" I turned and faced Fogg. "Once we render her unconscious, can you pull her back?"

"I'm not going to lie to you, Jimmy." Fogg pulled a syringe out of his pocket and held it up. "This is a very potent mixture and I have no idea of Miss Martin's physical or psychological history. I might be able to pull her out in five minutes or we might waste the next five years trying to make any kind of progress. There are huge risks with this strategy, but the only other alternative is to leave her to Natasha's whims."

I wasn't sure what to do. I'd put my life on the line more times than I cared to remember. Some of them for Lucius Fogg, others for Uncle Sam. But it was my choice to do it. Emma wasn't getting to choose. She was never given an option. She was just sucked into this battle of good and evil that had surrounded me since the day I started working there. The brownstone was a chaos magnet and I was an idiot for bringing Emma anywhere near it.

"I don't want to rush you, but we don't know when she might get out of the Random Room."

"That's okay." I stood up and was ready. "As my elementary teacher used to tell me, when you have no choice it's easy to make up your mind."

"I'll do everything in my power to bring her back." Fogg put his hand on my shoulder.

"I know you will." I looked at the concoction in the syringe. "How do you want to play this?"

"First we have to let her out." Fogg grabbed his cane and headed out of the office. "I think it's best we face her here in the foyer. More room to move."

"Let her out the kitchen door?" I asked.

"Yes." Fogg stood by the candied apples. "You open the door then duck into the bathroom. When she comes out she'll see me first and we go from there."

"All right, let's do this." I walked over and stood by the kitchen door. I spoke in my best Welsh accent. "Agorwch y drws!"

I waited long enough to see the handle change from brass to black. I took a deep breath, pushed the door open and then spun back into the bathroom. I expected to hear yelling, energy bolts flying, cursing of Fogg's name. None of that happened. I looked over to Fogg. His shocked expression mirrored my own. I slowly poked my head into the room and looked around. It was completely empty.

"She's not in here." I turned back to Fogg. "You think she knows Welsh?"

"I have a better question." Fogg looked around. "Where is she?"

CHAPTER SIX

I made my way down the long back hallway. Twenty rooms in total to check. Fogg headed upstairs to check the two upper floors and the attic. He said to yell if I found her. I asked if screaming like a little girl while she flung lightning bolts at me counted. He frowned at me. Being the only one in the house with a sense of humor was difficult at times.

I was told to check each room thoroughly if the door opened. Some of them were spell protected and that should've been enough to have kept Emma out. The Random Room opened its door into whatever room you were thinking of in the house. Since she was alone in the place for a while it was possible she could be in any of the rooms she might have come across when she was looking for us earlier. At least that's how Fogg was trying to explain it to me. I told him to stop and I'd just check inside any door I could open.

The first knob was locked so I moved on to the second. This one turned and opened into a library. It was no wider than any other room in the house, but it stretched up all three stories and every inch of wall space from floor to ceiling was covered in shelves filled with books. A thin, slatted landing went around where the room would be separated into both a second and third floor and ladders allowed you to go up and down between them all. Besides the books and a few comfortable looking cloth chairs, the room was empty.

After two more locked doors, I came across one that opened onto a stairwell leading down. Odd since we were on the first floor. I figured it was best to see where they headed, so I quickly moved down the first flight of stairs, hit the landing and started down the second. At the next landing I found myself looking at what appeared to be the same door I entered through and another set of stairs going down. The door was ajar exactly the same as the one I had entered through. I dug my knife from my pocket and cut an 'x' into the jamb. Then I turned around and went back up the two flights to where I started. The 'x' in the jamb was right there. I went back into the hallway and continued on.

I checked a few more rooms including the memory viewing room we had used on a previous case and a gallery room where some of the most amazing pieces of art hung. I had already decided that the concept of space inside the house was irrelevant to the size of the house itself – and then I found the store room. I stepped in and found rows and rows of pallet racking full of miscellaneous items. The room was bigger than all the warehouses down at the docks combined. It would take me hours to search the place. I wondered how Fogg found anything in there.

I heard a scratching sound to my right and turned to discover a green chalkboard on the wall with words just appearing. "Ask me for what you need."

"Can you tell me what's in this room?"

The word 'Yes' appeared on the chalkboard.

I decided to try it. "How many vases are in this room?"

The words on the board vanished like they had been erased, and then a second later they returned as if each letter was being written individually. "There are three hundred and forty-seven vases in the room. Would you like a listing?"

"No, thank you." Figured it was worth a shot. "How many humans are in the room and where are they located?"

Words wrote out on the board, 'Living or deceased?"

"Deceased? Living humans, please." I tried to ignore the creepiness of dead bodies being stored there.

"There is one living human in the room. James Michael Doyle. He is located at the entrance."

I thanked the board for its help, not knowing if it was necessary but there was no reason not to be polite even to a magical object. And it had kept me from having to search that room row by row. I was about to close the door then changed my mind and leaned back in.

"How many deceased humans are in this room?" I asked.

The board wrote out, "There are twenty-three deceased humans in the room. Would you like a listing?"

"No, thanks." I closed the door, regretting I had asked. Damn creepy.

I crossed the hallway to the next door in the line. I took a deep breath and prepared myself for whatever strangeness I was about to find, yet I was still surprised by what I saw. I stepped out onto a dirt path surrounded by trees and vines. I could taste fresh air and hear the sound of running water. I took a few steps forward and then turned to look back at the door. The jamb was wedged into the side of a cliff that went up for a hundred feet easily. If it wasn't for seeing the hallway through the open door, I'd have sworn I was outside.

"I heard the door open." Emma's voice called out. "You should come join me. The water is perfect – as always."

I made my way through the trees towards her voice. A few feet ahead I could see a clearing where the sun was breaking through the canopy. A waterfall crashed down from the rocks above and into a steaming pond of crystal clear water. A hot spring under a waterfall, that was something that only magic could create.

"I'm surprised. I figured Lucius would come looking for me here." Emma stepped through the falling water. Her naked alabaster skin was glistening in the sun, her long wet hair cascading down her back, the water tracing along every curve of her body until it spilled out onto the rocks below her. She looked more beautiful than ever. Only the hollow sound in her voice reminded me of the dire situation.

"Sorry to disappoint you." I glanced away, feigning disinterest.

"I'm not disappointed." She lowered herself into the hot water of the pond. "Emma and I are both very excited to see you. Why don't you slip off that suit and climb in here with us?"

"Because it's *us* and not just Emma." I took a seat on a large rock to the side of the hot spring. "You've been in this room before? With Fogg?"

"Didn't he tell you?" She moaned and stretched out seductively. "This was one of our favorite rooms when I'd come to visit. Have you ever made love in a waterfall, Jimmy?"

"He told me you came here to get away from your abusive husband, Kieran."

"That's right." She stretched her arms over her head, making her bare breasts bob up out of the water. "I got away from him once or twice a week for six months before I decided to leave for good."

"So that night, sixty-five years ago, you came here to be with Fogg?"

She sat more upright in the water as the subject of that night came up. "Kieran and I got into another fight. I couldn't tell you about what, we were fighting over everything then. I had enough, took my coat and told him I was leaving. He grabbed my arm and wouldn't let me go. Screaming at me that I belonged to him and I wasn't going anywhere. In his rage, he must not have thought I'd use a spell. I blinded him, just long enough to get away. I came here. What I didn't know was that Kieran had suspected something was happening between Lucius and me. He immediately came here."

"I know the rest." I had gotten her talking, figured I'd try defusing the situation. "You loved Fogg, didn't you?"

Melancholy washed across her face. "He was always there for me, no matter how many times I went back to Kieran."

"Then why do you want to kill him?"

She looked down at the water for a second. When she raised her head again her look had changed to something very stern and serious. "Sixty-five years. I was trapped in that room alone for sixty-five years. He just accepted that I was dead. He never even entered the room. He never even tried to make contact. I waited for him for sixty-five years!"

That backfired on me, badly. I had hoped to re-connect her to her feeling for Fogg. Instead she was angrier than ever. Her body floated up out of the water and hovered over the spring. A dark purple cloak appeared out of mid-air and wrapped itself around her naked body. Energy started crackling at her finger tips and her eyes glowed with power. She started moving forward, right towards me. I stood up as she got within five feet of me.

"This vessel cares for you deeply, Jimmy." Her voice was even colder than before. "If you care for her, tell me where to find Fogg and I will release Emma once I am done."

"And do what, find someone else to possess?" I asked.

"Does it matter as long as you get your love back?"

There was only one thing I could do. I had to save Emma. "He's searching the upstairs for you. We're supposed to meet back in the foyer to regroup if we don't find anything. He should be there any minute now."

"You made the right choice." She started floating past me. "Leave now and don't come back. This is your only chance. I am going to kill Lucius Fogg and if you interfere in any way I will not hesitate to kill you as well."

"Natasha!" I called after her, making her turn back around. "Know this. If you break your promise I will hunt you down no matter how long it takes and I will kill you regardless of whose body you are in. You won't be able to hide from me."

She glared at me for a moment and then finally responded, "Funny. For a moment there, when you were threatening me – you sounded just like Kieran."

CHAPTER SEVEN

She moved quickly for someone not touching the ground. I had to sprint out of the room to keep up. She was out of the hallway and into the foyer before I got by two doors. A few seconds later I heard the sound of breaking wood and something falling. By the time I caught up, part of the railing was gone and Fogg was lying at the bottom of the stairs. Natasha stood a few feet away with energy crackling around her entire body.

"Did you really think a random room would hold me for long?" Her hollow voice was now filled with rage. "No more games of hide-and-seek. This ends now, Lucius."

Natasha fired a lightning bolt. Fogg was up on one knee and thrusting his cane forward. The handle of the cane appeared to catch the bolt. The wooden shaft glowed for a split second and then went back to normal. She fired off two more blasts as Fogg was getting to his feet. He spun his cane, catching both of the bolts and absorbing them into the wood.

"Is this what you truly want, Natasha?" Fogg took a step toward his attacker He was calm, but his muscles were tense and ready to move. "It doesn't have to be like this."

Fogg looked at me for a brief second and then down. I followed his gaze and realized his right arm was at his side and held tightly in a fist. He jerked it once to make sure I noticed. A closed fist was a silent military sign to hold. He wanted me to stay out of it. Either that or he wanted me to deck her. I decided to go with the former.

"Yes, it does!" Emma shouted. "All of this is your fault!"

"You're right. I should have been better prepared for Kieran that night." Fogg moved a little closer. "And I should have known you were still here."

"I would have found a way to tell you, but you never came into the room." Tears started flowing down Emma's face.

"I couldn't go in there." Fogg closed his eyes for a second. I'd never seen him like this before. "I couldn't stand to be in the room where you died. Even if it was all a lie."

Emma backed away from him a few feet. "What do you mean?"

"Kieran had always been cruel to you and every time he crossed a line, you'd come running to me." Fogg's features hardened as he went on. "But no matter how bad he got, you always went back to him. You always excused his actions claiming deep down he was a good person. Well, that good person was just using you. You think it was by chance he ended up here so quickly that night? He knew if he pushed you this is where you'd end up."

"No!" Emma backed away some more, obviously shaken by Fogg's words. "He loved me! He always loved me!"

"You were a pawn in his game." Fogg wasn't pulling punches. "He kept you around because you had an effect on me. It's the same reason why he killed you that night. He came down the stairs taunting me. Telling me how he had taken your life and how he enjoyed doing it. He wanted to rile me up, fill me with rage so I'd fight emotionally instead of logically."

"You're lying! He did it because I'd come here. I'd always come here and he'd take me back. He'd be better." Natasha was almost in hysterics. "He was supposed to come get me. I loved him. I never loved you!"

"I know you didn't. I knew you never would." Fogg put two fingers down from his right hand. I nodded. "Yet any time you showed up here I'd open the door. I let you use me as much as he used you. But you could never have loved me anymore than he could ever have loved you."

"He DID love me!" Emma lost control.

Fogg's words had pushed her over the edge and she just started throwing bolt after bolt at him. He swung his cane about like an expert swordsman, grabbing each electrical charge out of the air with the handle and harmlessly absorbing them. I knew it was my time to move. I dove into the kitchen and then into the office through the side door. I moved quickly and quietly, positioning myself near Fogg's desk.

"I'm more powerful than you think, Lucius!" Emma's body was lit up like a Christmas tree as Natasha pulled together all the energy she could and fired it in one huge bolt of lightning.

I feared this was too much for his cane to absorb, but Fogg didn't even try. He met the bolt with the handle as he did before, but this time he spun the cane over his head and hurled the energy back at Emma. She was blasted off her feet, thrown through the office doors and into the chairs by Fogg's desk.

30

I didn't hesitate. I leapt across the desk, landing on the floor next to Emma's body. She was groggy but coming back quickly. I pulled the syringe from my coat pocket and injected the serum into her neck.

Emma looked up at me with tears in her eyes. In her normal sultry voice she said, "What have you done?"

A second later, her body went limp in my arms. I put the third necklace on her then looked up to see Fogg standing in the doorway. I waited for him to tell me what to do next.

"Her spirit has to be here, somewhere." Fogg crossed over to the big safe and opened it. "I need to capture it quickly while I can. There is nothing for you to do at the moment, why don't you take Miss Martin up to one of the bedrooms and make her comfortable."

I scooped Emma up into my arms and carried her up the stairs. Inside one of the guestrooms I placed her gently on the bed and covered her with a blanket. I sat on the edge holding her hand for a few minutes. Hoping she'd just wake up. I'd put her there. I brought her to the brownstone knowing all the insanity that happened there. I was the one that put her into a coma. And there was nothing I could do but watch her sleep.

After a few minutes, I decided to go back down and see how Fogg was getting along. I found him standing by his desk staring at a very odd looking item he had assembled. A green-tinted bell jar sat upside down on a small metal frame. Inside the bell jar sat three lit candles, each on the curve of the glass making the candles point in toward each other creating a single flame. Just above the bell jar hung what looked to be a child's mobile made of metal. Hanging from the mobile were a half-dozen twelve-pointed stars and the whole thing was spinning slowly counter-clockwise.

"What is that?"

Fogg looked up at me having just realized I had returned. "It attracts disembodied spirits. I was hoping it would bring Natasha out, but so far nothing."

He went back to staring at the bell jar. I started looking around the room. Something was off. I wasn't sure what, but I knew we weren't alone. She was there with us regardless of what Fogg's device was telling him. Something was definitely different and I had an idea of what.

"You said she could only leave the house in a body, correct?"

Fogg looked back up at me. "Yes. A spirit alone couldn't break through the spell on the house. What are you thinking?"

"You said she couldn't go into Ariel and we have protection." I slowly moved towards my desk. "But there is one more body in the house that we forgot."

"Of course!" Fogg figured out what I was thinking and began moving toward my desk as well. "That's why I can't find her disembodied spirit."

I went to the opposite side of the desk as Fogg. "Because she's not disembodied, she's in the cat."

Sitting on my office chair, claws out and hissing was Mr. Whiskers. I reached out to grab the furry creature, but he dove under the desk and out the front. He raced across the office towards the side door, but Fogg used a spell to slam the door shut before he reached it. We had him or rather Natasha, pinned in with the only exit at our back.

"She can't cast anything in that form. But she can use it to get out of the house." Fogg took off his coat and held it in front of him. "We need to get…"

At that exact moment the front door burst open. Both Fogg and I spun around at the sound of the commotion. Ryan and Ernie were coming in with guns drawn. Neither had gotten a second foot into the house before they were swept off the ground and slammed up into the ceiling, pinning them fast so they couldn't move. This was Fogg's home protection spell at work.

It was enough of a distraction for Natasha to make her move. She raced towards the door. Fogg tried catching the cat with his coat, but she moved too quickly. I made a diving effort and caught her by a back leg. She raked her claws against my hand, slicing me open from wrist to knuckle. The pain was enough to make me release my grip. This left her a clear path. Mr. Whiskers raced out the front door and into the night.

I scrambled to my feet to give chase. By the time I got out the door and onto the street the cat was gone. Natasha wouldn't keep the feline body for long. Her spirit could take over any human she came in contact with, meaning she could be anyone. After sixty-five years of being trapped inside a room in Fogg's brownstone, Natasha Drake was back on the streets of New York.

CHAPTER EIGHT

When I got back into the brownstone, Fogg had let Ryan and Ernie down from the ceiling. They had put their guns away and were both looking pretty nervous. Fogg has that effect on people.

"No sign of the cat." I turned to my friends. "What were you two doing?"

Ryan got to tell the story. "We sent Patches over to check on you a second time. No one answered the door and he came back and told us he heard loud noises inside. That's when we decided to find out what was going on."

"Gentlemen," Fogg addressed them in a way I never would have. "We appreciate your concern, but the danger has passed. If you'd like to take a moment and recover from your ordeal, feel free to have a seat in my office. Help yourself to the Scotch. Jimmy and I must head upstairs to deal with one last thing."

"No, we'll stay with Jimmy, thanks." Ernie snapped back.

"Very well." Fogg started for the staircase.

"Emma?" I asked.

"Yes. There is no time to lose."

We all headed up the stairs to the bedroom. She was, of course, lying where I had left her. Fogg checked her wrist for a pulse and then leaned in to listen to her breathing. He gently slid her lids open and checked her eyes.

"What the hell happened to her?" Ryan asked.

"We don't have time for answers right now." I didn't want to be harsh but time was of the essence. "If you and Ernie want to stay, you'll have to just sit back and watch."

"Physically, she is fine." Fogg pulled a small leather pouch out of his jacket pocket. "Hopefully she'll only need a little nudge to bring her back to the surface."

The pouch was filled with a sticky gray powder that he used to draw a few symbols on Emma's forehead. The first was an inverted letter C,

33

the second a wavy line and the third looked like a W without the final up stroke. He leaned over her and placed his hands on each side of her face.

"I'll need complete silence." He looked more at Ryan and Ernie than me. "This might take some time."

Fogg closed his eyes and his brow furrowed as he began trying to make contact with Emma's consciousness. I watched intently, trying to read what he was doing in the motions of his forehead, but I couldn't tell anything. Ryan and Ernie were quiet as church mice, though both looked completely confused. The silence hung so thickly it felt like I could touch it. Even the air in the room didn't seem to move. Then Fogg finally spoke.

"I can't reach her." He stepped back from the bed.

I felt my heart drop. "What do you mean?"

"She's far deeper than I can go." He put the pouch back in his pocket. "Miss Martin went through a great tragedy of some kind in her past and now that she has entered this state, she doesn't want to leave."

"You're not giving up?" I grabbed him by the arm. "You can't just leave her in a coma!"

"I have no intention of doing that." He pulled his arm away. "I said I can't reach her, but maybe you can."

"Me? What can I do?"

Fogg turned to the others. "Mr. Aquino and Officer Psikla, if you go into the room across the hall you'll find a blue recliner by the window. Can you bring it in here please?"

"Sure." Ryan nodded and they headed out.

He wiped the symbols off of Emma's head. "I'm going to help you project your consciousness into her mind. You have to find her and convince her to come back. You're emotional connection with her is the only way."

"Do you think it will work?"

"It has to." Fogg looked at me eye to eye. "If you can't, she will never wake up. But there is a danger. You could get pulled in too far and then you'd be trapped in there."

Ryan and Ernie returned with the recliner. Fogg had them place it next to the bed. He then instructed them to stay back and again to keep quiet. Neither of them had dealt with Fogg too much, but both knew to do what he said with no question in a situation like this.

"It's up to you, Jimmy."

I took a seat in the recliner. "Let's do this."

"I need the Celtic pendant that I sent you in Europe."

He meant the one that helped me out of my coma during the war. The one I wore around my neck every day except for the short time I had loaned it to Emma to help her sister recover. I took it off and handed it to him.

"Hold her hand." He then wrapped the necklace chain around our combined hands, placing the pendant on top facing up. "Now close your eyes and just focus on the darkness in your mind."

He put his hand on top of ours and I heard him whisper something I couldn't quite make out. He had said to focus on the darkness but I didn't know what that meant. I realized that when I closed my eyes I could see different shades of emptiness. I tried looking into the darkest spot. Focusing on it like I was trying to see something in the distance. It oddly felt like I was moving forward, getting closer to something. The darkness began to engulf me, like it was tangible.

I kept moving forward, like passing through a tunnel except there was no light at the end. The darkness became foggy, thick and damp. My clothes became soaked in an instant and clung against my body. The air changed as I walked. I could taste it and it wasn't pleasant. Copper and ash mixed together, My stomach started to turn and I gagged. But worse than the taste was the smell, burnt wood and charred flesh. An aroma I learned in combat and could never forget.

I could see the ground beneath me, uneven dirt and grass curving off into the distance. The fog was still thick but I could see through it and followed along the horizon as it rose up and over my head like I was standing at the bottom of a ball. And as I looked up to the apex of the arc I saw myself looking back down at me. I saw in front of my double a blackened area of grass which I assumed was also in front of me, so I continued forward.

Not far ahead I found the foundation of what was once a home but now was charred rubble. Everything was destroyed but a bathtub with a running faucet. I could hear it going, filling the tub beyond capacity, causing it to overflow. But it wasn't water that gushed forth from the tap, too thick and red. The blood poured over the edge of the tub and ran across the tiled floor. I followed it out of the ruins and into the dirt beyond.

The flow of blood had been so heavy that the ground had turned to mud and my first step landed three inches below the surface. Each step forward took me just a little deeper into the muck, but I could see where I was going. A hundred yards ahead of me I saw a podium with someone crouched on it. I kept moving forward and sinking deeper. Each step became more laborious as my mass got mixed into the mud. It rose to my waist, then my chest, my neck, my chin until I was under it completely, it surrounded me but I kept moving forward.

The mud began to take shape. It became a matter of sliding past the solid lumps. The thick muck became a sea of humanity as I continued pushing my way through the floating masses of flesh. Squeezing past each person in the crowd until I could get to the base of the podium. If I stretched my arms straight up I could just reach the bottom with my finger tips. I looked up and saw Emma, crouched down and held in place by chains. Her arms stretched out to her sides and shackled in place. Another shackle fastened to her neck keeping her head forward and down. The crowd around me began to murmur. The sound increased until they were all shouting at once, their words becoming flames that engulfed Emma, her bare skin blackening as the fire scorched across every inch of her body. She let out a scream so drenched in agony that it appeased the crowd and they fell silent.

I leapt up and grabbed the edge of the podium and strained every muscle in my body pulling myself up. Once on the platform, I got in front of her and kneeled down. Her skin was healing before my eyes. A moment later she was completely whole and the crowd began to murmur again.

"Emma. It's Jimmy. I have to get you out of here." I grabbed the chain holding her hands out and realized there was no lock. The last link was embedded into her wrist as if it was part of her. The shackle around her neck was the same.

"No. I belong here." Tears rained down from her eyes as she spoke.

The crowd was starting to get louder. I figured they were going to shout soon and the whole thing would play out again and again. Emma was torturing herself over something and I had no idea what or how to get her to stop.

"Why? What did you do to deserve this?"

"It's my fault." She sobbed out the words. "Everything is my fault."

"Tell me what happened. Why is it your fault?"

The crowd began to shout and I had a split second to decide what to do. I covered her as best as I could with my own body just as their words burst into flames and surrounded us. She screamed out again as the fire passed through me with no effect but burnt her to a cinder once more. I stood up as her skin began to heal.

No matter how much I asked, she wasn't going to tell me anything. I had to figure it out myself. I started looking at our surroundings. The only thing there was the crowd, thousands and thousands of people in every direction. Except it wasn't thousands of different people – it was just two, a man and a woman. Thousands of the same man and woman. But who were they? When I had met Emma, I knew she was Diane Martin's sister because of similar facial features. I saw those features mixed into the couple.

"These are your parents, aren't they?" I was trying to put the clues together. "They're burning you with fire, the burnt down home. Did your parents die in a fire?"

"Leave me alone!" She shouted at me. "This is how it's supposed to be!"

The crowd started murmuring again. I didn't know if I could take seeing her suffer like this for too much longer.

"You think the fire was your fault." I grabbed her by the shoulders and shook. "You have to tell me what happened."

"No! Get out of here!"

"I'm not going anywhere." I sat down on the podium in front of her. "If you're staying here then so am I. I'll sit here for all eternity if I have to."

The crowd shouted again and the flames circled around, avoiding me but searing Emma's flesh off. Then it all began to heal again once she screamed.

"What happened to your parents?" I asked again.

"Yes, they died in a fire. Now go," she pleaded.

"I'm not leaving without you. Tell me the rest of the story." She was still resisting so I played my last card. "It's up to you. I will stay in here forever if necessary. My life is in your hands."

Everything went silent: Emma, the crowd, everything. Even the sickening copper and ash taste of the air lessened.

"I was in my senior year of high school. Diane had already moved out. I wanted to spend some time with my boyfriend Doug, but my father said no, it was a school night. My mom went off to bed, my dad was up reading. I went in and drew a bath but never took off my clothes. I climbed out the window and met Doug at the side of the house. I just wanted to see him for a second. I must have knocked a towel onto the heater on my way out. I was only outside for five minutes when we smelled the smoke. The fire spread so fast. They never made it out." Her final words were broken up by sobs that wracked through her entire body.

"It was an accident." I put my arms around her, trying to comfort her. "You didn't mean to do it."

"They're still dead! It's still my fault!"

"And look at what you've done since. You're a nurse, you help people every day. You've dedicated your life to it."

The crowd began to murmur again. I wasn't getting through to her. I had to try something different.

"Do you think this is fair? You're hiding in here, beating yourself up over an accident." I grabbed her face and made her look at me. "This isn't what your parents would want. They loved you and wanted you to be happy, and this is what you give them? What about Diane? You're her only family. You think it's fair to leave her completely alone in the world?"

She lifted her head and I noticed the chain attached to her neck was gone. I was making progress.

"And the people at the hospital that count on you. What about them? What about the lives of those people you have yet to help? You can't do that in here."

The crowd fell silent again and appeared to be thinning out.

"What about me? You think I dove in here on a whim? I came to get the woman I love. And I'm not leaving without you. What's it going to be? Selfishly torture yourself over and over again or live for the people who love you and need you? You can't change the past, but you can make a better future every day. It's time to choose."

The chains on her wrist were gone. I lifted her to her feet and pulled her in close. She clung to me harder than ever.

"I miss them so much…"

"I know." I held her tight. "But it's time to go home."

Fogg never told me how to get out, but deep down I knew. I reached into my shirt and found my pendant hanging on my neck as usual. I pulled Emma in close, grasped the pendant in my fist and yelled.

"Fogg!"

CHAPTER NINE

I opened my eyes to see Fogg staring back at me.

"A satisfactory job, I think." Fogg almost smiled.

"Then she's back?" I turned quickly toward the bed. "Emma?"

She sat up and wrapped her arms around me, tears streaming down her cheeks.

"Thank you." She held me for a moment and then pulled back. "Does this kind of stuff happen to you often?"

"Which part?" I kissed her, which she gladly returned.

"Is that it? Everyone is fine?" Ryan spoke up from the corner.

"So it appears." Fogg handed me back the pendant. "The crisis is over."

"I don't understand any of this. How did she? Where did he? Oh hell, how about that Scotch you offered?" Ernie gestured towards the door.

"Of course. Follow me, gentlemen." Fogg headed out the door with Ryan and Ernie right behind him.

I kept Emma in the room for a moment. I wasn't concerned about the other two. They only saw a bit of the evening and being my friends they knew to expect the bizarre when it came to Fogg. But Emma saw it all.

"You don't have to remember this night."

She looked at me with disbelief. "You think I can forget this?"

"Yes." I took her by the hands. "Fogg can make the memories of this night go away. Not everyone can deal with knowing the things we know. It's difficult to find out that the world as you know it is only a guarded lie within a terrifying reality. This isn't a burden you have to carry."

"As opposed to the burden I've been carrying for years?" Emma put her hand on my face. "Emotionally I feel better than I have since before the fire thanks to you and I don't want to lose it. But that aside, you're part of my life, Jimmy, and I'm part of yours. I don't ever want you to feel like you have to hide anything from me."

39

I kissed her once more before we headed down to join the others. As we reached the bottom of the stairs, the doorbell rang. I opened the door to see quite a sight. Patches stood there wearing a gray jumpsuit and a glass fishbowl on his head. He had a pair of plastic fangs in his mouth and he was holding Mr. Whiskers.

"You have no idea how many questions I have right now." I shook my head. "Let's start with, what are you supposed to be?"

"I'm a space vampire!" he said proudly.

"The fishbowl is for air I take it?" I tapped the glass. "Vampires are supposed to sleep in sealed coffins and underground. I don't think they need air."

I obviously threw him for a loop with this new information. Before he could come up with an answer the cat leapt from his arms and sauntered into the office. We followed him in where he hopped up on my desk and took his customary spot. Fogg had just released Ariel from the Mason jar when he saw the feline's return.

"The boy found the cat?"

"He found me." Patches plopped down in the chair behind my desk and petted Mr. Whiskers. "It was weird. I saw him come out of your door. He wandered into the diner a little while ago and hopped up on my table. The waitress was going to pet him but suddenly she started laughing instead and just left. The cook was yelling for her to come back. I got tired of waiting for you guys, so I grabbed the cat and came here."

I stroked the cat's back and it purred. "I think it's just Mr. Whiskers."

"Agreed." Fogg sat in his chair and started straightening up the books. "But that is something to deal with on another evening. I think we've had enough adventure for one day."

Ryan and Ernie finished their Scotches and headed out taking Patches with them. I saw the boy grab the last two candied apples on his way out the door. It made me smile.

I walked Emma upstairs to the room Ariel had prepared. The one Natasha had been trapped in. She looked into the room, but didn't enter.

She shook her head. "I can't go back in there."

I opened the door to the room across the hall. I made sure Emma had everything she would need then kissed her goodnight. After closing the door, I headed back down to my desk. I couldn't quite shake the thought creeping up the back of my brain.

"What's on your mind, Jimmy?" Fogg always knew when I was havering on asking a question.

"Earlier tonight you said you underestimate my detective skills occasionally."

Fogg looked up. "I did."

"I don't know just how good of a detective I really am." I leaned back and looked at him. "There were an awful lot of coincidences tonight. A good detective wouldn't accept that. I mean, what are the odds that the new owner of Emma's apartment building would decide to paint her place on the very same night you say is too important for me not to be here? A good detective would find out who the new owner is."

"Yes, he would." Fogg answered without looking at me. "What other coincidences did you notice?"

"That you just happened to put Emma in the very room Natasha died in. A room that you've refused to go in for sixty-five years." I started petting the cat again. "It's also not like you to forget something like she'd be able to use the cat to escape. Or even that a spirit could exist in this house for all that time without you knowing it."

"You're correct. A good detective would investigate all those coincidences. A good occultist on the other hand always tries to be a step ahead." He pointed at an envelope at the edge of his desk. "Before you start your investigation, perhaps you should look at that."

I got up and crossed the room, taking the envelope from his desk and opening it. Inside was the deed to Emma's apartment building dated a week before. The new owner's name was written clearly on the top line: Kieran Drake.

"Loeb at the hall of records has a list of names he watches for and lets me know if they pop up. Drake is the first name on the list." Fogg gestured towards the paper. "I got that a few days ago."

"You said Drake was dead."

"It's what I truly believed until I saw that paper."

"Then you knew this was going to happen?"

"Of course not." Fogg finally faced me. "I wouldn't willingly put Miss Martin in danger. But it was obvious to me that Drake planned to use her as a pawn somehow and when you mentioned her apartment being painted I didn't believe it a coincidence. I could only protect her myself if she was here. Drake probably knew that would be my move though. Perhaps his plan was to flush Natasha out all along."

"For what purpose? You said he didn't actually love her. Why would he want her free? Was she supposed to kill you or were you supposed to kill her?"

"I honestly don't know." Fogg folded his hands together on the desk. "Only time will tell if we helped or hindered him this evening."

I turned back to my desk to see Ariel placing a pot of tea and a plate of biscuits out for me. I sat down and poured myself a cup. I took a big drink, the hot liquid stung against my throat as it went down. I took a second drink, held it in my mouth for a moment to savor the taste and then gulped it down. The Earl Grey always helped me relax, but not this time.

Kieran Drake was Fogg's rival, equally as powerful and now it seemed he was back from the dead and putting my girlfriend at risk.

"Any chance that this is over?" I asked, knowing the answer already.

"No. Whatever tonight was, I think it's just his opening move." Fogg turned to look out the window. "Drake is as intelligent as he is power-hungry. I can guarantee that he has more up his sleeve and we'll be seeing it very soon. We just have to be prepared for the worst."

CHAPTER TEN

Morning came too quickly even in a house where time doesn't pass. Ariel had a huge breakfast waiting as Emma came down the stairs. She was showered and changed but I could tell she hadn't slept much. I couldn't blame her. I didn't sleep for a week after my first case with Fogg. My mind kept trying to make logical sense of the illogical. Years worth of indisputable facts were suddenly in question. The look I had on my face that whole time was now hanging on Emma.

"Good morning, I think." Emma gave me a slight smile. "I have absolutely no idea what time it is."

I checked the clock on the mantle. It wasn't an actual clock, but a glass that showed the face of the large clock at city hall. "It's just about seven."

"Did you sleep?" She leaned in and kissed me on the cheek.

"Like a log."

"You're a horrible liar." She sniffed the air. "Is that bacon?"

"Yes, ma'am. Ariel has been a busy girl. Care to join me in the dining room?"

Emma looped her arm under mine and I led her to the other room. Table conversation consisted of basic small talk. We danced around anything that might have brought up the previous night's events. When we finished, Emma went up to get her things and met me in the foyer.

"Is Mr. Fogg around? I'd like to say goodbye."

"He turns in as soon as the sun comes up." I opened the front door. "He said to apologize for last night and that it was a pleasure meeting you."

"Up until my body was hi-jacked and used to try to kill him?"

"Yes, right up until that point." I was glad to see she still had her sense of humor.

43

In all the commotion the night before I had not put the Studebaker in the garage, so it was at the curb waiting for us. Our original plan had been to head over to the Upper East Side and visit the Guggenheim for a few hours. That understandably changed. The painters had told her the apartment would be ready by that morning so Emma asked if I'd just take her home. I fired up the car and headed out.

Traffic seemed abnormally light even for a Saturday. There still should've been people rushing to work or to whatever destination they had. But there were no other cars, no buses, not even pedestrians. I was about to mention it to Emma when I made a left and it all changed. The parkway was suddenly a parking lot and thousands of people were walking towards the steps of City Hall.

I couldn't move forward because of all the people. A glance into my rearview mirror showed me that more were coming up from behind. Any direction I pointed the Studebaker would have me running over someone.

"What is going on?" Emma looked around confused.

"I have no idea." I rolled down the window and grabbed the arm of someone walking by. ""Hey, pal. What's with the parade?"

"Haven't you heard?" The guy looked at me like it was Christmas morning and Santa had brought hookers. "He's going to make an announcement!"

He pulled away before I could ask him 'who?' Since it was obvious we weren't going anywhere, Emma and I got out of the car and started following the crowd. A few blocks up we reached City Hall and the madness continued to grow. People poured into the area from every possible angle. All of them seemed to know exactly why they were there. Unlike the two of us.

We continued to move with the crowd until it stopped at the base of a makeshift stage. There were red, white and blue banners hanging all around and a podium set dead square in the middle of two large speakers. This didn't appear to be an official city set up. No seal on the podium face, no flags and no sign of security or police. It appeared that someone just put up a pulpit and the people flocked to see it.

The crowd was buzzing with excitement and it seemed to be building. They were eagerly awaiting someone but not one of the people I asked could say who. It was just, "He's going to say something important." It wasn't too much longer before a man in a very expensive suit walked out of City Hall and headed straight for the platform.

The man walked with an attitude, complete confidence and poise. From his appearance I could tell he was used to being in charge. He was comfortable in his clothes so he had money. I guessed he was in his early forties but wore every year well. His sandy blond hair had a bit of a bounce to it but remained perfectly in place. He didn't move like an athlete, more like a dancer and his physique matched. Add in his perfectly chiseled and clean shaven jaw and you had a man that could be on the cover of any magazine in the country.

The man approached the podium and tapped on the microphone. A thumping sound leapt out from the two large speakers on either side of him. He then looked down for a moment, giving the appearance of either praying or preparing for what he was about to say. Perhaps he did it just for that appearance. After a minute he raised his head and began to speak.

"Citizens of New York City. I come before you today saddened by the news I must share. There are things going on here that you need to know about. Things that will affect every aspect of your lives. Things that I don't think you can go another day without knowing. But these things are being kept from you by your duly elected officials. The very people whose salaries come from your hard earned tax dollars." Emma gripped my hand. She was nervous and I wasn't sure why. "Now I can't say what their motive is. I can't tell you if it's corruption or ignorance that has them quiet on these issues. But either way, their silence speaks volumes!

"Well, I cannot allow that to continue. So I have come here today to let you judge for yourselves. Let you decide if your politicians should tell you the truth no matter how scary it may be. We are not children! You don't need to have them decide what is in your best interest. You deserve the truth and I'm going to give it to you." The crowd was completely quiet, hanging on every word the man said.

"You tell your children to stay out of Old Town because of the monsters. And they believe you. You tell them this so you don't have to explain to them about criminals and lowlifes that inhabit the area. Well, your city officials from the mayor to the chief of police tell you to stay out of Old Town because of the criminals and lowlifes. They do this so they don't have to explain about the real monsters down there."

I was not liking where this was going. Whoever this guy was, he seemed to be on the verge of spilling the beans to one of the most important secrets in the city. The secret that allowed people to continue living normal lives. And I could do nothing to stop him.

"As hard as this may be to believe, Old Town is invested with real monsters. Vampires who feed on your blood. Werewolves who eat your flesh. And a slew of other hideous creatures too numerous to mention. These unholy being have taken over a part of your city and feast on any of you that accidentally happen into their domain. As long as it happens in Old Town, the police do nothing. Why is that, do you think? I'll tell you. Because the politicians that run this city made a deal. Humans stay in their areas and monsters stay in theirs. If a few citizens get killed in the wrong part of town, so be it. It's all part of the bargain."

I looked around for anyone giggling or shaking their head in disbelief. This was a grown man telling a hoard of people that the stuff of monster movies were real and everyone was accepting it like he had just said that property taxes were too high.

"They let you live with a lie. There is a huge difference between the chance of getting mugged and the chance of being torn to shreds. How many lives would have been saved if the truth was known? How many of those who have died in Old Town would have never been there in the first place if they knew what monstrosities were really waiting for them?

"Well, I for one don't think these creatures should be bargained with. They have weaknesses that can be exploited. If a courageous mayor stood up and ordered the police into Old Town, they could take back that part of the city. They could eradicate the threat to every man, woman and child of New York. A courageous mayor wouldn't make back alley deals with monsters. But this city doesn't have a courageous mayor. At least not yet."

He was working the audience like a magician, keeping everyone's attention right where he wanted it. He played to their emotions and fears, and now he was going to go in for the kill. The crowd was just waiting to be led.

"I came here today because I love this city. I came here today to make a difference. In three days you could change all of this by electing a new mayor. One that will stand up for you. One that will lead the charge against the dangers of Old Town. But you won't find that person on your ballots. I went into City Hall today to declare my candidacy for mayor and I was told that I was too late. It was past the filing time. I don't think I'm too late, do you? The horrors of Old Town still exist and the corrupt officials do nothing. I think I'm just in time!"

The crowd cheered and applauded. They'd vote for him right then and there if they could. It didn't make sense though. There was no dissention. No one shaking their heads in opposition. Rallying the majority of a group is tricky but can be done. Getting everyone on your side so quickly is impossible.

"So if you're tired of being lied to, if you're tired of this fine city being run by cowards, you can make a difference. You can make this city a safer place. When you walk into the voting booth on Tuesday, stand up for a better tomorrow. Grab your pen and write in my name. Cast your vote for someone with your best interest at heart. Make your life better, your streets safer and make your children's future brighter."

He walked out from behind the podium and stood before his cheering followers with his arms raised high. "Remember my name! Kieran Drake!"

CHAPTER ELEVEN

Drake exited the stage and the crowd began to dissipate. Emma held fast to my hand. She handled some of the worst accidents to roll into an emergency room, very little phased her. But the look of fear in her eyes told me this was something more.

"Are you okay?"

It took her a moment to find her voice. "That was Kieran Drake. He is something far beyond evil."

"How do you know?"

"Natasha could see my memories. Well, it worked both ways. I saw the things he did to her. The things he talked about doing. He'll only be happy when the world is suffering under his heel."

I lead Emma back to the Studebaker. Enough people had left the area that I could drive her home. She didn't say another word until we reached the curb in front of her apartment.

"Is what he said true? Is Old Town filled with monsters that we just haven't been told about?"

She gave me a look that begged me to make her feel better. I couldn't.

"I won't lie to you. What you saw last night was just part of the world that most people are saved from knowing. What Drake said is true. And by telling everyone, he has risked putting this town into a mass panic that could cost far more lives than the few that get lost because of the pact."

"So the mayor has been lying to us?"

"I don't think the mayor knows too much more than you did. The pact was created years ago between the most powerful among both the humans and the creatures. Only a handful of people know it exists and they do everything they can to keep it that way."

She shook her head in disbelief. "Why is he doing this?"

I didn't have an answer for her. It was just as confusing to me. She leaned over and rested her head on my shoulder. I kissed her on the forehead and listened to her breathe for a moment. She finally sat back up and opened the car door.

"I'll come by and check on you later."

"No." She leaned down to look at me. "I'll be fine, but this city won't be as long as that man is out there. So go wake up Fogg and the two of you figure out how to stop Drake."

I watched until she was safely into her building. What Emma had gone through in less that twenty-four hours was more than most people could take. But knowing her, she'd be at work on time that evening. I had never met a stronger woman.

As I pulled away from the curb, I decided I needed more information before I went back to the brownstone. I wanted to see just how the police were going to react to Drake's announcement. Were they going to consider him a lunatic or take him seriously? The best place to find out was police headquarters.

With a next step in my mind, I returned my focus to the road. As I turned onto Lexington I noticed the new sign taped up in a store window. It simply read 'Trust Kieran Drake.' Two shops down had a sign up saying "We need a stand-up Mayor. Kieran Drake." More signs appeared as I drove, all of them touting the accolades of Drake without really saying anything. It appeared he was more focused on getting his name out there than who he was. Then again, 'Vote for me, I'm an evil bastard' isn't a great campaign slogan.

I pulled into the parking lot of police headquarters and found Detective Sebastian Lee standing at the curb waving me over. I pulled up and rolled down the window.

"I was about to head over to see Fogg when I saw your car." The detective was obviously not happy. "What in the hell is going on?"

"You want to talk about it here in the parking lot?"

He curled his lip as he thought it over. It made him look like a hooked fish. Yet another reason why he got the nickname of 'Sea Bass.' He finally sighed and jerked the door open. He was no gentler with how he got in or shut the door.

"Drive."

"Where to, Chief?"

"The bar your friend owns." His face showed his frustration. "I'm going to need a drink."

Ten minutes later we sat in the back corner of Howard's with two glasses of single-malt on the table. Sea Bass ran his hand through his thinning hair and gulped down a swig of Scotch. Ryan looked up from the bar, saw the almost empty glass and decided to just give us the bottle. Once he left, the detective started talking.

"It's like a rickety house of cards and Drake just kicked over an ace." He took another swig. "The mayor and sixteen other city officials were all screaming at the chief of police and he in turn was screaming at me. It seems that all the creepy stuff is my responsibility to clean up and now that it's out in the open, everyone wants to know either why they weren't told or how I let it happen."

"Why are they pinning it on you?"

"Because every time Fogg's name shows up on a police report, mine's somewhere on it as well." He poured himself another glass. "Guilt by association."

"Fogg hasn't been in on every case involving Old Town. How did you handle the others?"

"The chief had a friend, some guy named Ravenstorm. He'd make a call and the rich guy would pay off the right people or something. But Ravenstorm got himself killed not too long ago. Mauled by some kind of animal."

I looked away for a moment. I didn't want the detective to see how much about Ravenstorm I really knew. The fact that I was the animal that killed him. I had also killed Ravenstorm's daughter.

"I think this is even bigger than the chief's friend could have dealt with. I don't know who this Kieran Drake guy is, but he didn't just open a can of worms, he ripped off the top and tossed it away. The whole city knows about the creatures in Old Town and the mayor is demanding we take care of it now, before it costs him his job."

"What exactly are they telling you to do?"

"I have been ordered to take every available officer, including the cadets from the academy, and set up barricades on the edges of Old Town. I'm to detain anyone trying to leave until their humanity can be verified. Then I'm supposed to sweep through the area building by building. Anyone found will be drug out into the daylight. If they turn out to be vampires we are ordered to stake them in the heart immediately."

I was stunned. "You can't do that, Sebastian!"

"I don't have a choice!" He shot the rest of his Scotch and poured a third glass.

"You have any idea what will happen after that? The vampires you don't find will come out into the rest of the city and feast. They'll get revenge for their fallen brethren. And what about the werewolves?" I had gained a soft spot for their kind in my brief time being one. "The full moon starts Monday night. They won't go to Old Town because it's not safe. They'll run loose through the streets killing at will."

"I don't want to do this, Jimmy. But it's going to happen whether I'm in charge of it or not. At this point, the best thing I can do is use the knowledge I have to try and keep as many of my officers alive as I can."

We both fell silent. I swirled the lone cube around in my glass trying to think of something we could do. A way for us to stop the dominos that were falling on a path to chaos. Nothing was coming to mind. The pact that held the city together was created by Lord Erik Ravenstorm, Conrad Black, Dennick Shaw and Lucius Fogg, four incredibly powerful men. It was going to take more than a cop and a private eye to keep it from exploding.

"Who is this Drake anyway? I checked out files and this guy didn't seem to exist until this morning." Sea Bass pulled a paper out of his pocket. "The only thing I could find related to the name was a birth certificate that would make him a hundred and seven. No death certificate though."

"First I heard of him was last night as he had my boss and I jumping through hoops. Fogg called him a rival, though arch-enemy seems more appropriate."

"He went after you last night and then the public announcement this morning? That can't be a coincidence." The detective pushed away his glass. "This guy is obviously making a play. You have any idea what he might be after?"

"I'm starting to think last night was to distract Fogg so Drake could do something big. Revealing Old Town and running for mayor is probably just another part of it."

"I don't care what this guy's plan is. Come dawn tomorrow I have no choice but to take the entire NYPD into Old Town. Which means Fogg has around fifteen hours to make all of this go away. So you better head back. I don't think he has the luxury of waiting until sunset to get started."

"I'll drop you at the station." I finished my drink and put the lid back on the bottle.

It was time to get to work. Sea Bass had to do what he could to keep his men safe. I appreciated that. I also knew how much it drove him crazy to have to count on Fogg and me. This was bigger than anything the detective or I had dealt with before, which meant he had to put everything on Fogg saving the day. I just wished I knew what the hell we were supposed to do.

CHAPTER TWELVE

I'm not a fan of politics. It's a mindset I've just never understood. As a detective your sole purpose is to find the truth. As a politician your sole purpose seems to be to avoid the truth. What I knew about the state of politics was I didn't like it. That and the current Mayor's name was Edward Harris. Anything more and I would need to talk with an expert, which meant a trip to go see Pops.

I swung by the five and dime and picked up a bag of butterscotch candy. Sometimes you've got to pay for information. I walked the half a block down from the shop to the corner newspaper stand. Sitting on his throne, a small wooden stool about two and a half feet high, sat the most connected man in the city.

"Heya, Pops."

The old man's face lit up as he turned. "Jimmy! How are you, boy?"

I gave him the customary hug and slipped him the bag. He opened it up, saw the gold discs and smiled wide.

"Man, I love butterscotch. You're a good kid, Jimmy." Pops slid back onto his stool. "So how's tricks?"

"Can't complain, but then again who'd listen?"

"With the guy you work for, who'd believe ya?" He patted me on the back. "Now, what can I do ya for?"

Pops was a seventy-five year old man who'd lived more life than four people his age combined. Started off as a kid driving for the mob. He got the nickname 'Blackie' for his mop hair that always needed brushing. He never got involved in the nasty side of the business, always just on the outside but close enough to know what was going on. When prohibition rolled in, he ran one of the speakeasies. When it was gambling, he took book. And when the black hair began to gray and thin, they started calling him Pops and allowed him to do what almost no one else did. He retired.

Bought himself a newsstand and now spent his day talking with whoever came by. Pops had become the hub of information in the city and if you were a friend and brought the right kind of candy, he'd let you in on what you needed to know.

"I saw the announcement at City Hall this morning."

Pops nodded. "Got a feeling you won't be the only one come by asking about this Drake character. I have to be honest, Jimmy. I've got nothing on him. He just popped up out of nowhere."

"It's not him I need to know about. It's the other players. I know Harris, I've heard the name of his opponent. But I need to know who the real power players are here. Who's pushing the buttons and what winning the job is worth."

"There have been rumors about Old Town for years. I figured some of it was drunken exaggeration. I wasn't sure what to make of what Drake said this morning. If you're here for Fogg then maybe what he said is true. That's something I'd like to know."

I thought on it for a second. I could count on Pops' discretion. No one needed to know what I was looking into. But this time was different. I figured Fogg's reputation might work in our favor here.

"I can't say what is or isn't in Old Town. But it can't hurt if people know that Fogg is looking into Kieran Drake. He'd even be appreciative of any information brought his way."

Pops nodded once more. "I'll put the word out. As for the other candidates, it's a matter of picking your poison. Neither one of them are worth a damn if you ask me. Harris is the incumbent. He takes credit for anything good that happens and distances himself from the bad. Been mayor for twelve years and it will take a crowbar to get his butt out of that seat. He panders to the press and voters in public then avoids actually doing anything in private. He's got enough friends in rich places to keep him in office all these years. This seems to be the first time he's actually in danger of losing."

Pops stopped long enough to sell a copy of the Times to a guy in a cheap suit and a comic book to a little red-headed kid very excited to be reading about cowboys. The old man unwrapped one of the candies and tossed it in his mouth.

I pushed to get him started again. "Who's his opponent and what does he have to challenge the Mayor's friends with deep pockets?"

"That would be Gilbert Morgan and he has friends of his own. The same people I used to work for."

"The mob is backing a candidate? I thought they already had half the officials in their pockets?"

"They got tired of paying kickbacks and bribes to get things done. It's cheaper for them to just buy the seat itself. Morgan gets in and he'll rubber stamp anything the Made Men want."

"And the interest of the actual citizens of the city gets lost in the shuffle." That was why I hated politics.

"It's the nature of man, my boy. Those with power want more power." Pops handed me one of the comic books. "You want a world where the good guys wear white and the bad guys twirl their mustaches, you need to be reading these."

As I was about to head out, a truck pulled up and tossed a stack of special editions onto the sidewalk. Pops grabbed the stack, cut the twine and started putting them up. I took one off the pile and dug in my pocket to pay.

"You pull a coin out of there and I'll be insulted," Pops said without even looking up. "The butterscotch covers everything. Now it sounds like you have a lot of work to do, so you get going. Let me know if you need anything else."

I thanked the old man and headed back to the Studebaker while glancing over the front page of the Times. There was a photo of Drake along with the headline 'Candidate Reveals City's Secret Horrors.' Next to the picture was a story that told of the day's events and included some stats on how many people had gone missing in or near Old Town. The reporter made a jump in logic and began referring to them all as victims of brutal murder. I knew that in most cases he was probably right, but there was the possibility that some of the missing actually left on their own. It wasn't unheard of for a guy wanting to get out of his debts or his marriage to leave his car on the edge of Old Town, hop a bus and never look back. In those situations the police did very little. I could understand how the reporter made the connection, but it seemed a bit irresponsible to assume that all the cases were the same.

Below the fold were two more stories related to the incident. The first one was about the reaction to Drake's announcing his candidacy by the other two men running. The article included quotes. Mayor Harris took the announcement in stride saying he thought it was a great example of how our democracy worked and he had complete confidence in the voters of New York to choose the best man for the job. Morgan on the other hand condemned Drake for his fear mongering tactics and accused him of fabricating the whole thing just to get himself votes. He felt that any man who would align himself with intimidation and deceit had no business running for state office. The irony of that coming from a mob-controlled candidate was not lost on me.

The other article was far more interesting to me. It had almost nothing to do with Drake or the elections. Instead the reporter, Eric Fiallos, decided to focus on previous reports of monsters in the city and how many times those reports included the name Lucius Fogg. He gave specifics about police investigations that Fogg and I had gotten pulled into that he shouldn't have had access to. Fogg had gained a certain celebrity status over the years with some of the cases he solved. But this reporter was tying together those cases and others with the existence of vampires, werewolves and the like. And he was doing a very good job of it. He maintained that Fogg was the one behind the existence of Old Town and that he should be arrested for endangering the public. The reporter claimed to have hard evidence that Fogg knowingly hid these supernatural monsters from the citizens of New York. He called for the police to investigate Fogg's connection immediately.

This just kept getting worse and worse. If the mayor wanted to show he wasn't connected to Old Town, he could use his influence to open the investigation that the reporter called for and the odds were they would find evidence that Fogg was involved. Even if he wasn't arrested, he could be called in for questioning which wouldn't work very well for a man who couldn't leave his home. This now gave us two headaches to deal with. First, we had to figure out what Kieran Drake was after and stop him. Second, we had to find a way to shut Fiallos up before he pressured the mayor into moving on Fogg. And we couldn't forget that somewhere out there was Natasha Drake running around in a borrowed body and up to who knew what kind of trouble.

I tossed the paper onto the seat and slid in behind the wheel. The Studebaker roared to life and I pulled out into traffic. A glance up at the clock on the corner told me the bad news. It was two in the afternoon, four hours away from sunset. Fogg might not have liked starting work before nightfall, but in this case I didn't think he really had a choice.

CHAPTER THIRTEEN

I pulled up across the street from the brownstone to find a crowd of people gathered by the front door. There were enough note pads and cameras visible to tell me this was the press on a feeding frenzy. Fogg had always been an enigmatic figure in the media. The press never got the full story on our cases no matter how deep they dug. They didn't even have a photo of Fogg. That had to be incredibly frustrating for a group used to finding out everything about everyone. But the press had been on good behavior so far as Fogg's publicity had always been positive. Now that there was a negative story, they could use every trick in the book to get what they wanted. That included staking out Fogg's house.

I drove around the back and parked in the garage. There were a few more reporters set up in the alley but none of them could find the door to the kitchen. If you didn't know where to look, you'd swear there wasn't a backdoor at all. It was another little security feature Fogg had set up. You had to be looking straight at the door to see it. If you were at even the tiniest of an angle you'd just see past it. I knew the mark on the ground where to stand and which way to look to find the door.

The door being hidden was great except as soon as I walked up to it, they'd see it as well. I had to get them looking the other direction. I had no spell for that. What I had was a small oil can and the knowledge that most of the reporters working would have spent some time covering the war.

I poked my head out the door and tossed the can of oil at the feet of the collected press. Then I shouted, "Grenade!"

Cameras and notepads went flying as the reporters dived for cover behind trash cans and car fenders. I dashed through the chaos straight for the kitchen door and inside before any of them dared raise their heads. Once inside with the door closed, I looked back out the window and watched as they realized they'd been had. They didn't look happy about it.

Ariel was inside waiting for me. She pointed upstairs. I had hoped Fogg would have sensed something was wrong and been waiting for me in the office. It looked like only half of that was true. I had never been summoned to his room before. I had no idea what it looked like. I knew he didn't eat, but did he sleep? Was there a bed, a big comfy chair or maybe a giant wooden rocking horse? I honestly had no idea what to expect.

As I reached the top of the stairs and approached his door I heard his voice. "Come in, Jimmy."

I opened the door to Fogg's room and was a little disappointed. It was just a very nice, relaxed room. There was a king-sized sleigh bed in one corner and a dresser to the side. The bed was neatly made and there wasn't a single item on top of the dresser. The other corner had a small table and two chairs. On the table was a chess-set with the pieces moved to show a game in progress. White seemed to be winning, but the truth is I knew nothing about chess. Poker was more my game. Next to the chess board was a stack of letters I remembered coming in once a week with no return address. I guessed Fogg was playing chess with someone through the mail. In the center of the room was a small reading area with a high-back leather chair and Tiffany lamp.

Fogg was sitting in the leather chair closing the latches on a hard-sided suitcase. The case was about two feet by three feet and a foot deep. On the table next to the chair sat a few pieces of cloth along with a spool of thread and a needle. I didn't even try to guess what he had been doing.

"How bad is it?" He sat back in his chair and waited for my report.

"Drake told the world about Old Town and wants to be mayor. Sea Bass is being pressured to take the whole police force in to clean up the area. The house is surrounded by reporters who think you're part of the problem. Oh, and the Studebaker needs a tune up."

"Any chance we can convince the Detective to hold off his raids?"

"His hands are tied. Drake called out everyone from the mayor to the chief of police. If he tries to stop it, they'll just replace him with someone who'll do it."

Fogg leaned his head down and began rubbing his temples with his thumb and middle finger. "What is he after?"

"From what I understand, both the current mayor and his opponent are pretty much shills for power. Maybe that's what Drake wants, the money and influence that comes with the office?" It sounded good to me at least.

"He has more money than he could ever need and the power of an elected official is a joke."

"Then you tell me what he wants. He's your old friend."

Fogg snapped at me. "I don't know!"

We had been through a lot of cases over the years, dealt with very intense moments including my quitting, but never once did I see Fogg lose his cool. This was different. I could see the frustration on his face. He'd always been three steps ahead of his opponents but now he was playing from behind. I wasn't sure Fogg could work like that.

"I'm sorry." He let the words sit out there for a second before continuing. "I can think of no reason why he'd want to be mayor or why he'd want to clear out Old Town. I have no idea what he is hoping to gain."

"Maybe that's the whole point."

Fogg looked confused, not a look I was used to from him. "What do you mean?"

"Maybe all of this is just to get you so focused on what he's doing now that you don't see what he's really doing behind the scenes." I pulled a handkerchief from my pockets and waved it about. "Like a magician distracting you with the flamboyant so you don't see the slight-of-hand, he's doing all of this so you won't see his true purpose."

Fogg thought on that for a moment. "Even if you're right, that doesn't change the fact we need to stop the potential slaughter before it starts."

"How are we going to do that?"

"We need to meet with Conrad Black and Dennick Shaw immediately. Perhaps between us we can come up with something."

"I can get a message to them to meet here…" Getting a message to Black would mean a run into Old Town. My day just kept getting worse.

"No, not here." Fogg stood up and walked over to the chess board. "We can't risk either of them being seen with the press outside. There is a place where the four of us would meet to discuss the terms of the pact. A neutral location we could all get to securely."

"You have a way of leaving the house?" I was a little surprised.

"In a manner of speaking." He pointed to the suitcase on the floor. "You'll go in my place and take that. Once Conrad and Dennick are present, you will set it up and we'll see if we can find a solution. Be warned though, Conrad won't be in a good mood and may be rather resistant to any plan we come up with."

"Why is that?"

"I stopped him from killing Kieran Drake over seventy years ago. He's bound to blame me for all of this."

Fogg gave me the location of the place and the name of the person to ask for. It all sounded odd to me, but odd was part of my job. My next trick was to get back out of the house and away without the press following me. Fogg started rambling off some spells that might get me out unseen but I told him to forget it. I had a plan.

I made a phone call and then waited by the kitchen door with the suitcase in my hand. It wasn't too long before I heard the blaring of a car horn echoing through the alley. A pale green Chevy Coupe sprang into view, knocking over trashcans as it approached. Some of the reporters dove out of the way as the Coupe flew by. They yelled a few profane comments at the trunk but stopped immediately when the brake lights flared and the car began to turn around. The Coupe was making a second pass, charging towards the huddle of reporters once more. They began running away en masse.

The car slammed to a stop right where I had told Ryan to pull up. I raced out the door, tossing the case in through the back window and slid behind the wheel as Ryan shifted over to the passenger side. I floored it immediately and raced past the screaming press. I had no idea that such educated men could use such filthy words.

I drove around a bit until I was certain we weren't followed, then I headed back over to Howard's to drop Ryan off. I had bought the Coupe a few months back and didn't see a reason to sell it, so I made a deal with my friend that he could use it when I wasn't in exchange for letting me park it behind the bar. You never knew when you'd need a second car.

"You need help with anything else?" Ryan asked before he got out.

"We're kind of flying by the seat of our pants on this one. I'll let you know if we do."

"I'm just a phone call away." Ryan smiled and climbed out of the car.

Everyone should have the friend that you can call at a moment's notice. A guy who will do whatever you ask of him without a single question. I was lucky I had that in Ryan Aquino. Plus he poured a generous Scotch. As I pulled away from the curb I could see Ryan in my rearview mirror. He was watching the street, double checking that I didn't have a tail.

CHAPTER FOURTEEN

I drove past the address Fogg gave me twice before finally finding it. The place was a tiny little hole-in-the-wall store front that you'd miss if you blinked. I must have blinked twice. Wedged in-between a hardware store and a haberdashery was a shop barely wider than the Coupe. Two things hung out front: a small wooden sign just above the door that said 'Tea Time' and the Union Jack. In the spotless front window was a sign that said 'Open.' I parked the car, grabbed the suitcase and headed in for tea.

The interior of the shop was a long, stretched out area filled with small tables for two and four. The tables were of various shapes and designs and I couldn't find a matching set of chairs in the place. Even the table cloths were a hodgepodge of colors and designs. The wallpaper was the one consistent thing, a white background with a pattern of yellow flowers and wooden barrels on patches of green grass. Hanging throughout the room were various framed black and white photographs of things associated with the United Kingdom: pictures of the Queen, Big Ben, Buckingham Palace, Westminster Abbey and so on. It almost felt like a library without any books.

The one thing I didn't find was any people. There wasn't a single customer in the shop. If it wasn't for the noises coming from the door in the back I'd have thought the entire place was deserted.

"Hello!" I called out loud enough to be heard but not too loud as it still felt like a library.

A few seconds filled with clattering and shifting went by before a tiny woman of advanced age came through the door. She wore a blue gingham dress with a white apron tied around it. Her purple-gray hair sat in curls upon her head and a large pair of glasses clung to the very tip of her nose.

"Oh, hello, dearie. I didn't hear you come in. I'm afraid we're going to be closing in a few minutes."

"I was told to ask for Dorothea. Is that you?"

"Why, yes. That's me. What can I do for you?" She tilted her head slightly and gave a warm friendly smile like your grandmother would give.

"I work for Lucius Fogg."

Her smile faded. She walked straight past me and flipped the sign over to 'Closed.'

"I had a feeling he'd be needing my place. You must be Jimmy." She patted me on the back as she passed by again. "Lucius speaks highly of you. Glad we could finally meet. Wish it was under better circumstances."

"Then you know what's going on?"

"Not all of it, but enough to know that a meeting was called for." She led me to a round table in the back, one with four chairs. "I'll let the others know you're here."

I put the suitcase down on the floor and sat in the most comfortable chair of the set. I had my back to the wall and could see the back door to my left and the sun setting through the front window on my right. Tea Time was on Fourth Street, the edge of Old Town. Fogg said this was a safe haven where they could meet. I brought my .45 anyway.

I settled into my seat just as Dorothea returned with a pot of tea and a small plate of scones. "A little something while you wait."

The tea was a popular British blend, not my usual Earl Grey but still tasty. The scones were served with clotted cream and strawberry preserves. I made a mental note to return sometime when there wasn't a crisis and I could really enjoy the place.

Out of the corner of my eye I noticed a form pass across the front window and reach for the door. The height and weight gave me a good idea who it was, but seeing the salt and pepper colored hair and beard enter the door made it obvious. Dennick Shaw headed straight through the shop to the back table and took the seat opposite of me. He was a good-sized man, a few inches over six feet with a big barrel chest and about twenty pounds of excess weight. His long hair was pulled back tightly into a ponytail draping down the back of his black t-shirt.

"Hello, Jimmy. How goes the high-brow world of Lucius Fogg?"

"As fun as always. How are things down at the Dawn? Still shooting pool with the Neanderthals?"

"Of course. They send their love."

Dorothea came in with a second tea pot and cup for Shaw. She kissed him on the cheek as she put the cup down. Shaw seemed genuinely pleased to see the elderly woman.

"Ah, Dorothea, my love, why do I see you so rarely?"

"Because you'd rather sit in that filthy bar of yours drinking beer than come to a nice place like this." She put her hand on his shoulder.

"Not all of us can be cultured." Shaw let out a hearty laugh.

Without making a sound, Conrad Black entered the room through the back door and took the seat to my left. As always he was dressed in a three-piece gray suit perfectly fitted to his muscular frame. His short cut, brown hair and goatee added the only dash of color in contrast to his almost white skin. His sudden appearance startled Dorothea.

"Oh my, you gave me quiet a fright there, Conrad."

The vampire kissed the back of her hand. "My apologies. It's a pleasure to see you again."

"I would offer you some tea, but I know you won't have any." She turned back towards the kitchen. "If you need anything, I'll be in the back."

As Dorothea left the room, both Black and Shaw turned their attention to me. I had instructions to follow. I pulled the suitcase over and opened up the latches. Fogg told me to take what was inside and set it up on an open chair. I was truly not expecting what I found inside. It was a ventriloquist's dummy like Charlie McCarthy, except this one was done up to look like Fogg, down to the gray hair and walking stick. Even the suit looked like one of his and was probably more expensive than all the suits I owned put together.

I put the dummy into the open chair, sitting like he was a guest. I then pulled out my notebook and said the words Fogg had given me. The eyes on the dummy immediately opened and were far too human looking for my comfort.

"Well done, Jimmy." The dummy complimented me. "Thank you both for coming on such short notice."

Both Shaw and Black nodded. They were obviously less creeped out than I was. The little wooden body moving on its own and talking with Fogg's voice was just weird. I wondered if this was something he created that night or if Little Lucius had been somewhere in the house all along. That thought really disturbed me.

The meeting began with me catching the others up on all we knew. Conrad Black was the eldest vampire in the city so all the others answered to him. Dennick Shaw was the leader of the werewolf pack. The two of them were the unofficial leaders of Old Town. We would need their help to keep thousands of both humans and the supernatural from being killed in the next few days.

"The police are heading in first thing tomorrow morning," I finished up. "There won't be any werewolves there yet, but the vampires will be completely vulnerable as they go to sleep for the day."

"If the police kill some of my kind, I will not be able to stop the others from going out at nightfall to get revenge," Black admitted. "They obey the pact because it works for them. If the police are going to hunt us during the day, they'll return the favor at sundown."

Little Lucius' head turned toward Black. "Do you have any safe locations to sleep that the police won't be able to find?"

"Enough for maybe ten percent of the vampire populous."

"If the police are going into Old Town to hunt, why don't we just move the vampires?" I refilled my cup as I explained. "Sea Bass doesn't want to do this anymore than we want it to happen. So what if we play three-card Monty with the undead? We get enough trucks and trailers for those vampires that don't have safe locations. We then drive them out of Old Town on one end as the police go in at the other. Move them around the city until it's clear and then drive them right back again."

"You want to move my people around like cattle?" Black was offended.

"Of course not, Conrad." Little Lucius jumped in. "But Jimmy's idea is plausible if we could come up with enough trucks and drivers. The important thing is to keep this from becoming a bloodbath for anyone."

Shaw leaned forward, "How many trucks are we talking?"

Conrad thought for a moment, "Two or three dozen if we packed in tightly."

"I can get that many and the drivers. But the police won't be fooled if they get into Old Town and find nothing."

"On the contrary, Dennick." Little Lucius jumped in. "If the police don't find anything then they can go back to their superiors and claim the whole thing was a hoax. This may even prevent them from doing the sweep again."

"Can you trust the cop to work with us?" Shaw didn't trust the police at all.

"The Detective is a good man and doesn't want to see anyone hurt. He'll do what we ask." Little Lucius assured them. "Worst case scenario it buys us a day, maybe two to figure out exactly what Drake is up to."

"Why only two days?" I asked.

"Because all those drivers I'm getting for tomorrow will have full moon issues of their own." Shaw got up. "I need to make the arrangements. Let me know where to have the trucks set up."

"Wait!" Conrad started in on Fogg. "This is your personal battle with Drake spilling over onto the balance of the city. He and his actions are your responsibility. How do you plan to stop him?"

"This is just the start." Little Lucius' plastic eyes locked onto Black. "Drake doesn't do anything without a long range plan. This is obviously just his opening move. We can't figure out how to stop him until we know what he is truly after."

"And how many of my kind will have to die before you know? His personal vendetta against you is going to cost a lot of lives: humans, vampires and werewolves. You should have handled this years ago."

"I know you never trusted Drake and tried to convince me of his evil ways. I can't change that. I honestly thought he was dead. I can't change that either. All I can do now is try and keep this all from blowing up and prepare for whatever endgame Drake has." The dummy's head turned away as he finished. "I made mistakes, but I'm trying to fix them."

Conrad didn't look happy, but he nodded. "I'll get the information out to my people. Hopefully most of them will listen."

Shaw left through the front door, Black by way of the kitchen. I noticed the eyes on Little Lucius were closed again so I felt it was safe to pack up the dummy. I finished my cup of tea and was about to head out when Dorothea came back into the room.

"Do you know why the British stop for tea?" She started clearing up the table.

"I'm not exactly sure."

"It's so that no matter where they are, what they are doing or how stressful the world is, they can take a moment and remember who they are and just breathe. If you spend all your time running from one fire to the next trying to put them out, you lose sight of why you are doing it in the first place. That's why I opened this shop exactly where I did, so no matter how insane the world gets there would be one place everyone could go to catch their breath and have a cup of tea."

I smiled at the woman, thanked her for the hospitality and headed for the door with my dummy in hand. I would need to visit Sea Bass and solidify the plans for the morning and I wanted to stop and check on Emma before heading back to the brownstone. The next few days were going to be hectic and our plan was nowhere near foolproof. But at least I had a moment where I could stop and catch my breath.

CHAPTER FIFTEEN

I'm not much of a flower buying guy. I understand the sentiment, but I also see the reality of giving your gal a bunch of weeds that will be dead in a few days. I think there are far better ways to show someone you care than a fist full of thorns. That said, on my way to go see Emma, I stopped and picked up a dozen roses. With all Emma had gone through the night before I felt she could use something beautiful to look at. Something simple and natural to take her mind off of all that she'd learned.

There was a flower shop on the corner next to Emma's building which made my decision even easier. I couldn't help but notice the 'Trust Kieran Drake' poster in the florist's window. Just about every shop I passed had one up. I decided to ask the guy behind the counter some questions as he put my order together.

"Why'd you put the poster up?"

The florist stopped and looked at the window. "I'm not sure. It just seemed like the right thing to do."

"You're not happy with the current mayor?"

"He seems okay for a politician." The guy grabbed some string to tie the bouquet. "I'd forgotten that an election was coming up."

"So why are you supporting Drake?"

"He seems trustworthy." He smiled and handed me my roses.

I headed out of the shop and walked the thirty feet to the apartment building's front door. I could still smell the paint fumes as I entered the lobby and started up the stairs. Whoever Drake had hired to do the painting wasn't too bad. They'd gotten the entire place done in one day. It was nice to know that evil sorcerers still hired good workers.

I knocked on Emma's door. We had a few hours until she'd have to get ready for work, so I figured I could take her to dinner or a drive. When the door opened, she was standing there in nothing but her robe. This wasn't the see-thru, sexy one that she'd worn on more than one occasion. This was the thick dark-green terry-cloth robe that she wore on cold nights before getting into the shower.

I held up the flowers. "For you."

She took them out of my hand and tossed them onto the couch without a second thought. Then she grabbed my hand and dragged me towards the bedroom. I was just able to kick the door closed with my heel as she pulled me away.

Once in the bedroom, she dropped the robe. I could see every inch of her alabaster skin as it shown in the three-quarter moonlight coming in through the window. Her jet black hair cascaded down her shoulders and across her chest, ending just shy of her ample breasts. Her body had curves that I couldn't resist putting my hands on and that night was no exception. She stepped forward and pressed her lips against mine. Our tongues met and intertwined. Her fingers found the seams of my shirt and yanked them apart, sending buttons flying. I quickly undid my own pants, knowing I'd need them to function later.

Within a few seconds we were both naked and she pushed me down on the bed. My body reacted well to the intensity as she slid on top. She straddled my hips and took me inside of her. Over the months we'd been together, there were nights I was the aggressor. Other nights, like this, she was in charge. I put my hands on her hips as she ran her nails down my chest. She rolled her pelvis, thrusting down on me over and over again. Quickly at first, then slowing down when it was obvious the pressure was building.

She tried prolonging the inevitable until she knew it was too much and let me finish. Then, sweat covered, her body collapsed against mine. Her breasts pressed against my skin as she laid there on top of me. Nothing was said. She would just move and stroke things occasionally until I was ready for a second round. The moment I was, she sat back up and took me in once more.

After the repeat performance, she slid off me and curled up in my arms. The silence hung over us like a blanket. I didn't want to say anything that would ruin whatever sense of normalcy she had gotten from our being together. I'd wait until she spoke, but I wasn't prepared for what she said when she did.

"You're a good private detective, Jimmy." She snuggled in close as she spoke. "Why don't you quit Fogg and go off on your own?"

I stared at her, slack-jawed and eyes wide. The question lingered in the quiet, demanding a response. It wasn't a conversation I could have lying naked next to her. I sat up on the edge of the bed and reached for my clothes.

"You're not going to answer me?"

"I'm not going to give you one you're going to like."

She slid out of bed and grabbed the big green robe. She had it on and tied shut by the time I got my belt fastened. She walked into the living room and poured herself a drink. It wasn't her first of the day.

"There is no reason for you to do the work you do." The plop of an ice cube added emphasis to her statement. "There are thousands of normal people in the world who need help. Thousands of normal lives you can make a difference in. Why must you work for someone who is constantly surrounded by unnatural and dark forces?"

"That's the exact reason." I tucked my shirt in to keep it shut. "Vampires, werewolves, demons, wizards and the like, they all have power so far outside our comprehension that sometimes humanity gets lost. Someone has to be there to remind them that the average man still matters. That we are more than just pawns on a chess board. Someone has to speak up for you, your sister, Patches, Ryan…"

"Why does it have to be you?" She gulped at her drink like it would make the bad go away. "How many times do you have to risk your life before someone else can take over?"

"You want me to let someone else take the risks? That's not who I am. I did my duty in the war and for all I know I'd still be in a coma in Europe if it wasn't for Fogg. I owe him."

"That damn necklace he gave you is becoming a noose."

She threw her glass into the wall. It shattered into a dozen little pieces and sprayed across the carpet. I grabbed the dustbin from the kitchen and started cleaning it up. She just stood there, staring at me. Once I was done, I put the bin back and grabbed my coat.

"I didn't mean to upset you. I should go."

She grabbed my arm with both hands, digging her fingers into my elbow. Her eyes locked with mine and I could see how lost she was feeling. She was desperately trying to cling to anything that made sense to her and right then all the insanity was tied to Fogg. So she wanted me to quit. To leave all the chaos with him and start a life she could better understand. There was something very attractive about that idea.

She finally spoke, "I tried to sleep when I got home, but I was afraid to close my eyes. Afraid that Natasha would suddenly take control again. That I would be trapped again, watching as someone tried to hurt you."

"She tried, but I'm still here. I can be pretty tough when I need to be."

"But that's the thing. You need to be tough constantly. How many times have you been in danger since we've met? How many times have you had to face down something a hundred times more powerful than you? What happens the day when you aren't tough enough?" Streams of tears began rolling down her cheeks. "I have lost far too many people in my life. I can't lose you, too."

I pulled her into my arms and held her tightly. She was shaking. "I know your whole world has been blown apart. Things you thought were just fantasy are suddenly real and very dangerous. But most of the time everything co-exists quietly. Fogg and I will stop Drake, we'll find Natasha and things will calm down. It won't go back to the way it was, but it will become something you can live with."

"Live with?" She gazed up at me with watery eyes. "I love you, Jimmy. And as long as I know you work for Fogg, I'll worry about you. I will think every ring of the phone or knock on the door will be bad news. I'll be constantly waiting until the day some freak of nature takes you away. The balance you talked about is great, unless you're the one that has to keep that balance."

"Are you giving me an ultimatum?"

"I'm sorry, but I am." She put her hands around my neck and pulled me in close. "If you want me in your life, you need to quit working for Lucius Fogg."

I hadn't had the easiest life. Growing up an orphan didn't create much stability. Nor did it give me any sense of love. Loyalty, honor, responsibility, those were all things I'd had in my life, but love had been rare. When I went into Emma's head, she didn't emerge for herself. She did it out of love for me. It was the first time in my life I knew without a doubt that someone loved me. Fogg had guided me back to life after I was shot, but Emma was showing me how to live.

"I can't leave him now, not with everything going on." I kissed her gently on the forehead and stroked her back. "But the last thing I want is for you to worry about me. Once this is handled and Drake is stopped, I'll make a change. I'll talk to Fogg."

"Thank you, Jimmy." She clung to me tightly. "Thank you."

CHAPTER SIXTEEN

I dropped Emma off at work in time for her shift and then drove over to Howard's bar for a drink. I didn't feel too chatty, so I took a seat in the last booth in the back. The one that once doubled as my office. I could have gone back to Fogg's, but that would mean another dash past the waiting reporters. I just didn't have that in me right then. I drank in a swig of twelve-year old Scotch and let the familiar burn trace down my throat. I leaned my head back and shut my eyes for just a second.

When I opened them again, it was because Ryan was shaking my shoulder. "Jimmy. It's five a.m. Are you still planning to go into Old Town with the cops?"

I had slept for four hours, but it felt like I had just shut my eyes. "Yeah. Thanks. I better get down there."

"You want some company?"

"Not on this one. My hope is that absolutely nothing happens today." I slid out of the booth. "You should get some sleep."

I found the Coupe out by the curb where I'd left it. On the drive down, I thought about the conversation with Emma. She was right, working with Fogg was incredibly dangerous and that had started to spill out into the rest of my life. Besides her, my cases had pulled Ryan, Ernie and even Patches into harm's way. So far nothing too bad had happened, but one day my luck was bound to run out.

My soul searching stopped as I came upon a large grouping of police cars. This had to be their command post. Cops loved using terms like that instead of 'meeting spot.' When I spoke to Sea Bass the night before, I suggested I go along with them on their sweep. He was hesitant at first, but I assured him my goal was for no one to get hurt and he gave in. I parked the car and got out to find myself greeted by the last cop I wanted to see.

"What are you doing here, Doyle?" Officer Jim De Carlo approached me with a swagger. "This is where the real men go in and take care of the mess you and Fogg created."

"Really? When are the real men getting here?"

A few officers behind him snickered. He wasn't happy about that. De Carlo and I had clashed quite a few times in the past. For every good cop like Ernie Psikla or Detective Lee, there were incompetent cops that just liked the gun and the badge. That was De Carlo. I probably could have played nicer with him, but he was the type that didn't honor the uniform and demanded respect because he wore it. That didn't work for me in the army any more than it did on the streets of New York.

"I could arrest you for obstruction." De Carlo slid his hand to his belt where his cuffs sat.

"You couldn't even spell obstruction." I started walking past him. "I'm here with permission from Detective Lee."

I turned my back on him. Not something you do if you considered a person a threat. He wasn't. I continued walking and could tell he was about to act. The sound of his quickening footsteps behind me, the gasp from one of the other officers. I took a deep breath and got ready to roll with whatever attack he made.

"Put that baton away, De Carlo!" Sea Bass' booming voice rang out. "Unless you want to be the first one hauled in this morning!"

"But Detective!" De Carlo's response sounded more like a child upset that he was caught by his mother. "Doyle doesn't belong here!"

"He's here at my request. Get over it. Or you'll be the one who doesn't belong here."

I caught up with Sebastian as he was looking over a map of Old Town with a few other officers. I could tell by the markings on the map that he was going to do the sweep pattern exactly as we had discussed, giving enough time for Shaw to get the vampires out in the trucks. I could also tell that he assigned Ernie to cover the street Shaw would be using to leave Old Town. Things were set up perfectly. Which almost always meant something was about to go really wrong.

"Would it kill you to be nice to him, just once?"

"Yes." I gave my best innocent smile.

The detective checked his watch and the sun. "I think it's time. Any last words of advice?"

I shrugged. "Don't do this."

"Let's go!"

The cops moved out down Eighty-Second Street and began a building by building search. Six officers would go into each building and search it in pairs. Another six would go into the building on the other side of the street. Three buildings on each side would be searched at the same time while a dozen waited on the street with Sea Bass ready to rush in if they found something. Another thirty officers spread out on different street corners to keep people from entering or exiting the area. Another twenty officers were set up in a bus back at the command center ready to roll at the first sign of trouble. With a hundred officers assigned to this sweep, I wondered how many were left to patrol the rest of the city.

The first hour passed somewhat quietly. There were a few false alarms. De Carlo just about lost it when a cat jumped out at him. But that was the worst of it. A good number of the buildings were abandoned and wide open. Some of them could've been resting places for vampires. The hope was that any resting place that wasn't completely secure would've been abandoned for the truck caravan. Not all of the buildings in Old Town were empty. There were a handful of establishments that catered to those that frequented the area, like Black's club or clothing stores. For werewolves, waking up naked after a full moon was a regular occurrence and a clothing store with a line of credit was a must. But all of those places were in a small area in the center of Old Town.

Every time a building was cleared, Sea Bass would call it in on the radio. I imagined a guy checking off each address on the big map back at the command base. I was starting to wonder why I was there. Either the vampires were great at securing their resting places or Black had done an excellent job convincing them to leave.

We had reached the end of Eighty-Fourth and were about to work over to the next street when I heard a noise. It was from a small alley between two buildings just ahead of the search teams. The detective had been calling in another cleared building at the time, so I was the only one who heard it. I waited until everyone was looking the other way and dashed into the opening between the structures.

The first thing I noticed was the smell of burnt flesh. Then I saw a lump under a blanket, tucked in behind a dumpster. I could hear the police getting closer behind me. I didn't have much time. At the back of the alley was an old wooden door that led into a building over on Eighty-Fifth. I ran over to it and slammed my shoulder against the door. It popped open immediately.

"Get up and come to my voice." The lump didn't move. "I'm a friend of Conrad Black. I will get you to safety, but you need to move now."

The blanket rose and moved quickly. Once in range, I guided it through an opening and closed the door behind us.

"How bad are your burns?" I started looking around for the best way to exit.

"They'll heal."

The blanket slid off and revealed a beautiful, pale skinned woman with wavy shoulder-length brown hair, green eyes and soft-pouty lips. She wore a long leather coat over a dark-blue velvet dress. A pair of black calf-high leather boots matched the coat. She had the body of an athlete mixed with the soft curves of a woman. Another dangerous creature in a pretty package. The skin on the backs of her hands was cracked and charred like a log burnt through to its core.

"What are you doing out here? Didn't you know about the police raid?"

"I was on my way to the trucks with my friend Rollo, but we got separated. I tried to find him but the sun came up before I could get over there." She rubbed one of the burn marks as it healed. "I've been blindly trying to keep ahead of the cops."

"We don't have much time." I glanced out the front window to get my bearings. "We're about four blocks up from Black's club. If anyone has a safe hiding place it will be him. If we go now, we might be able to make it before the cops turn the corner."

I was about to open the front door when she grabbed my arm. "You're a human. Why are you helping me?"

"My name is Jimmy Doyle. I work for Lucius Fogg. That will have to be enough explanation for now."

"I've heard of you. I'm Caitlin Ryder." She smiled and her fangs poked out between her lips.

"Pleasantries can wait. Get that blanket back over your head. It's time to run."

I wrapped my coat around her arm so she could hold it out without her hand being exposed. I grabbed the wrapped limb and lead her out into the street. There was nothing between us and the club. The moment the cops turned the corner, they would see us running. We had no other choice.

I ran, pulling Caitlin along behind me. The heels of her boots tapped loudly against the cement sidewalk. Every hit sounded like a thunder clap that would alert the officers. I didn't look back. I focused on the front door of the club and kept moving. It was just a half a block ahead of us.

We reached the front door and I tried the handle. It was locked. The door was solid wood. I could break it down with a battering ram, but I didn't have one and I didn't think I could go back and borrow Sebastian's. I started looking around for another option. We couldn't just keep jumping into abandoned buildings hoping to keep ahead of the sweep.

"Hey, I see something! Over there!"

Not only had we been spotted, but I could tell by the whine that it was De Carlo. He was frantically waving for back-up and pointing in our direction. I wasn't sure what to do when I heard a voice call out from the side of the building.

"Mr. Doyle! This way, quickly!"

CHAPTER SEVENTEEN

My stone-skinned friend had a habit of turning up to save my bacon. Tiny was a golem that worked at Black's club as a bouncer. Who better to handle unruly vampires than a man made of rock? He was also one of the most well-read and philosophical beings living in the city. And he loved waffles.

"I hope you've got room for a party of two."

I pulled Caitlin by the arm and made for the open side-door. Just before we reached Tiny, the blanket got caught under Caitlin's heel and was pulled off. The sunlight immediately began frying her exposed skin. I flung her by the arm into the open doorway. She crashed into something in the shadows, but it was better than watching her burn up outside. I dove in after her and Tiny slammed the door shut.

"There's no time to get you into the tunnels. You'll have to hide here for now."

Tiny moved over to a large oil painting of a Victorian woman hanging on the wall and swung it open. Behind it was a space about three-foot square. Caitlin and I could squeeze in there, but it would be close quarters. There was no way Tiny was going to fit.

"Where are you going to be?"

Tiny pointed at an open space against the wall, just to the side of the painting.

"I'll be right there, making sure they don't find you." He helped Caitlin to her feet. "You should go first, Mr. Doyle."

I climbed up in and sat down. Tiny lifted Caitlin up and placed her gently into my lap. She looked bad. The sun had done a real number on her. Her face, neck, legs all looked like third degree burns. Any part of her flesh that wasn't covered by clothing got barbequed. She weakly fell against my chest and was completely still. As I looked at her, I noticed that her wounds weren't healing as I would have expected.

Through the door I heard voices. "They went in there! Get the ram!"

Tiny swung the painting back into place, cutting off all light to the hole in the wall. It also cut off the air flow, making the tiny little space fill up with the smell of burnt skin. It was quickly getting hard to breathe. Caitlin remained motionless, pressed against me. I had no idea how she was doing. None of the normal things you'd look for on a human were valid here.

It took three hits with the ram before the door gave way. Black had obviously paid well for it. I could hear a parade of footsteps flood into the room. From what I had seen it was a lounge area, maybe for private parties. It wouldn't take them long to search and then move on to the rest of the club. I suddenly worried about Black. Had we led them to his resting place?

"What are we looking for, De Carlo?" I had a good ear for voices and could tell Sea Bass was there.

"They were a few blocks away, but I saw two people. One was definitely a man. The other was hiding under a blanket or coat. They tried to get in the front door then moved to the side."

The detective barked out orders. "Spread out in teams of two. Sweep through this building quickly. Look for any place that someone could hide. And be careful!"

I could hear as the officers ran out of the room in different directions. I had hoped they'd all leave so I could check on Caitlin, but two voices I didn't recognize stayed.

"Hey, you think this is the Queen of England?"

"No, that's not the Queen. The woman in the painting is much more attractive."

"Well, you're not going to get attractive people if you keep marrying your cousins."

"Are you speaking from experience?"

"Look at this thing!"

"It's a statue. What the big deal?"

"It's in a suit. A very expensive suit. Who would do that?"

"That's called Modern Art. They throw out the conventional for the experimental."

"It's a waste of a good suit if you ask me."

As much as I was enjoying the episode of art-talk, I was very happy to hear Sea Bass return.

"You two, stop gawking at the statue and stand guard outside. No one gets in or out that door unless they're wearing a badge.

"Yes, sir!"

I waited a few more minutes, listening for movement. Tiny tapped once on the wall to tell me the room was empty. I reached up and ran my fingers over Caitlin's face. I could still feel the sharp edges of her burn.

I talked as softly as I could, "Why aren't you healing?"

"The wounds are too severe." Her voice was barely a whisper and broken by pauses. "And I haven't fed in a few days. Don't think I'm going to make it."

I wasn't an expert on vampires, but I knew there was a point where they became too damaged to heal and without blood immediately, their bodies would just shut down. I feared Caitlin was at that point. I slid my hand slowly into my front pants pocket. I had my keys and change in there and didn't want to make any noise. I grabbed what I was searching for and pulled it out just as slowly.

"I just want you to know, I don't do this for every vampire."

I flipped the blade out on my pocket knife and cut small incision across my wrist. Not an easy thing to do in the dark. Once I felt the blood start to flow, I put my arm against her lips and told her to drink. It was slow at first. Like the blood was just trickling into her mouth and running down her throat. But after a few seconds, her natural instincts kicked in and she began to suck the liquid from my vein.

It wasn't the first time I had a vampire drawing blood from my arm. Black saved me from my own curse once by draining me. But this time was different. I could feel her lips against my skin, her tongue dancing over the open cut. Each time she swallowed, I felt a pull from somewhere deep inside me. I could feel the strength leave my body with each drop she took. The darkness that surrounded us seemed to be getting blacker. I felt like I was leaving my own body. I knew I had to stop her, but I couldn't. My arms wouldn't move.

Then she pushed my arm away. I don't know if she could tell how much she had taken or if she sensed my building panic. Either way, it was over. I felt dizzy and tried to regain my composure. She wrapped a cloth of some kind around my wrist and tied it off to stop the bleeding.

I felt her lips brush against my ear as she whispered, "Thank you."

She then laid her head back down on me and I could feel the soft skin of her cheek against my neck. I allowed myself to drift off for a moment, hoping to regain my strength.

"This building is clear. Everyone back out to the street so we can continue the sweep." Sea Bass came into range. "And someone tell De Carlo he's got a mandatory eye examination next week."

I heard the cops move out of the room, but I wasn't going to budge. Wasn't sure I had the strength to push back the painting if I wanted to. A few moments later the point became moot as Tiny let us out. Caitlin sprang down to the floor looking a lot healthier.

"Are you well, Ms. Ryder?"

"Yes, Tiny. Thanks to our friend here." Caitlin reached out and helped me down.

I was a bit unsteady, but I could stand. I looked around the room. The police had moved things about but didn't do much damage. Tiny led us through the club to the far back corner. He moved a mirrored panel that revealed a passageway.

"This will take you to one of Mr. Black's resting places. It's perfectly secure." Tiny gestured towards the opening.

"One of?" I was curious.

"He has seven at the moment."

"Okay. Caitlin, get to safety." I took my coat back from her and slipped it on. "I'd better meet back up with the police or they'll start to think De Carlo actually saw something."

"You're still weak from the feeding." Caitlin seemed to be truly concerned.

"I'll manage. Now get going."

Caitlin looked at me for a moment, then ducked into the passageway. Tiny replaced the mirrored panel and walked me towards the other side of the club.

"Are you sure you're okay, Mr. Doyle?"

"I'm fine. When this is all done, we'll meet up for waffles."

"I'd like that." He pointed to another door I hadn't seen before. "This will let you out into the back alley. No one should see you leave."

"Thanks, Tiny."

I patted him on the shoulder, forgetting he was made of stone. My hand stung from the gesture. I headed out into the alley and he closed the door behind me. I few unsure steps later I was back on the main street and I could see Sea Bass about a hundred yards ahead.

"Find anything?" I asked as I approached.

"No. Where did you wander off to?"

"You know me. Can't help but find trouble."

He looked at me closely. "You definitely found it, didn't you?"

He grabbed me by the arm just as my legs began to buckle. He then looked down and saw the cloth around my wrist. It turned out to be a handkerchief. He grabbed his radio and opened the channel.

"I need a squad car to the corner of Eighty-Fifth and Second Avenue."

"On its way, Detective." The radio chimed back.

"What happened?"

"I found one. She was trapped. I had to get her to safety."

"And she needed to feed on you?" He looked worried.

"Yeah, she did. It wasn't my brightest idea." The strength returned to my legs and I stood on my own. "Are you going to arrest me?"

"No, I'm sending you home to rest. You look like hell."

The squad car pulled up and Sebastian opened the passenger side door for me. As I got in he told the driver to take me back to my car. I nodded my thanks and leaned my head back against the seat rest. It had just turned eight a.m. on what was going to be a long day.

CHAPTER EIGHTEEN

I was in no condition to deal with the press outside of Fogg's place and the bar was closer. Ryan had given me a key to the place when I had stayed in the apartment upstairs for a while. He'd never asked for it back. So I drove there and crashed out in the back booth again. About two o'clock Ryan woke me with one of Willie's cheese steaks and a beer. I couldn't remember the last time I'd eaten, so I wolfed it down and asked if Willie could make another. The food was making me feel normal again.

Ryan dropped the second sandwich in front of me. "Ernie stopped by a little while ago. Said you'd be happy to hear that the police found nothing."

"That's good news." I bit into the second sandwich, the melted cheese oozing across my tongue.

"He also said the police chief was going to have a press conference downtown at four to try and alleviate some of the people's fear."

"I should probably be there."

"I figured you'd say that. Ernie will be back in a half hour and we can all go together."

"Don't you have a bar to run?" I held up my half empty glass to emphasize my point.

"I've got someone coming in to cover for me." He grabbed my first empty plate and walked back to the bar. "Besides, Ernie has to be there anyway. And I'm starting to feel left out."

"Well, we don't want you to get your feelings hurt."

Ryan came back over and tossed a first aid kit on the table. "Here, put a proper bandage on that wrist or Emma will kick your butt."

I unwrapped the handkerchief as Ryan went back to work. The cut had stopped bleeding, but was still raw. I poured some antiseptic on it then covered it with gauze and a few strips of tape. It wasn't the first time I'd had to patch myself up, but never before from a self-inflicted wound. Which made me wonder why I had done it that way. Was it the most efficient thing to do or was explaining a mundane knife gash easier than a bite mark? Twenty minutes later I was no closer to the answer, but both my beer and second sandwich were gone. I tucked the handkerchief into my jacket pocket just as Ernie arrived.

Ryan grabbed his coat and headed for the door. "Let's go."

On the drive downtown, Ernie filled me in on how well the truck convoy had worked.

"Sea Bass ordered us back to the station around three. I signaled Shaw's man that it was clear for the trucks to return. The Detective also told us that continued sweeps were not likely since we found nothing. Seems the police chief is good friends with the mayor and he plans on reading Drake the riot act for trying to spread panic in the city."

"Couldn't happen to a more deserving guy." I started looking for a parking spot as we got close. "I might actually enjoy this. Let's hope this finishes whatever Drake is up to."

Normally any press briefings done by the police were held in a small room on the first floor with a couple chairs and a table where they put out donuts and coffee. This was different. Between the press, visiting officials who wanted to be seen as part of it and regular people off the street who wanted to know firsthand what was going on, the whole thing had to be moved outside. The podium was set up on the top of the stairs that led to the front doors. There were more than a few thousand people about. How many more I wasn't sure and I didn't feel like counting.

It wasn't long before the police chief, the mayor, a few other men in suits who I'd never seen before and Sea Bass walked up to the podium. The chief stood at the microphone and addressed the assembled audience.

"Thank you all for coming. As many of you know, an absolutely incredible allegation was made yesterday that vampires and werewolves not only existed, but resided in an area of the city called Old Town. Now I could have assured you then that we had seen no evidence of that. But I'm certain that the same person who made these wild charges would also claim that my word was not enough. So this morning I ordered one of my best men, Detective Sebastian Lee, to take one hundred officers and sweep through Old Town. They did a building by building search and found nothing out of the ordinary. No vampires. No werewolves. No zombies. I want to assure you that there is nothing to worry about. The city is a safe place to live and will remain that way."

The chief opened the floor to questions and the first one was about the man who started the rumors.

"I don't know this Kieran Drake. But it's obvious to me that he is attempting to use panic and fear-mongering to try and steal this election away from Mayor Harris, a man who has worked tirelessly for the benefit of the people of New York. I also want to warn Drake that any continued attempts to rile up the city into a panic will force me to look into the legal ramifications of his actions. As it is now, I am thinking of sending him a bill for the man hours we wasted today on his accusations."

A man shouted from the back of the crowd. "I hope you don't pay these incompetent dolts you call the NYPD much then, because they're not worth more than a penny a day."

The crowd started to buzz. I couldn't see who said it, but the reaction was obvious. The reporters backed off, clearing a path. Then I saw him, at the base of the steps. Kieran Drake half addressed the police chief and half the crowd. Behind him was a man rolling a large crate on a dolly.

"You've got some nerve showing up here, Drake." The chief was furious. "I have half a mind to…"

"Half a mind? Well that would explain a lot." Kieran instructed his man to put the crate down. "You just said that your best man took one hundred of your officers into Old Town and found nothing. Is that correct?"

"It most certainly is!" the chief growled. "And I don't appreciate you coming down here and accusing my men of incompetence!"

"Well, that's fine. Let's let the work speak for itself. Before your hundred man march through the town, I took two men in with me and look what I found."

The front panel of the crate dropped open and I could see someone inside. He was hiding in the back desperately trying to stay in the shadows. I had a good guess what Drake was about to do. I began pushing my way through the crowd. The sheer number of people made it difficult to move.

"My friend Rollo here is a little shy. Not one for the spotlight you see. Let's bring him into the light. Help him out won't you."

The man with Drake popped the top off of the crate. The vampire in the box let out a horrific scream as the sun beat down on him. I pushed past the last few reporters and into the opening just as Rollo's skin burst into flames. Before I could take another two steps, he was turning to ash before all of our eyes.

Drake waited for a moment. He let the shock race through everyone, getting the full effect. Then he kicked the pile of ashes up into the air causing them to spread out over the crowd.

"I spent five minutes in Old Town and I found a vampire. Yet the police want you to think you're perfectly safe. Why? So you'll go to the polls and re-elect the lazy, good-for-nothing mayor you've been saddled with for years. And if Detective Lee is one of the best men on the force, then you all will want to lock your doors tight this evening."

He walked the crowd, working each and every one of them like a professional. Then he saw me. A smile slid across his face like he had just found a hundred dollar bill in the street. Whatever his plan was, I had just given him a new piece to play.

"And look who came rushing forward to help the vampire. Jimmy Doyle. You all know Jimmy, right? The trusted right-hand man of the enigmatic Lucius Fogg. All those bizarre cases Fogg has solved, how many of them do you think were involving the supernatural? My guess is all of them. Then he and his city official friends covered the truth up over and over again. You think I'm wrong? Well, ask yourself this. How many of you would try and help a dying vampire? Maybe that's why they found no vampires. They told their friend Lucius Fogg about the raid so he could get them out. That sounds like the worst kind of corruption, the kind that puts the people in danger!"

He then walked directly over to me and spoke so only I could hear. "Are you enjoying the show?"

I wanted to answer him with my fist, but I knew that would just make matters worse. Not that they hadn't already gone to hell.

"In the next few days, I'm sure stories will start to come out about me." He was speaking to the people now and not the podium. "They'll try to tell you some things to make you think I'm not trustworthy. But I'm all about honesty. So let me tell you before they do. Let me tell you my big secret. Ladies and gentlemen, I am a sorcerer!"

The crowd fell silent again. Drake took that moment to create a small series of magic butterflies made out of light. Then the butterflies began to interweave, around and around until all of the movement took on a shape of its own. The light formed an eagle that suddenly soared into the sky then exploded out like a Fourth-of-July firework. He really was putting on quite a show.

"I have studied the arcane arts and I can perform some magic. I did this to protect myself from the evil in this world. The evil that has been kept from you for years. I have the ability to defend myself, but I want to help defend you as well. I want to rid this city not only of the supernatural, but of the corruption and dishonesty that put you all at risk in the first place. I want to make New York City the safest and most secure place in the world to live. And with your help, I can make that happen. With your help, we can make this a world where humans are in charge again. All you have to do is to go into the voting booths on Tuesday, skip over the printed drivel and write in the name Kieran Drake."

Drake then walked up to the podium, pushed the police chief aside and spoke into the microphone.

"I'm not going to wait for Election Day though. I am going to start making changes now. The head of the vampire community in Old Town is named Conrad Black. I call for Black to come meet me at midnight tonight just outside of City Hall. We can discuss how his kind can leave the city peacefully by Tuesday. If he fails to show, then I will use the magic I know to rid this town of vampires once and for all."

CHAPTER NINETEEN

After the show at police headquarters and Drake calling out Conrad Black, I knew it was time to check in with Fogg. I headed back to the brownstone and parked a few blocks down. I figured keeping the Coupe a secret from the press was probably a good idea. I'd hoped some of the group camped out around the place had moved on. I wasn't so lucky.

I got to the corner and was trying to come up with a way to get in when I heard a tap on a window behind me. I was standing in front of the corner diner and the tapping came from Patches. He waved me inside and I followed.

"Heya, Boss." The kid pointed to the seat opposite of him. "I've been watching for ya."

"You got news for me?" I sat down.

"Not so much news, but someone you can talk to." He turned and gestured toward the waitress behind the counter. "That's Ethel. She was here the other night when Mr. Whiskers showed up. She's the one that suddenly went for a walk."

Ethel strolled over with her notebook in hand to take an order. She was a cute girl with a roundish face, big eyes and a friendly smile. A few freckles danced across her cheeks and a bob of brown hair framed her face like a heart. The uniform they made her wear wasn't flattering at all, giving the illusion that she carried ten pounds more than she did. She flashed an innocent smile as she stood next to the table.

"What can I get ya?"

"Let me have a cup of hot tea." I looked over at Patches, he was anxious. "And anything the boy wants."

"Let me have an egg salad sandwich and a root beer." He practically said all the words at once.

"I'm sorry, sweetie. The cook just discovered the egg salad has turned. Can I get you something else?"

"How about a grilled cheese?"

"Sure thing."

She was about to walk away when I had an idea. "Have you tossed out the egg salad yet?"

"Not yet."

"I want to buy it. All of it. Make as many sandwiches as you can out of it. On whatever bread you've got. It can be day old slices if you have them. Wrap them up and put them in a bag for me."

She looked at me funny but agreed to do it. She brought out my tea and Patches' sandwich and root beer first. He tore through both with abandon. When she came back with the sack full of egg salads, I handed them to Patches and told him what I wanted him to do. The boy laughed, grabbed the bag and ran off. I turned to Ethel.

"You mind if I ask you a couple of questions?"

She looked around at the practically empty diner and nodded. "Sure."

"My young friend was telling me about Halloween night, when the cat came in and you suddenly left. What do you remember?"

I could tell by the look on her face that she was still confused about what happened.

"This cute cat came in and hopped up on the counter. I tried to pet it and then things got kind of weird."

"Weird in what way?"

"It was like I was suddenly a passenger in my own mind." She sat down in the seat across from me. "I found myself walking out the door. Frank was yelling at me to come back, and I tried. I mean I really tried to turn around, but my body wasn't listening. And then..." She turned to look out the window.

"Go on."

"No. You'll think I'm crazy." She started to shift in her seat.

"I'm not going to think anything, Ethel." I put my hand out on top of hers. "You've seen me around here. You must know I work for Lucius Fogg. The weird is my specialty. There is nothing you can tell me that I haven't heard worse."

She relaxed a bit and her smile returned. "It'd probably be good to tell someone."

I sipped my tea as she collected her thoughts. I could see that she hadn't told anyone the whole story yet as she was trying to put the pieces in order in her mind. When she finally did speak, it came out like she was giving a witness statement to the police.

"I'm not exactly sure what time it was. Frank doesn't let me wear a watch with the uniform and I got too busy that night to check the clock. When the cat wandered in, it seemed odd. I grew up around cats. When a cat enters a room it doesn't know, it sniffs around a lot, moves slowly, checking for safety. But this cat just stormed right in, looked around once and headed straight for me."

"Were you the only woman in the place?"

"Let me think." She put her head to the side and frowned for a moment. "I believe so. Does that matter? Is it because I'm a girl?"

"I'm not sure." I tapped the back of her hand gently. "Please continue."

"Like I said, the cat came straight for me. I reached down to pet it and I felt something. Like a shock of electricity. But not just on my hand, like all over. And then everything felt weird. My body wasn't doing what I wanted it to. And I could remember things I had never done before. Like I remember this street before the diner was built, but it's been here since before I was born."

"Do you remember the names Natasha or Kieran?"

"Yes, both of them. What does that mean?"

"I'll let you know once you're done with the story. Go on, please."

"Okay." She looked around again to see if anyone needed her then continued. "It was like there was someone else in my head with me and they were calling the shots. As I, or we, walked away, I dug into my pockets and counted the tip money I had taken in. Then I hailed a taxi and went over to a YWCA and slept there for the night. I figured it was all some odd dream and I'd wake up in the morning in my own bed. But it was all the same in the morning."

"Did you sign in at the front desk?"

"Yes. I signed in as Natasha Drake. That's where I first came across the name. And the Kieran name the next morning on signs on the street. But the name was already in my memories. I could picture spending time with him through the years. It was all very strange."

"I'm sure it was." I tried to keep her on track. "What did you do the next morning?"

"I walked over to a thrift shop and found a pretty dress that fit me. Then I put it on along with a pair of pumps and used the last of my tip money to pay for it. It wasn't a color or cut I would normally pick, but it did look good on me. I still have the dress if you want to see it."

"No, that's okay. Where did you go in the dress?"

"I went downtown to the First Union Bank. When I got in there, I looked around until I found a woman working there. She handled new accounts. I went up, shook her hand and I felt the electricity thing again. Then I was back in control of my body. I was alone again in my head."

"What did the woman from the bank do?"

"It was weird. She smiled, thanked me for the ride and gave me two dollars for a cab home." Ethel shook her head. "I was so shocked I took the money and left."

"Do you remember what the woman's name was?"

Ethel looked to the side and frowned again. "No, I never got her name. Can you tell me what all of that meant?"

"A lot of strange things happen in this world, Ethel. Not all of them can be explained." I held her hand once more. "It could be anything from something spiritual to you happened upon another bad batch of egg salad. The important thing is you didn't get hurt and you ended up with a new dress."

"I'm still a bit worried."

"I'll tell you what. I'll go speak with my boss. Tell him what you told me. If he thinks it's anything serious, I'll come right back here and tell you what to do about it. And if I don't come back then you know everything will be okay. How does that sound?"

This time she smiled wide enough to show off her dimples. "That sounds good. Thank you."

Ethel got up and left just as Patches returned. He slid back into the seat and pushed a paper over to me.

"I did what you asked." He looked like he wanted a pat on the head. "Also, one of the guys had the late edition. I thought you should see it."

The headline read 'The Vampires Have A Leader.' It wasn't shocking since that was what Drake had told everyone. The interesting one was the second story, the one just below the fold: 'Fogg's Connection to Black.' The story intimated that Lucius and Conrad went back for more than a hundred years. Which might be true, but there was only one way they could have that information. Drake had to give it to them directly. He was feeding the media the stories he wanted printed. He was controlling the narrative and doing a damn good job of it.

"Thanks." I reached in my pocket for some cash to pay the bill. "You want another sandwich and soda?"

"That would be great, Boss."

I told Ethel to give the kid another round and left her enough for the bill and a good tip. I then headed out the door to see if my ploy had worked. I had Patches run the egg salad sandwiches over to the reporters as a gift from someone who admired their dedication to journalism. I waited until it was exactly sundown and then I made my way right for the crowd at the front door.

"Jimmy Doyle! Have you met with Conrad Black? Did you know he was a vampire? Is Lucius Fogg a vampire?" The questions just kept coming.

I put my hands up to make them stop. "Hold on. I'm here to tell you guys something."

I walked over to the front steps and turned around to face them all, giving myself a little stage to stand on. They had their pencils out and cameras at the ready for some juicy bit of news.

"Your papers have claimed a lot of things about Fogg. Some have suggested he's a warlock, others that he taps into the spirit world. You all seem to think he's a very powerful person. Yet you stand here on his front porch, pestering him. Not a good idea. The last time this happened, was a reporter who wanted an exclusive. After Fogg put up with the man for a while, something happened. He suddenly got very ill. Not life threatening, but any time he got near the house he would become sick to his stomach. He couldn't get within ten feet of the front door without having to vomit."

I could see the worried faces begin to spread through the crowd. One or two even put their hands on their stomachs.

"Now, Fogg has been more than tolerant of your staking out his house, but I think that tolerance is coming to an end. I would suggest you leave now before you start feeling ill. Unless, of course, it's already too late."

I watched as the reporters looked at each other. A few seemed to turn a bit green. They were all trying to understand what I had just said and what it meant to them. And then the first one threw up. What followed would only have been more brilliant if it had been set to the old Keystone Cops music. The reporters scrambled back to their cars, some stopping to be sick which would in turn cause others to be sick. It took a good five minutes until all of them had reached their cars and left. I felt bad for the street cleaners that would be coming by in the morning.

I turned to make my grand exit into the house, the end of a perfect scene. Except I had to play with the damn key in the lock again. I thought about the spell Fogg had given me, but decided against it. Magic was for emergencies, not for convenience. I was even more determined to find out why Fogg wouldn't let me change the lock. At least I was home and the press was gone. Back to the real problems.

CHAPTER TWENTY

I was about to close the door when I noticed a sea-green Morris Minor sedan pull up at the curb. It wasn't the small car itself that caught my eye but rather the giant-sized figure in the passenger seat. I watched in awe as the stone golem unfolded himself and squeezed through the door of a car I would have trouble getting in and out of. Once he was out, I could see Dorothea sitting behind the wheel giving me a friendly wave.

"I don't think I've ever seen you this far up town, Tiny."

"Mr. Black had a message for Mr. Fogg he needed delivered right away." The golem closed the door to the car.

"Black could just get a telephone." I tossed out the line I always used on Conrad.

"I don't see that ever happening."

Dorothea called to me from the open window, "Jimmy, I need to go pick up some supplies for tomorrow. Would you be a dear and see that Tiny gets back home okay?"

"I'd be happy to."

"Thank you. Give my best to Lucius."

With that the engine of the Morris whined back to life and Dorothea sped off on her way. I stepped back, holding the door wide so Tiny could enter. Once inside the foyer, I asked him to wait while I saw if Fogg was in his office. Tiny was a friend, but even still, I didn't take anyone in without the letting my boss know beforehand.

I entered the office and found Fogg at his desk. He was putting together what looked to be an Erector Set. My natural curiosity wanted to ask what he was building, but the urgency of the day, the stone man in the hallway and my uneasy fear that I wouldn't like the answer prevented me from inquiring.

"Jimmy, glad you are here." Fogg looked up from his work. "I assume you have news to report?"

"Quite a bit actually, but first we've got a guest with a message from Conrad."

"Please show them in."

I stepped back out to the foyer and motioned Tiny inside. I realized at that moment I had no idea if Tiny had ever met Fogg before. He'd never been to the brownstone since I'd been there and I knew Fogg hadn't left in sixty-five years. But I also had no idea how old the golem was, or at least how long he'd been animated. I was about to introduce them just in case. It turned out I didn't need to.

"Hello, Father." Tiny stood with his head slightly down and his hands crossed in front of him.

"Timothy!" Fogg rose quickly and came around to meet his guest. "It's so good to see you. How have you been?"

"Up until these recent events, things have been wonderful. Thank you for all the books you've sent." There was a small smile on his stone face. "I've read each one, cover to cover."

"I will send some new ones on to Dorothea in a few days then."

I was floored. Father? Timothy? Fogg sending books? With all the time I spent chatting with Tiny never once did he say his name was Timothy or mention any kind of connection with Fogg. I knew that he was a voracious reader, but I never thought to ask where he got his books. Stunned, I walked over to my desk and sat down while watching the two of them interact.

Fogg pointed toward the red leather chair. "Have a seat. Would you like anything? I could have Ariel make up some waffles."

"No, thank you." He sat. "Mr. Black asked me to come see you."

"Yes, Jimmy said you had a message." Fogg sat back in his chair. "Is Conrad okay?"

"He is. But there are some things that happened today you may not know about yet." He looked over to me. "Maybe Mr. Doyle should fill you in first."

Fogg turned to me without a word, a silent signal to begin. I pushed my confusion about the two of them aside and caught him up on the police raid of Old Town and my meeting with Caitlin. I told him about the press conference and how Drake allowed a vampire to burn in the sun in view of the media and then called out Conrad specifically. I threw in the part about meeting Ethel and the egg salad sandwiches and then I turned the floor back to the golem.

"Mr. Black wanted to let you know that he will not be confronting Drake. He figures its best to give you another day to resolve this issue."

Fogg nodded, "I appreciate that."

"There is a problem though." Tiny looked over at me. "The young lady you helped this morning, Ms. Ryder, she and the vampire that Drake killed were friends."

"You mean Rollo?"

"Yes. He was very popular with the newer vampires and word is they are going to defy Mr. Black's orders and go after Drake themselves."

Fogg glared at me. "It seems one taste of your blood makes even a vampire rebellious."

"What can I say? It's genetic."

Fogg leaned back in his chair. "I still don't have any idea what Drake's end game is. This can't all be about becoming mayor. It's too pedestrian a job to matter to him."

"You can keep looking at the big picture, but that doesn't solve the initial problem about tonight." I pulled my Old Town bag of tricks out of the drawer. "Now I can go down there and try to keep things from getting out of hand. But in this case, the vampires are on the side of right and my bag here doesn't have anything to stop a warlock. At least not one on your level."

"No. I don't want you going tonight." Fogg shook his head. "We're not ready to confront Drake yet."

"Whatever his plan is, it's been going off like clockwork." I got up and crossed over to his desk. "And I'm certain that his plans don't involve a peaceful exodus of the vampires. Black isn't going because he knows it's a trap. Which means the vampires who are going have no chance. We can't let them walk into a slaughter."

"That's a lot of pure speculation. And you said it yourself, you have nothing in your bag to stop a warlock on my level. And Kieran Drake is definitely my level. So what could you possibly hope to accomplish by going other than your own death?"

"At least I would be trying." I glared at him for once. "Instead of sitting back in my chair and trying to guess at Drake's next move. You can't win if you don't play."

"This isn't a game!"

"I know!"

We both fell silent. Fogg and I were very different people, but we always wanted the same outcome. His approach tended to be more cerebral than mine. He wanted to outthink his opponent like in a chess game. I was more of a force of nature type, pick a direction to go and damned be anything in my way. Which made it even harder to admit when his way was the right way.

"You're right." I turned and leaned against his desk, my back to him. "There is nothing I can do to change whatever is going to happen and it drives me crazy to admit it. I've felt like a Chihuahua trying to pull down a Mastiff since Halloween night and I don't like it. It's not in my nature to stop trying, but even I have to eventually accept when there is nothing I can do."

Fogg stood and put his hand on my shoulder. "We will stop Drake. We just need more time."

"That's not something we have a lot of. So I hope you figure this out soon."

Fogg walked over to Tiny. "I wish I had more time to spend with you, Timothy. But I need to get back to my research. When this is all over, will you come back and visit?"

Tiny got up and lowered his head again. "Of course, Father."

"I'm going to my library. Jimmy, please drive Timothy back to the edge of Old Town." Fogg stopped in the doorway and looked back. "With any luck, I will have figured this out by the time you get back."

I dropped my bag of tricks back into the drawer, but slipped my revolver into my pocket anyway. I then led Tiny to the front door where Ariel was waiting. She stepped up and wrapped her arms around the golem, giving him a hug. It was one of the oddest and cutest things I had ever seen. I grabbed my coat and hat as we headed out the door.

The walk to the Coupe went quietly, but once inside the car I had to ask. "I wasn't sure you even knew Fogg. Why do you call him 'Father'?"

"He created me and sent me to watch over Mr. Black."

"Wait. You work for Conrad at Fogg's request?"

"I'm told that when Mr. Fogg could no longer leave his home, he still wanted to help Mr. Black control Old Town and keep him safe. So he made me to do what he couldn't."

"And your name?"

"My name is Timothy. Tiny is just a nickname one of the vampires at the club gave me."

"Because of your size I take it?"

"No. When Mr. Fogg sent me to Old Town, he gave me a stack of books to read so I wouldn't get bored during the day time when everyone was asleep or gone. The first book I read was *A Christmas Carol* by Charles Dickens."

"Of course. Tiny Tim."

"So when someone calls me Tiny, it reminds me of the first gift my father gave me."

"And he continues to send you books?"

Tiny smiled. "Every other Tuesday I walk up to Dorothea's and pick up three or four new books from him. We also play chess through the mail."

Even after all the years I'd been working for Fogg, he was still able to amaze me. Here I learned that not only was he capable of being in love, he was also capable of parental feelings. I was seeing parts of him that he had kept well hidden. And with enemies like Kieran Drake, I could understand him keeping those things a secret.

I fired up the Coupe. "Let's get you home."

Tiny reached across and put his stone hand on my arm. "No. I'm going with you."

"What?"

"You and I have talked a lot and I think I know you pretty well. I know you have no intention of going back to the brownstone after you drop me off." He lifted his hand. "I consider you my friend. I also consider protecting Caitlin and the other vampires part of my job. So, I'm going with you."

I knew arguing with him was going to be a waste of time. I weighed the benefits of having a stone juggernaut with me against the hell I would get if anything would happen to him... from both Black and Fogg. But in the end, his insisting on going was no different than mine. I fired up the car and we took off toward Howard's.

"Okay. You win. We'll need a place to hang out for a few hours." I smiled at him. "Have you ever tried single malt Scotch?"

CHAPTER TWENTY-ONE

I parked the Coupe in the alley and went in through the back. A quick move into my favorite booth and I didn't have to explain to any of the patrons why a statue had just come in for a drink. With his back to the other customers, Tiny just looked like a really big guy squeezed into a booth. I caught Ryan's eye and signaled for him to bring two Scotches. A minute later he carried over a bottle of fifteen-year old and four glasses.

Ryan slid into the booth next to me and put the bottle and glasses down. Ernie was right behind him. When the cop saw how little room there was on the other side, he grabbed a loose chair from one of the tables and sat on the outside edge of the booth. He picked up the first glass, poured three fingers worth of alcohol and slid it to me. It was then that he finally looked at Tiny.

"Uhm. I have no other way to ask this." Ernie tilted his head a little as he stared. "Are you made of stone?"

"I'm a golem."

"Of course you are." Ernie turned to me. "Good guy or bad?"

"Definitely good."

"Works for me."

Ernie poured a glass and gave it to Tiny. I did the usual introductions, letting them know that Tiny worked for Conrad Black and the rest. The golem took a swig of the Scotch and his eyes got huge.

"You drink this? On purpose?" Tiny tried to hold back a cough.

I laughed. "It takes a few sips before it wins you over."

Ernie got us back on topic with some interesting news of his own. "We've been ordered to stay clear of City Hall tonight."

"Ordered by who?" I asked.

"Well, it came from the police chief, but everyone knows that Harris is behind it." Ernie took a drink. "I think he's hoping that Black shows up and kills Drake for him, putting an end to all of this."

"I'd love to see that. But it won't be Black. He knows it's a trap and is skipping it."

Ryan laughed. "It's going to be a boring night for Drake."

"No, it's not. A couple of young vampires have taken great exception to Drake letting one of theirs burn up. They're going after him tonight."

Ernie's eyebrow rose. "Is Fogg sending you two in to stop it?"

"Nope. I am currently driving Tiny to Old Town and then I'm racing back to the brownstone. We were both told to stay out of it by our bosses, just like you were."

Ernie shook his head a bit. "What time are we heading to City Hall?"

"Now wait…" I began to protest but Ryan stopped me.

"We can go through the whole song and dance where you tell us it's too dangerous and not our responsibility and so on. But you know in the end that we are going to go. Do you really want to waste all that time and effort?"

I knew it was useless. They wouldn't listen to me any more than I did to Fogg. If I tried to leave them behind, they'd just show up there anyway. For some men doing the right thing is almost impossible. For others, it's impossible not to do it.

We had a few hours to kill and the boys found Tiny to be a great audience to tell stories. Especially stories that made me look bad. Both Ryan and Ernie had their fair share of tales like that to tell. We also introduced the stone giant to the joys of a Philly cheesesteak and fries. I knew these wouldn't replace waffles on his favorites list, but he seemed to like them very much.

"Officer Psikla, do you mind if I ask you a question?"

"Go for it."

"Mr. Doyle told me in the past about having served in the army with Mr. Aquino. But he's never told me the story of how you two met."

Ernie stopped and looked at me for a minute. He knew I hated hearing the story. He hated telling it. We'd ducked this question a few times before. Even Ryan didn't know the full truth. I nodded to him to let him know it was okay to tell if he wanted to.

"We met on a case a few years ago." Ernie sat back a bit in his chair. "I'd been on the force a couple years at most. I think Jimmy had just started working for Fogg. A kid went missing on his way home from school. Keith Brooks. He was nine. He was a good student, didn't cause any trouble. When he didn't make it home, the parents started looking for him. When no one had seen him by the next morning they called the police. I was dispatched."

Tiny seemed confused. "By yourself? Why would they send just one officer to find a missing child?"

"Because he wasn't from the right part of town. He didn't have white skin, blue eyes and blond hair so one officer was all the higher ups would send. I coordinated with the family. Figured out where they had searched, made of list of places he might have gone, talked to a few people at the school. After a few hours I knew something was really wrong. The boy had just vanished. So I called in to request more officers to help expand the search. I was told my shift was over and to return to the station.

"I didn't leave, though. I had just decided I would continue searching on my own when Jimmy showed up out of nowhere. He introduced himself and told me he worked for Lucius Fogg. Even back then Fogg had a reputation of dealing with weird things. Jimmy had a map of the city with circles on it."

I decided to jump in at that point. "Fogg had been tracking reports of missing children in the area. Keith was the seventh. Fogg figured that it was a single person doing the abductions and that whoever it was would have a hunting ground not far from their base of operations. We'd mapped all the abductions and created a five mile perimeter around them. With each abduction we were able to narrow down the suspected area. With Keith, we'd gotten it down to a two mile stretch of homes and apartments."

Ernie picked it back up from there, "I wasn't sure what to make of him at first, but Jimmy was there offering to help. He and I started going door to door looking for Keith. I called in sick the next day so we could keep going. After hours and hours of walking and knocking, we'd found nothing. I was almost ready to give up when Jimmy started asking me about the people I had seen. A lot of them had become a blur at that point, but he kept trying to focus me in. Describing to me the type of person we'd be looking for. I wasn't sure where he'd gotten his facts from and I was too tired to ask. I just kept thinking as he talked. It would be a person living alone. A very well cared for place, maybe too well cared for. It would most likely be a house as apartments would be hard to get a kid into without someone seeing you.

"As he kept pushing, my mind would flash back to one particular old man with a perfectly manicured lawn. He was a bone skinny guy with thinning gray hair and yellowish skin. He didn't stand up straight, his head was always down and his back hunched. I met him at his door and I could see the living room. The furniture all had plastic covers on them. There were no pictures on the walls. The recliner still had the price tag hanging from it. As I described it all to Jimmy, I could see by his face I was on the right track.

"We drove around looking for the house. It took a little while as again, a lot of stuff had blurred together. Once I found the house we made a plan. I would go to the door with some follow up questions. Jimmy would sneak around back and try to get a look into the other rooms. When the old man answered, he wasn't happy that I was back. He grumbled about my wasting his time. I was scrambling to make up questions when the old man suddenly spun around and ran into the other room yelling. 'Get away from them!' I followed."

Ernie stopped at that point and poured himself another drink. Neither of us had talked about that day since. I could have gone my whole life without ever hearing the story again and been happy. But he'd gotten to that point, so he was going to finish.

"I followed him through a door and down a set of stairs into the basement. Jimmy stood in the center of the room having climbed in through a small window. He stood on a white sheet that had been laid on the ground. The sheet was stained with both dried and fresh blood. The floor was littered with bones and skulls, all too small to be adults. In his arms Jimmy held the body of Keith Brooks. Part of the flesh from his legs and chest were missing. They'd been bitten off.

"I called it in. Detective Lee was the first on the scene. Jimmy and I were sitting on the front porch. Inside the detective found the old man's body filled with both .38 and .45 caliber bullets. The coroner found eighteen different bodies in the basement. No one knew if that was all of them or if he had already disposed of some corpses. I heard Jimmy tell Sea Bass that the old man was a fiend. I didn't know what that was, but I knew it didn't need to exist. I was never questioned about what happened. Never disciplined for disobeying an order. Never even asked to fill out a report. It was just never mentioned again."

When Ernie had finished, we sat silently for a while finishing our drinks. Ernie stared at his glass so intently I thought it would melt. Tiny finally broke the silence.

"Thank you for telling us, Officer Psikla."

"Why do you do that?" Ernie looked up. "Why do you refer to everyone as Mr. Doyle, Mr. Aquino, Officer Psikla? You can call me Ernie."

"I appreciate that, but you have the honor of having a surname. A lineage that you are connected to. I want to show proper respect to that."

Ryan looked puzzled. "You don't have a surname?"

"No. I was given a first name only."

"Well, we can't let that stand." Ryan smiled. "Let me think about it and we'll find you a good surname."

The clock above the bar told me we should head out. We piled out of the booth and headed through the back door to the Coupe. We were about to get in and go when Ryan stopped.

"This isn't fair. Tiny is disobeying Black. You're disobeying Fogg. Even Ernie is disobeying the Police Chief. I feel left out again."

"Fine. Ryan, go back inside the bar and wait for us. I don't want you going."

"To hell with you, Jimmy. You can't stop me." Ryan jumped into the back seat.

I got behind the wheel and looked at him in the mirror. "You feel better?"

"Much. Let's go."

CHAPTER TWENTY-TWO

We parked a few blocks away and approached City Hall on foot. Ernie knew of an office building across the street where the tenants had recently been removed by the police for illegal bookmaking. They thought it was funny to sit across from the mayor committing crimes. We were able to enter though the service entrance. Ernie and the night watchmen were on a first name basis.

"Hey, Ernie. What you doing here so late?"

"Evening, Paul. We wanted to keep an eye on this thing over at City Hall."

"You mean the Kieran Drake guy calling out the vampires? Sounds like a bunch of hooey to me."

"I hope you're right." Ernie patted Paul on the back as he walked past. "But it's better to be safe than sorry, right?"

"You know it, my friend."

Paul tipped his hat to the rest of us as we headed up the stairs to the second floor. We were a night away from the full-moon, but that was still more than enough light pouring in through the windows for us to see where everything was. Not much in the office to worry about. A couple desks and a few chairs. Most everything else had been taken by the police. I grabbed one of the seats and rolled it over to the window looking out over City Hall. I could see the sidewalk and the front steps. There was no activity but we were still a half hour until midnight.

Ernie grabbed another chair and sat near me. Ryan hopped up on one of the desks and lay back with his arms behind his head. He wasn't great at waiting. Tiny stood looking out the far window. I wasn't exactly sure where he was looking but it was in the direction of Old Town. I hoped that somehow Black was able to convince Caitlin and the others to abandon their plans, but I didn't think it likely.

We, on the other hand, didn't have a plan. I had my .45, Ernie his .38 and Ryan brought the shotgun he kept behind the bar. None of these would do us any good against vampires. But we weren't there to kill vampires. Mainly we were there because we couldn't not be. We'd wait, watch and hope that if something did happen we'd find a way to help.

The wait wasn't too long. At about ten minutes to midnight two very large men carried out a black leather club chair and placed it at the bottom of the steps. They walked off, returning again with one carrying a small side table and the other a bottle of wine and a glass. Once the table was in place, the other man removed the cork from the bottle and placed it and the glass onto the table. Then the two men positioned themselves on either side of the chair.

At two minutes to midnight the man on the table side of the chair reached down and poured a glass of the wine. It was a red. I kept visually sweeping the area, looking for Drake to approach. The sound of the clock bell announcing midnight distracted me for just a second, but when I looked back at the chair Drake was already seated and taking a drink.

"Mr. Doyle." Tiny pointed to the rooftops to our left.

I looked to where he was indicating and couldn't see anything at first. Then I saw just a glimpse of movement. The vampires were there as well.

"How many?"

His stone eyes squinted. "Four or five. Hard to tell from here."

Drake had picked a good spot for the meeting. It was well lit at night and far enough away from any shadows that even with the speed of a vampire you couldn't approach unseen. But you didn't have to give away your numbers either. Three vampires dropped down onto the street in front of City Hall. There were two males and a female. I had never seen either of the males before. The female I knew. One of the males had long blond hair down to the center of his back and seemed to be the leader. The other was a smaller guy, slicked-back black hair and a denim jacket. The leader approached the warlock and was doing the talking. We couldn't hear anything from where we were.

Ernie broke the silence. "Do you know the players, Tiny?"

"The woman is Caitlin Ryder. The vampire speaking to Drake is Kurt Pine and the other one is Guillermo Torres." Tiny looked around. "I haven't seen enough of the others to recognize them yet."

Ryan was on his feet and looking out with the rest of us. "This looks like it's going to get very ugly. You think we should go out there?"

"Not just yet. Let's see what's going to happen before…"

I didn't get a chance to finish my sentence before I saw Drake raise his hand and the two men at his side let out a growl so loud that it rattled the windows in front of us. These two were already big, but suddenly they were getting bigger. Their skin and clothes began to stretch and tear. The pinkish flesh began to fall to the ground at their feet as horns grew from their foreheads and wings spread out of their shoulder blades. Their newly exposed faces and bodies were covered in a black layer of almost leather looking skin that matched the club chair between them. In the blink of an eye Drake's two men became a pair of eight-foot tall winged obsidian demons.

The vampires attacked immediately. Caitlin and Guillermo went after a demon each while Kurt leapt for Drake. Caitlin went in low, cutting across the demon's midsection with her claws. Guillermo went for the throat, which cost him. The demon grabbed the vampire in mid-leap and held him by the throat. Drake barely moved. He gestured with his right hand and Kurt went flying across the street, slamming into a light post.

Two more vampires dropped down from the roof of City Hall and went to help Guillermo. They leapt on the demon's back, but he brushed them both off easily with his wings. He then grabbed Guillermo's legs and pulled, ripping them both off. The creature did the same to his arms before leaving a still alive but limbless Guillermo helpless lying on the sidewalk.

Drake cast a spell that caused a bubble to appear around one of the unnamed vampires. It had a reddish tinge yet was still clear enough to see through. The vampire pushed against the walls of the sphere but couldn't break it. It started to contract around him. He struggled uselessly as the shape changed and began to form around him. Soon it was so close it looked like he had been covered in a layer of paint and even then it contracted more. Tighter and tighter until his bones gave way to the pressure and snapped before being ground down to powder. And in a few seconds from when it was first cast, the sphere had disappeared having compressed the vampire into nothing.

"They're getting the crap beat out of them. We should get out there." Ernie started for the door.

"No." I grabbed his arm. "If we go now, we'll just end up collateral damage. The only chance we have of helping is to wait it out."

Looking back out the window I found Caitlin. She was holding her own against the demon. She had managed to claw him a few times, always staying just out of his reach. She was fast and agile while the demon was stronger but more lumbering. She sliced across his back while he yanked a chunk of wrought-iron fence up from the cement. The next time she dove at him, he swung the fence, just catching her leg. The blow was enough to knock her off balance and send her spinning to the ground. The demon pounced, wrapping the fence around her, pinning her arms to her side and her legs together. She was helpless, but the demon didn't finish her off. He simply tossed her out into the street near Guillermo.

Kurt raced back at Drake with no change in strategy. And once again the warlock gestured with his right hand sending the vampire into the air and slamming into the third floor of City Hall. He hit so hard that an outline of his body formed into the stone building. One of the demons pulled a lamppost out of the ground and flung it. The metal shaft impaled Kurt and buried itself into the wall, sticking the vampire to the side of the building.

The final vampire was a fierce fighter. He kept moving and hitting and over time he might've been able to kill the winged monster, but Drake wasn't taking any chances. He nodded to the demon who then left himself open for a kill shot. The vampire took it. He drove his hand through the demon's chest and tore out the creature's black heart. This move made the vampire stop for just a second. More than enough time for Drake. The warlock cast a spell that set both the vampire and the demon ablaze. Both creatures were turned to ashes before our eyes.

Drake looked pleased. Caitlin struggled to get free. Guillermo lay motionless on the street. Even Kurt who had tried to slide himself down the length of the lamppost was rendered helpless when the remaining demon flew up and bent the pole preventing Kurt's escape. The warlock poured himself another glass of wine and sat back in his leather chair.

"That's it?" Ernie was anxious. "We just sat and watched them get slaughtered!"

"I agree with Office Psikla. We should have gone and helped. Our standing here allowed Ms. Ryder and the others to be beaten."

"Even with our help, the vampires didn't have the power to take out Drake. All we would have done is gotten ourselves killed." I pointed out to Caitlin. "But, we can try to rescue them."

"Why bother to trap them if you're just going to kill them?" Ryan asked.

"Simple. If he kills them all now, he doesn't get the press coverage. It wouldn't surprise me if he has the press scheduled to show up here at sunrise to watch more vampires burn up. Everything he's doing is about popularity and convincing the city it's in danger. Killing five vampires in the middle of the night while no one is watching gains him nothing. He needs an audience."

"You think we can go do what five vampires couldn't?" Ryan stared at me. "Is that metal plate in your head getting rusty?"

"We don't need to fight him. We just need to distract him long enough to get Caitlin and Guillermo to safety. Not sure how we'll get Kurt down."

"And you have a plan on how to distract him?" Ernie looked out the window. "Because he seems pretty calm and in charge of the situation."

"Simple. I'm going to go out there and do what I do best."

Ernie's eyebrow rose. "And what's that?"

"I'm going to piss him off."

CHAPTER TWENTY-THREE

I walked out of the office building and headed straight for Kieran Drake. He had just taken out five vampires and still had a demon at his side. I was hoping he wouldn't see me as a threat. I made sure to step into the light at the first chance and to draw attention to myself.

"Trust Kieran Drake." I said it loud enough that he would hear me. "That's what your sign says, right? Trust Kieran Drake. What are we supposed to trust you to do?"

"Jimmy Doyle. I had a feeling I'd be seeing you again." He held up his bottle of wine. "Care for some Merlot?"

"I'm not much of a wine drinker. It just seems too elitist for my taste."

"Your loss." He poured the rest of the bottle into his glass. "Did you come down for the show? If so, you just missed it."

"No, I saw enough. I was a little surprised you brought hired muscle."

"Oh, you mean my demon friends. Well, I have to admit that I thought there would be far more vampires to fight. I'm disappointed that Conrad Black didn't come. I guess raiding his territory and killing one of his kind wasn't enough to get his attention. I'll just have to go bigger. Luckily tomorrow night is the full moon. If I can't get Black to play, then I'll just have to go after Shaw and his clan."

"Is this your big plan? Scare the hell out of the city so they'll make you mayor? Seems kind of low-brow, even for you." I walked closer, passing Guillermo. "To hear Fogg talk, you were like a junior version of him. Like the minor league version of the Yankees. But this seems like child's play to someone of your supposed stature."

"This is interesting. You're trying to get a rise out of me." Drake moved forward in his seat. "I assumed you were just a legman, doing exactly what Fogg ordered. I may have underestimated you. Not that it will change anything. But it is fascinating."

"Oh, I'm just a big ball of entertainment once you get to know me." I stopped a few feet in front of him. "On the odd occasion I even dance."

Drake stared at me like he was looking over a chess board trying to see the next move. His demon hung in tight to his back and stared at me with flaming red eyes. I had positioned myself so I would be slightly off to the side, opposite of where Caitlin was. I just had to keep their attention.

"Why would Fogg send you here to confront me? I am sensing only faint traces of magic on you. And that's just defensive and very limited." He leaned his head into his hand as he tried to figure it out. "He may have taught you a spell to use, but he'd have to know I'd counter it before you could finish the incantation. He wouldn't just send you out here to talk."

"You seem to know Fogg fairly well. Were you his apprentice?"

"As if Fogg had anything he could teach me. We studied under the same master. But I outshone him quickly as he lacked the imagination to fully utilize what we were learning."

I risked a subtle glance past the demon and saw that Caitlin was no longer there. I took a few steps up the stairs and sat down. This made Drake turn in his chair, but he did so with that continued stare of a scientist trying to figure out why the mouse is running backwards through the maze.

"You'll have to forgive me, it's been a long day and I'm tired." I stretched my back a bit to sell it. "Now, you and Foggy studied together. Then you met a girl and what? Did you let a woman get in the way of your friendship?"

"I never said Fogg was a friend." Drake had turned sideways in his chair now. "He was barely even a rival. And I only took an interest in Natasha because she seemed useful and was good for passing away the boredom at times."

"But you knew there was something between her and Fogg?"

"He showed a weakness towards her, yes. I noticed it as something I could manipulate to my advantage."

"It all sounds pretty petty to me. For a bunch of all knowing warlocks you guys spent a lot of time doing the same juvenile things the rest of us did. The only differences being none of us know magic tricks on par with an atom bomb. Did your master never think to teach you guys a little bit of humility or compassion?"

"Humility and compassion only make you weak. Allowing others into your life only creates places for your enemies to attack you. Lucius was weak and I exploited that every chance I got."

He raised his hand, spreading his fingers out as far as he could and cast a spell. Little circles of light raced around each digit from knuckle to tip and back again getting brighter as they went. When it became too bright to see individual movement, bolts of lightning leapt from his fingers and spread around me. I could hear the crackling of energy and feel its warmth. They circled around my chest and arms.

"Now, your working for Fogg makes you another weak point for him. He sent you here for a purpose and you're going to tell me what that is. Do you know why you're going to tell me?"

"Because you asked so nicely?"

The lighting suddenly contracted around me and I felt my skin burn. The pain seared through my chest and I thought my heart was going to explode. It was like every wound I ever had brought back at once and then tripled. The pain was so fierce that I couldn't help myself and screamed.

Then it stopped. The lighting pulled away from me but didn't dissipate.

"Now, that is the lowest intensity that I know how to do this spell. You can save me the time and you the agony and just tell me what I want to know."

"Fogg didn't send me." I couldn't hide the quiver in my voice.

"We both know that's a lie. You wouldn't come out and face me without Fogg's approval."

The lightning wrapped around me again and I gasped for air. Every muscle in my body was contracting over and over again, the pressure in my head kept building. I felt like my eardrums were going to burst. And just as quickly it stopped again. The lightning dissipated. But my body felt wrong. It couldn't take another blast.

"Why did Fogg send you?"

"He didn't. I came here against his wishes." It was hard to speak.

"And what was your grand plan? Were you going to try to kick my ass?" Drake laughed.

"Kicking your ass is the last thing I want to do." I forced myself to my feet. "But it's definitely on my list."

As I figured, the lightning followed with me, even as I took a couple steps toward Drake.

"Impressive." Drake continued to chuckle. "You are quite the entertainer after all. So what's your big plan?"

"I don't have a big plan. I have a small one. You might even call it… TINY!"

I yelled the final word and as I hoped, the stone golem came running from behind them. Both Drake and the demon turned at the sound of the rock hard footsteps. The demon went after Tiny and the two began to fight. The mammoth creatures locked arms, each trying to out-muscle the other. Neither one giving ground. I took the moment to push my luck. I leapt toward Drake while his attention was turned. The lightning that circled me now hit him. He let out a scream that made mine sound manly. He rescinded the spell and pushed me away. I hit the ground hard and lay there trying to catch my breath.

In the distance I saw Ryan and Ernie race across the ground and head for Guillermo. Ernie had his .38 out and pointed at Drake as he ran. The first shot took out the wine bottle. This got Drake's full attention. The next five shots were headed right for the warlock. He raised his hand and stopped the bullets in mid-flight, then turned them around and sent them hurling back at the cop.

The first two bullets hit Ernie's leg, one in the knee and the other in the thigh. The third bullet missed all together. The fourth clipped him in the shoulder, turning his body toward us. The fifth bullet buried itself dead center into Ernie's chest. He crumpled to the ground like a puppet with its strings cut.

Drake then turned to Ryan. He was crouched down trying to grab Guillermo. Drake flicked his hand like he was swatting an insect. Ryan went flying backwards, slamming head first into the marble door frame of an office building. The ex-soldier slid down the polished marble leaving a blood trail behind him.

Tiny was holding his own against the demon. The leather skinned creature had sliced open the golem's shirt, revealing a series of symbols etched into his chest. I had no idea what they meant. The demon tried to claw at the golem's face but it had no effect on his stone skin. Tiny grabbed the winged nightmare by the head and began to twist. The demon struggled fiercely but the golem's strength was too much. With one last pull, Tiny decapitated the creature and its body dropped hard to the ground.

"There's something you don't see every day. What a wonderful creation." Drake got up from his chair and walked over to where the lamppost had been pulled up. "Seems Fogg has a little more imagination than I gave him credit for. Writing the word on his chest instead of his forehead was brilliant. I wouldn't have thought to look there. Oh well."

Drake picked up a chunk of cement that had come up when the lamppost was pulled out. He crumbled a bit of it into his hand and blew on it. The concrete dust flew from his fingers directly over to Tiny. The particles of rock poured into the first symbol on the golem's chest. It continued until the symbol vanished. And Tiny stopped moving. Whatever signs of life you could see in his stone features were now gone.

I struggled to get to my feet. I wasn't going to go down like this. Drake had hurt too many people I cared about. I couldn't let him win.

"You just don't know when to quit, do you, Jimmy?"

I had gotten to my knees, but Drake kicked me in the stomach, flipping me onto my back. He moved over and stared down at me. I looked up, not at him, but at the wall behind him. I then glanced back out to the street. And then I did the last thing he expected. I laughed.

"What? Why are you laughing?" He genuinely looked confused.

"Because... you lost."

"How did I lose? I just took out your golem, I took out your friends and now I'm about to kill you. How exactly is that losing?"

"You asked why I'd confront you. Simple. It was to distract you."

"Distract me from what? There's no one else here."

"Exactly." I laughed again. "But you're so damn smart, figure it out."

He looked around. Out at the street, back at City Hall, down at me. He kept circling between the three until he finally saw it.

"They're gone!"

"About time. Thought I needed to draw you a map. You have no vampires. Nothing to show the press tomorrow morning. But what you do have are two ex-war vets and a cop. 'Candidate Slaughters Normal Humans' is going to make a great headline. How's that write-in campaign going to go now? Go ahead, finish me off. I'm sure the press will love that story just as much as a city filled with vampires."

"No! I won't let you ruin this." Drake frantically looked around for a way to salvage his plan.

"Come on! Kill me, you bastard! Let's be in the papers together!"

Drake kneeled down and grabbed me by the collar. "This isn't over Doyle. I'm going to go after everyone you ever cared about."

"You already have."

Drake stood up and then was suddenly gone. I was alone. I looked out and saw Ernie lying in the street. Ryan against the wall in the distance. I tried to get up but my legs wouldn't hold my weight. I could feel darkness creeping in around the edges of my vision. I tried once more to get to my feet, but the whole world went black.

CHAPTER TWENTY-FOUR

I regained consciousness in the emergency room. Emma was standing over me with tears in her eyes. My shirt was off and I had bandages around my arms and chest. They stung like crazy. Every part of my body was sore, even parts I didn't know could be sore. I reached my hand out and took Emma's. She squeezed it so tight that I thought I was going to scream again.

"So, how's your evening going?"

"It was going great until you rolled in here half burned to death and in the arms of another woman."

"I can explain that." I then shook my head. "Well, I can explain the burned part at least."

"Don't. I have a good idea of what happened already." She gestured to the window. "She's been sitting out there since she brought you in."

She walked over to the window and opened it. Caitlin climbed in and approached the bed. Emma headed for the door.

"I need to check on another patient. I'll be back."

I looked up at Caitlin and tried to read her face. "You came back?"

"I owed you one. Or two if you count that insane confrontation with Drake. For a human you seem to have a death wish."

"I appreciate what you did." I tried sitting up with only a minor amount of pain. "Do you know how the others are?"

"One of them is stable. The other is in surgery. I'm sorry I don't know their names to tell you one from the other." She seemed embarrassed by that. "I had Kurt get Tiny back to Black's club. I don't know what Drake did to him, but I couldn't just leave him out there like that."

"Thank you. How is Guillermo?"

"Angry as hell, but he'll be okay. It will take a while but he'll grow his limbs back." She headed over to the window. "I should get going. I just wanted to make sure you were okay."

"Be careful. Drake is still out there so this is far from over."

She nodded, put one leg out the window then stopped. "You know, growing up I bounced back and forth from foster home to foster home never really finding a place. It wasn't until I became a vampire that I felt someone actually cared about me. You are the first human to even give a damn, and you've risked your life for me twice on the same day we met. Thank you."

With that she was gone. With her out of the room, I swung my legs over the side of the bed and got up. It didn't take me too long, even with the pain, to get dressed. My shirt had seen better days and my tie was in shambles, so I just tucked my hospital gown into my pants and threw my damaged coat over it.

"What the hell are you doing?"

I turned to see a furious Emma standing in the doorway.

"Get back in that bed, now!"

"As much as I love it when you talk to me like that, I need to go check on Ryan and Ernie." I headed for the door.

She stepped in front of me. "I can physically put you back in that bed, you know."

"Again, under other circumstances I'd enjoy that. Not tonight." I looked straight into her eyes. "I need to see them."

She struggled with it for a moment, but gave in. "Ryan's two doors down on your right."

I made my way down the hall with my shoes in hand. The cold floor was oddly soothing to me right then. I slid into Ryan's room. A nurse was in there checking his blood pressure. She gave me a displeased look but I waved it off. Ryan's head was wrapped in bandages so far down they practically covered his eyes.

"How is he?"

"I can hear you."

I smiled. "You're still with us then?"

He opened his eyes. "Yeah, guess you're not the only one with a really hard head."

"What are the doctors saying?"

He waited as the nurse got up and left the room. He shifted a bit, trying to rise up in the bed.

"He recommends avoiding confrontations with warlocks for at least two weeks." He sat up some and I slid a pillow behind him. "He also said to keep vampires off my dance card."

"Those doctors can be strict."

"Cracked my skull pretty good. They stitched me up and want to keep me around for a day or two for observation. How are you?"

A voice from behind me took over. "Third degree burns on his chest and arms. Also indications of a possible stroke. And a cut on his left wrist that doesn't match any of the other injuries."

Emma stared at me again.

"What can I say? It was a long day."

"How's Ernie?" Ryan's thoughts turned to our friend.

"I'm told he's in surgery. Unless you've heard more?"

Emma shook her head. "Nothing yet. He's going to be in there for a while."

"I'm told I'm supposed to be getting some rest. And since at this moment I'm seeing two of both of you... not a bad thing in the case of Emma, but I think I need some sleep."

"All right, soldier."

"Hey, before you go." Ryan tried sitting up again. I leaned in closer to help. "I can't go with you on this one, but Drake has to go down."

"He will. I promise."

"I don't want a promise, I want you to do it right. No more half-assed plans. Go back to Fogg and work out a real strategy. End this with you still alive and then pick me up when I get discharged."

I shook his hand and then Emma and I left the room. We walked a few feet away. When we were definitely out of earshot, I turned to Emma. "Is he going to be okay?"

"He should be as long as he gets his rest. He's going to be here at least a few days, probably longer. I'll keep an eye on him."

"Thanks." I kissed her on the cheek. "Now where's Ernie?"

"He's down on the third floor." She hesitated for a moment, putting her hand on my arm. "It's not looking good."

I hugged her and promised I'd be careful. She went back to her rounds and I grabbed the first elevator to the third floor. I walked out expecting to have to ask for directions, but there was no need. The hallway was filled with cops all waiting for word. Even De Carlo who could never say a kind word to me if his life depended on it just nodded as I walked by.

Another officer approached me. "There's an observation room through there."

I thanked him and went through the door and up the small stair case. At the top of the stairs was a small, gray painted room with a half dozen seats set up theater style. A large glass window looked out over the operating room. A speaker on the wall allowed us to hear everything going on during the surgery: every doctor's order, every blip of a machine, every ting as a bullet got dropped into a metal bowl. It was a battle of life and death and these were the box seats.

The only other person in the room with me was Detective Sebastian Lee. He nodded to me as I entered and then went back to watching his man struggle to live.

"The shots to his shoulder and knee are bad. He'll never be able to walk without a limp and he won't be able to fire his weapon with his right hand. If those were it, his career as a cop would be over. But the shot in his leg hit an artery and he lost a lot of blood. Even that isn't the worst of it. The bullet that entered his chest pierced his heart. They are desperately trying to get in there to repair it. Blood is coming out of him as fast as they pump it in. Every officer out there is volunteering to donate in hopes they're a match."

"This wasn't supposed to happen."

"You don't get it do you, Jimmy? If it wasn't tonight, then it would be next week or next month. Anytime you needed help, Ernie was going to be there for you. Just as Ryan Aquino was. People like you. They like you so much that they want to help you. They know that you would take a bullet for them so they're willing to take one for you."

"I never asked him to…"

"You never needed to. You are just being yourself. And in most cases that would be just fine. But you don't live a normal life. You work for Lucius Fogg and all the insanity that comes with it. Just because you choose to put yourself in that kind of danger day in and day out, you put the people that care about you in that danger as well."

I didn't know what to say. He was right. I let Ernie and Ryan come along on more than one occasion. I'd put too many people in danger all in the line of doing my job. I had to change that.

"I know this is Drake's fault. And I'm going to work with you to get this guy. But you are to stay away from every other cop in the city. You don't talk to them, you don't look at them and for God's sake, you don't become friends with them. You need something from the NYPD, you call me. You get pulled over, you tell the officer that he needs to call me. You want to buy a ticket to the Policeman's Ball, you buy it from me. You don't get any more of my men. I will not sit here and watch another of my officers fight for his life because he had the bad luck to have met you. Do I make myself clear?"

"Yes."

I saw tears welling up in the base of his eyes. His rage was from his pain, but his rage was also justified.

We sat silently, listening as the doctors worked. The steady beep in the background was comforting in a way. Then the voices became more agitated. A doctor called out for suction. A nurse announced Ernie's blood pressure numbers as they declined. Someone said they were losing him. The beeps began to slow down. I leaned forward to see the face of my friend again. His eyes were closed. A tube hung from his mouth. I suddenly remembered the day we had met. How intently he worked to find that child. He wouldn't give up. It wasn't his way.

Someone yelled that he was crashing. The beep became a long constant squeal. More words leapt from the speaker: 'charging,' 'clear' and then a sound like a double hit on a base drum. More charging, more drums. The squeal just kept going, on and on. And then suddenly they all stopped moving. They stopped trying. No more charging or clears. Someone reached over and turned off the squealing machine. I wanted to scream out. I wanted them to keep going. Ernie was a fighter. He wouldn't give up.

The doctor called the time of death.

Sebastian punched the wall so hard the plaster buckled.

I stood, watching as they pulled the sheet up over Ernie's face.

I felt Sebastian's hand on my shoulder. "Come on, Jimmy. I'll drive you home."

CHAPTER TWENTY-FIVE

No words were spoken on the drive from the hospital to the brownstone. I wasn't looking forward to telling Fogg about Ernie. I wouldn't be surprised if he fired me. It wasn't the first time I had disobeyed him. Maybe deep down I wanted him to fire me so I wouldn't have to make the choice between the life working with him and the normal life I could have.

As the detective parked the car, I noticed another vehicle out front, one that I had seen before when all the press was there. It was almost four in the morning and I didn't see anyone around. So where was the owner of the car?

"I'm going in with you." Sebastian got out of the car without waiting for my reply.

I unlocked the door. It was a bit easier this time. Inside I took his coat and hat and hung them up with my own. By the time I turned around Fogg was standing in the doorway of his office.

"I'm glad you're here Jimmy. You, too, Detective Lee."

That should have clued me in that something was wrong, but I was so thrown by what had happened that I let his words slip by me.

"I went against your wishes and tried to help the vampires against Drake tonight." I waited, but he didn't respond. "It was a disaster. Ernie is dead. Ryan is laid up in the hospital and Tiny isn't moving. I don't know what Drake did to him, but he's just a statue."

"I am sorry to hear about your friend." Fogg looked at Sea Bass "And your officer. I didn't know Officer Psikla well, but I did know him to be a very good man. Detective, if it's possible, I would like to pick up the medical bills and funeral costs for the man. Also, the bills for Mr. Aquino."

Sebastian nodded his head. "I'm sure that can be arranged and it's appreciated."

"Is Timothy in a safe place?"

"He is. They got him back to Black's club."

"Okay, then I can fix that once this situation has passed." He gestured into his office. "I hate to burden you on a night like this, but I seem to have an urgent problem of my own that I need some assistance with."

The detective and I followed Fogg into his office and were stunned to find a bald man with a goatee slumped over dead in the high-back red leather chair.

"Who's the dead guy?" It seemed like the right question to start with.

"I know him." Sea Bass did what any cop would do, he checked for a pulse. "He's a reporter for the Times. I think his name is Eric Fiallos."

"Fiallos?" A chill ran down my spine. "He's the one doing the stories on you in the paper. Why is he here?"

"I invited him." Fogg walked around to his chair and sat. "But I didn't kill him."

I shook my head, disbelieving how things just kept getting worse. "You'd better tell us the whole story."

"And I need to call the meat wagon." The detective walked toward the door. "I'm going to use the radio in my car. Don't touch anything until I get back."

As soon as he was outside, I turned to Fogg half expecting a series of orders to rush through or something. But he didn't say a word. He just looked at the corpse.

"If you did kill him, tell me now and we can try to figure this out."

"I appreciate your loyalty, Jimmy." He looked me in the eyes. "I assure you I did not kill this man."

A minute later the detective returned and took out his note pad. He looked at the body sitting in his usual chair and then took the next one over. I sat behind my desk and grabbed something to write with as well. You never know what you might need for later.

"Okay. You said you invited him?"

"Yes." Fogg leaned back in his chair and started. "I had seen his articles about me over the last two days and figured it would be a good idea to tell my side of the story. I sent word to the Times that I wanted to talk to Mr. Fiallos. That I would answer any questions he had as long as he printed everything I said. His editor agreed and said the reporter would be by this evening. It was quite late when he finally showed up. Almost two in the morning. He apologized for being so late but said my reputation as a night-owl was well known. I told him it was fine and showed him into my office.

"He asked some very basic questions at first, some to get background on me and my past. I didn't go into too much detail but gave him enough to fill in his story. He then asked me about my connection to Conrad, the rumors about Old Town, et cetera. Once he had exhausted his questions, I told him it was my turn and I began to tell him about the real Kieran Drake. I was only a few minutes into it when he started coughing. Ariel brought him some water and we paused while he composed himself.

"After a minute or two he seemed fine and I went back to the story. His coughing started up again and we tried to push on through it. When I mentioned that Drake had killed his wife, Mr. Fiallos clutched his chest and began convulsing. By the time I got around my desk, he was dead."

"Wait, you said Drake killed his wife?" This was news to the detective. "When? Do you have any evidence?"

"I don't have any proof that would stand up in a court of law. It was also sixty-five years ago."

At that moment there was a knock on the front door. Two men from the coroner's office entered with a gurney. They gave the body the once over and reported to the detective.

"I don't see anything that doesn't say heart attack, but I won't know for sure until I get him cut open."

They put the body into a bag, strapped it to the gurney and rolled it out. Another officer appeared and dusted the chair and side table for prints. He took the glass and what water was left in it and put it into evidence bags on his way out the door. The whole thing took about an hour.

"As long as the coroner's report matches your story, we should be fine. But with all the heat coming down from City Hall, they might want you to come down for more questioning."

"I can't do that, Detective."

"I've heard the stories about you not leaving your house. Unless you can give me one real reason why, I can't stop them from dragging you downtown."

"Jimmy, please go check that the men closed the front door." Fogg was nicely asking me to leave.

I stepped out and closed the door to the office behind me. I walked over and checked the front door anyway even though I knew it was an excuse. I checked the hall closet while I was out there. Found my back up coat and took it up to my normal hook. My damaged coat was already gone. Ariel had probably taken it to start repairs. A moment later the door to the office opened again and Sea Bass came out.

"Remind me not to ask Fogg for real reasons ever again."

The detective grabbed his hat and coat and headed out the door. I stepped out on the porch as he left.

He looked back before he got in his car. "I'm going to do my best to keep things from exploding downtown. But tonight's the full moon and tomorrow's the election, so you know Drake has to have something else ready. You two need to come up with a hell of a plan to end this."

As he pulled away, I closed the door and locked it. I went back into the office and found a plate of biscuits and a pot of Earl Grey waiting for me. I didn't feel like any of it right then, so I pushed it aside and looked over to Fogg.

"What did you leave out?"

"It was no heart attack." He pulled the metal monstrosity he had been building earlier back out from under his desk. "I could sense the residual magic on him. Someone planted a spell in his subconscious."

"How would that work?"

"Like a hypnotic suggestion with a trigger word. For instance I could teach you how to make light come out of your nostrils by thinking of a spell. But I teach it to you subconsciously and plant a trigger so that when you hear a dog bark, you will think of that spell. End result, your nose would light up every time a dog barked and you'd have no idea you were doing it to yourself."

"If you can do tricks like that you should throw dinner parties." The humor was more for me than Fogg at that point. "So you think someone planted a spell in Fiallos' subconscious? A spell meant to kill him?"

"Not just someone. Drake." Fogg attached another piece to the Erector Set. "He's the one who had been feeding Fiallos the information about me, so it stands to reason that he's the one who would want Fiallos dead if he found himself talking to me."

"You think this was to keep the press from finding out the truth?"

"No, I think it's something bigger still." Fogg put the work down. "I have to assume that Drake knows I can't leave my house. But if he gets me accused of murder, the police will take me out by force if necessary."

"Thereby killing you in the process. Devious yet simple. So what is that thing you're working on?"

"It's kind of like the bell jar I tried to capture Natasha with, except this is more of a guidance tool. If you are attuned to another spirit then you could use it to find them.

"How does one become attuned with someone else's spirit?"

"I'm fairly certain that you and Ms. Martin are now attuned since you took a trip into her mind."

Fogg went back to working on the metal guidance tool. I waited until he put on the final bar and declared it finished. Once he placed it on the table by the window, I figured we could talk about a plan.

"Am I missing something? We have a lot of pieces to the puzzle, but none of them are fitting together. We still have no idea what the big picture is. He uses Emma to bring out Natasha. But we don't know if that was just to get her into play or to kill you. Then he declares he's running for mayor and exposes Old Town at the same time. I don't see what any of these things have in common. He's even using obsidian demons to help with fighting the vampires."

Fogg leapt from his seat. "Demons? When did he use demons?"

"Tonight when he set the trap for Conrad, he had two demons with him."

"And you are certain they were obsidian demons?"

"They had black leathery skin, big wings, and fiery red eyes."

Fogg quickly moved to the big safe in the corner, the one where he kept all the magical items. He pulled out a piece of wire and placed it on the table. I had seen it once before when he used it to look through a series of memory gems. He then dug through a few more things and dropped them into a small satchel. He closed the safe and asked me for my notebook where he wrote in three pages worth of spells and which item to use them with.

"What is going on? I've never seen you so frantic."

"You have to get out of here." Fogg handed me the satchel and the Erector Set thing. I just had time to grab my hat and coat before he pushed me toward the kitchen. "The house is not safe and I don't have time to explain why. I need you to take these items and use them when you think it's right. You have to find a way to keep Old Town safe so the werewolves can go there and you have to stop people from voting for Drake tomorrow."

"How the hell am I supposed to do all of that?"

"You will. I have faith in you." Fogg stopped just at the backdoor. "When all of that is done, I'll need you back here, but not a moment before."

"How will I know when that is?"

"Do what you always do. Trust your instincts."

And with that Fogg was gone. I loaded the things into the Studebaker and fired up the engine. I didn't know where to go or what to do. I was all alone with the weight of the world on my shoulders.

CHAPTER TWENTY-SIX

I headed up the alley from the garage to the main street and then slammed on my brakes as a squad car screeched to a stop right in front of me. De Carlo hopped out with one hand in the air and the other resting on his holstered revolver.

"Kill the engine, Doyle!"

After the lecture I'd gotten from Sea Bass, this didn't seem like a good time to mess with De Carlo. I shut off the engine and put both hands up on the wheel. The cop walked over to my window. He looked serious, which wasn't his normal expression. Not a hint of the cockiness he normally carried.

"I need to search your car. Open the trunk."

I got out, unlocked the back and stepped aside so he could give the car a once over. He checked it thoroughly. He searched for extra hiding places in wheel wells, the seats and even under the spare tire. In the end he found nothing.

"What were you looking for?"

He slammed the trunk down hard. "Your boss."

"Fogg can't leave his building. Sea Bass already verified that just a little while ago."

"Detective Lee has been suspended and I have orders to bring Lucius Fogg in for questioning."

"Suspended? For what?" I was confused.

"He's accused of tipping off Conrad Black about the raid and for giving preferential treatment to a suspected murderer."

"Murderer? You mean Fogg?"

De Carlo looked at his notebook. "Yes. He's the main suspect in the death of Eric Fiallos."

"The coroner said it looked like a heart attack and there is no way he could have done an autopsy in the last thirty minutes." I looked De Carlo in the eyes. "What's really going on here?"

He looked at me for a moment, then sighed and shook his head.

"Something isn't right. The Chief and that Kieran Drake guy were at the station house before dawn. We were being told about the suspension before Detective Lee even made it in. He was going to get it for anything short of bringing Fogg's head in on a stick. And it was obvious that Drake was pulling the strings."

"Do you have orders to take me in as well?"

"Drake was pushing for that, but just about every cop on the force saw you last night at the hospital with Psikla. He couldn't make that happen."

"Then I'm free to go?"

"Not yet. Let us into the brownstone and..."

Before he could finish his sentence, another officer came running over to us. This one looked barely old enough to be driving, let alone wearing a badge and gun. He also seemed too winded for his age.

"We're about to go inside," the young cop said between breaths.

My jaw dropped. "Did you break down the door?"

"No." He panted twice. "It's sitting wide open like an invitation to come in."

De Carlo looked at him funny. "Why are you out of breath?"

"I don't... know." He put his hands on his knees. "I stepped inside to see if anyone was there, then they told me to come get you."

The three of us walked the hundred yards to the front of the brownstone. Sure enough the front door was swung open so anyone could walk in. Seven other officers were standing around the stoop. All of them seemed to be gasping a bit for air. De Carlo pointed to the hood of one of the squad cars.

"Stand over there out of the way while we search the house."

I walked over, leaned back against the fender and saluted to show my compliance. He then turned and went into the brownstone with the other seven uniformed men. I didn't have a whole lot to do while I waited. I watched the sun climb higher into the morning sky. I listened to the radio broadcasts from inside the squad car. There was nothing about new sweeps through Old Town. I figured they'd give up on that one after we pulled the Three-Card Monty act on them the day before.

After about twenty minutes I saw the first officer come stumbling outside. He leaned against the wall and tried to catch his breath. A few minutes of rest and he went back in. Another fifteen minutes went by and De Carlo wandered out. He looked exhausted.

"How many rooms are in that place?"

"Depends on the time of day, I think."

He came over and leaned next to me, forcing himself to take long breaths. "There's a hallway in there longer than the house is wide. I had an officer go down eighteen flights of stairs in a three-story house and there's a storage area that may be bigger than the city of New York. Every one of the officers searching feels like he's run back to back marathons. What in the hell is that place?"

I gave him half a smile. "It's what Fogg calls home."

"There are locked doors we can't even bust open. Do you have a key or anything that might help us?"

"Do you know Welsh?"

"No."

"Then nope, I've got nothing that can help."

De Carlo stood up straight and took another deep breath. He then opened the squad car door and sat down inside while grabbing the radio.

"I'm going to call for more men. It's going to take us longer to search this than it did all of Old Town."

"Do I have to stick around?" I tried looking innocent.

"Get out of here." He waved me off. "Find some other place to be for a while... like a month."

I held my tongue as I walked back to the Studebaker. That was the longest period of time I had to deal with De Carlo and be nice. It was actually starting to hurt at the end. It was obvious to me Fogg left the door open to prevent them from breaking it down. He knew they'd be coming. With the random room alone Fogg could stay in the house indefinitely and no one would find him. I also guessed he put a spell on the place that lowered the oxygen level. That was the only way I could explain a bunch of decently built men being that far out of breath just searching a house. Well, except for the guy checking the infinite stairwell.

I reached the car and noticed I'd gained a passenger while I was away. I slid in behind the wheel and closed the door.

"Let's go kick Drake's butt."

I looked at my young friend and saw how streaks of tears had washed away some of the dirt on his face. He held his jaw locked tight to prevent it from quivering in front of me.

"I take it you heard about Ernie? A least Ryan is going to be okay."

"We can't let him get away with it." The boy was filled with rage and had no idea how to let it out.

I turned to Patches, placing my hand on his shoulder. "I won't let him get away with anything. You have my word on that. But I'm doing this one alone."

"No dice, Boss." He turned and I saw his rubbed red eyes. "He killed one of the team. You, me, Ernie and Ryan, we keep this city safe. With Ryan hurt, I'm the only back-up you got."

"No, we're not a team." I shook my head. "You were all people that I selfishly put into harm's way to help me get my job done. That cost Ernie his life and got Ryan severely hurt. I'm not going to let anything happen to you. This is my responsibility to finish."

"I get it, Boss. You're upset over what happened. I am, too. But you need me. We can take this guy down together. We just need to find his weakness. I could go hang around his campaign headquarters or…"

"Damn it, Patches. You're not listening." I grabbed him by the arm, harder than I intended. "You're just a kid. You already ended up in the hospital because of me once. That's not happening again."

The boy screamed at me. "This isn't fair! You can't cut me out!"

"I can and I am. We're done. Go find some kids your age to play stickball with. Stop following me around like a lost puppy."

He wrenched his arm away and I could tell it was hurting, but he didn't touch it. The tears were flowing again, but he wouldn't wipe them away. He just glared at me.

"This is how you want it? Fine! I won't help you. But you can't stop me from going after Drake on my own."

"You go anywhere near Drake or try to get involved in this in any way, I'll get one of those officers back there to throw you into Juvenile Hall."

"You wouldn't do that."

"Yes, I would. I'd rather see you locked up than on a coroner's slab next to Ernie."

Patches threw open the door and jumped out of the car. "I hate you!"

With that the boy slammed the door and ran off down the street. I felt horrible for treating him that way and even worse for hurting his arm. But I couldn't risk him ending up in the crossfire between Drake and Fogg. More than enough people had been hurt since Drake returned.

I looked back over to the brownstone. All of the officers including De Carlo were outside, sitting on the ground looking like they just reached the halfway point up Mount Everest. What De Carlo said popped back into my brain. Drake was at the station with the police chief before dawn and even before Sebastian called in the dead body. This confirmed to me at least that Fiallos was given the information he had and was set up specifically to die in Fogg's presence. I had no evidence to prove it. I also figured Drake wasn't counting on the police to arrest Fogg. Between the nature of the brownstone and Fogg's abilities, he'd be able to hide out there forever. Drake had to know that it wouldn't work.

The only other thing that would make sense is if Drake was just trying to take Fogg out of the game. If he was spending all of his time hiding from the police, he wouldn't be able to interfere with Drake's plan.

But that still didn't explain what the final prize was. If forcing Fogg into hiding, becoming mayor and revealing Old Town were all just distractions then whatever Kieran Drake was after had to be pretty big.

CHAPTER TWENTY-SEVEN

I headed over to Howard's bar and let myself in the back. The place was completely empty. I'd been in there at all hours of the day and night and Ryan was always somewhere about. He never seemed to leave the place unless he was heading off to help me. His father opened the bar a year before Ryan was born. He named it after Ryan's grandfather. When we were in the army together, Ryan talked about the place constantly. The people who drank there, the food his mother made and how I'd always have a free drink waiting for me.

When I was in my coma, Ryan got his orders to ship home. He got back three days after his father had passed. He tended bar that night and went to the funeral the next day. He ran the place with his mother for a few years before she also passed on. In the time I knew her, she treated me like a second son. As I sat alone in the bar, I silently apologized to her for letting her son get hurt.

I slipped into my booth and put the small satchel on the table in front of me. I dug through it until I found the memory gems Fogg had placed inside. He'd written in my notebook to start with those and which one to view first. He also included how to make them work. I had seen him do it once when he was scanning the memories of the recently departed. I wasn't exactly sure whose memories these were. He may have had time to get the reporter's before we showed up, but that would only have been one gem and there were three in the bag.

I dug out the head piece. It looked like a five-year old had been playing with a coat hanger and bent it into the letter C with two hooks at the end. I put it on my head and secured the hooks over my ears. The third wire that hung out in front of my face had the small net attached where I dropped the first gem. It dangled just above the bridge of my nose. I leaned my head back against the booth, closed my eyes and recited the words Fogg had written down for me.

Though I didn't open my eyes, I was now standing on the docks looking out into the ocean as a small ship approached. I could taste the salt in the air. I could hear the waves lapping against the shoreline and the cries of the seagulls. I looked around at the small seaport village. Everything looked old yet new at the same time, like recently made antiques.

My hair was blowing in the breeze and I could feel that it was longer than I normally had it. I looked down at my clothes. I wore a waist coat that barely reached my navel yet had long tails down the back. A pair of pants that were loose at top yet tight below the knees and tucked into my calf-high leather boots. The front of my shirt was a bit frilly and stuck out through my large collar. Wherever I was, it was many years in the past.

The ship had docked and the passengers began to disembark. The first few didn't seem to matter to me, but then a young man of maybe eighteen in a similar suit to mine appeared. He carried a medium-sized trunk at his side and came toward me. I took a few steps forward and reached out my hand.

In a familiar voice I spoke. "You must be Kieran. I'm Lucius. Welcome to Ipswich."

The young Drake didn't take my hand or even make eye contact. He looked around at the village with disdain.

"Why would such a powerful man live in such a pedestrian location?" He shook his head before turning to face me. "You must be Matheus' servant. You can take my trunk."

"I'm not his servant, I'm his apprentice." I turned and started walking away. "And you can take your own trunk."

As I passed by a shop window, I got to see my reflection. It was that of a very young Lucius Fogg. If I had to guess, I'd say he was in his early twenties at most. His hair was jet black, body lean and fit and a stride of confidence without being cocky. Even in his youth Fogg carried himself well.

I didn't wait for Drake nor do anything to help him with his luggage. I merely walked to the awaiting wagon and climbed up onto the seat. Drake struggled to get his trunk into the back before climbing up next to me. He didn't say a word. The silence continued the entire hour long ride out of the city and into the countryside. The homes were quite a distance apart and all seemed to have some kind of farming going on. The house we finally turned toward had rows of vegetables across one half of the land and a fenced in area with chickens and pigs on the other. I noticed a couple cows in the back, making it a fairly self-sufficient home.

I pulled up in front of the house and turned to Drake. "Get your trunk and wait here."

After leaving him on the front step, I drove the wagon into the barn and detached the horse, putting it back into its stall. I then returned to collect my guest.

"This is a joke, right?" Drake was looking at the house. "Why on Earth would Matheus live here?"

"You can ask him that yourself. Follow me."

The house was simple. A one story ranch style that looked like it maybe had two or three bedrooms from the outside. Once inside, it looked still simpler, even Spartan. The living room had three old wooden chairs, two in the center of the room and one over by the front window. Each of the three bedrooms had a single bed and a small dresser. The largest of the rooms also had two bookshelves packed full with dusty, worn tomes. The look on Drake's face told me he had never lived in such squalor.

There was a third person in the room with us. He sat in the chair by the window reading a book. He was an older gentleman, maybe late sixties or early seventies. He was bald except for the band of white hair that ran around the back of his head. His face was a bit round but not fat and his long, pointed nose made him look a bit like a sundial. He might have been athletic once, but now he looked somewhat frail and unimposing.

I cleared my throat to get his attention before speaking. "Matheus, our guest is here."

The old man looked up with a smile then hopped to his feet. He stood a good six inches shorter than either one of us. He reached out his hand as he walked across the room toward Drake.

"You must be Karen Drake."

"That's Kieran." The young man showed his offense at the mistake. "You can't possibly be Matheus."

"I can't?" The old man looked around the room. "Well, I know you're not Matheus. And Lucius here would have told me if he was Matheus... he's very good about things like that. There doesn't appear to be anyone else in the house. You think maybe one of the pigs is Matheus then? Or how about the horse that brought you here?"

"Matheus is the most powerful sorcerer of our time. He has kept the balance between order and chaos for over a century. The demons in hell tremble at the mention of his name." Drake sized up the man in front of him. "You would have a hard time making a rodent tremble."

"Demons in hell? Order and Chaos? This Matheus fellow sounds very impressive." The old man got really close to Drake. "Have you seen him before? Do you know what he looks like?"

"No. But I know that he lives here and I'm tired of these foolish games. Take me to Matheus now or else." Drake was getting angry.

"Or else what?" The old man prodded him. "Do you do magic? I love magic. Can I see your magic?"

"I'll show you my magic, imbecile!"

He began casting a spell. I raised my hand to counter it but I wasn't fast enough. Neither was Drake. The old man moved his hand so quickly that before I could get a word out, our guest had vanished only to be replaced by a pile of clothes. I wasn't exactly sure what had happened until I heard a pounding coming from the trunk on the floor.

The old man crossed over and lifted the lid. An even more furious Drake sat up and glared daggers. He quickly moved to put his clothes back on.

"You still want to see if one of the pigs is Matheus?"

"No. I accept you are who you say you are."

"Then that is a good start. Come outside."

The old man bounced out the front door. Drake climbed out of his trunk, putting on his shoes and followed. I went along as I still didn't trust Drake and I wanted to see what happened next.

"When Harry wrote me about you, he said you were powerful, young and undisciplined. I have now seen two of those. Would you like to restore a bit of your honor and demonstrate the powerful part?"

"Fine."

Drake said a quick enchantment and one of the chickens burst into flames. The creature ran around for a few second before collapsing into a burning pile of feathers and skin. Drake was now smiling.

"Impressed?"

Matheus shook his head. "You have just killed my best egg laying hen for no reason other than to show off. You could have done any number of spells that I am quite certain that you know, yet you chose to be destructive and take a life."

"A life? It was a chicken."

"It was my chicken." The old man scratched his head where the hair once was. "I am hesitant to continue on with what we corresponded about."

Drake's face changed. He no longer seemed cocky and arrogant. "I'm sorry. I was nervous about meeting you and wanted to impress. But I have obviously gotten off on a very wrong foot. It is my dream to study with you, to be your apprentice and learn at your feet. Please allow me that opportunity."

Matheus looked to me. I subtly shook my head, letting him know my apprehension. But the old man would make his own choice.

"Very well." He pointed toward the house. "The room on the back right is yours. Go put your things away and then come help Lucius and me with our chores."

"Thank you, sir." Drake ran off into the house.

"You don't approve of my training young Kieran Drake?"

"He is arrogant and self-righteous. Not good things for a sorcerer to be. He looks at everything about you with disdain yet wants your help." I lowered my head. "But you are the master and the decision is yours to make."

Matheus laughed. "I always liked that about you, Lucius. Your ability to disagree without being disagreeable. That young man is self-taught and already accessing spells on your level. Left on his own, he could become horribly dangerous to the balance between order and chaos. Or worse, he could fall into league with someone of questionable morals. I just hope I've gotten to him in time."

I went from looking at the old man's face to looking at the dark roof of Howard's bar in the blink of an eye, literally. It felt odd being inside Fogg's head like that. It wasn't the first time I had watched someone else's memory, but that was basically a stranger. This was Fogg's life. A part I knew nothing about. He had never mentioned Matheus before and to see the man who taught Fogg magic was interesting. He was nothing like I would've expected, obviously not what Drake had expected either.

The memory flashback was a bit draining and I could feel an emptiness in my gut. I decided I was going to go in the back and make something to eat and then continue on. I still had two more memory gems to go through.

CHAPTER TWENTY-EIGHT

After a quick sandwich and a glass of milk, I pulled out the next gem and placed it in the little net. I prepared myself for another trip through Fogg's life. The first bit seemed pretty straightforward, but I was watching these for a reason and that reason wasn't very clear yet. I leaned my head back, closed my eyes and said the words once more.

I immediately felt wet and chilled. My soaked clothing clung to my body. I could feel the rain pelting against my face and the bitter cold wind racing through my jacket. I looked out to my surroundings, having to shield my eyes from the elements before I could see anything. I was on a small island of jagged rocks. The waves were crashing over the small bit of land like it wasn't there. To my left I saw a lighthouse towering above me, its brilliant signal barely able to penetrate the storm clouds around us. The gale force winds and slippery ground made it hard to stand, let alone walk.

I turned away from the lighthouse and made my way toward the other end of the island. The land began to narrow as I went, allowing more and more of the waves to pass over it unfettered. If it was me walking out there and not a borrowed memory, I'd be inching along, bracing myself for every wave. But Fogg walked with an almost reckless confidence that I hadn't expected from him. In the distance I saw a figure sitting on a rock. It was only a silhouette from where I was, but it was definitely where I was going.

I raised my hand, palm up with fingers outstretched and recited a spell. A black spot appeared in front of me, hard to see in the middle of the storm, but it was there. As I focused on it, the spot stretched out to the left and right and grew until it became a long black walking stick. I snatched it out of the air and got a closer look. It was the same stick I'd seen Fogg carry for years. With each step forward I would strike the ground with the stick, not really knowing why at first. Then a large wave came crashing over the jetty, aimed straight at me. The water slammed against me with enough force to push me into the ocean if not for the walking stick holding fast. It was as if someone had cemented the tip to the rocks, giving me the handhold I needed to withstand the wave.

The going was slow as wave after wave swept over me. I could only move a few feet before I'd have to brace for another hit. The shadowy form on the rocks began taking better shape. I could tell that it was female and she seemed oblivious to the storm around her. She sat there on the rock like it was a warm sunny day and she was getting a tan. Another three strides and I noticed something else kind of important. She was naked. I kept going and to my surprise the winds began to calm. The waves no longer surged over the bank and the woman no longer gazed out to sea, but rather turned to look at me. There was a radius around us of maybe twenty yards where everything was peaceful. Outside of that circle, the storm continued to rage. Within the circle, even the sounds of the storm were gone. It was replaced by music. The beautiful naked woman sitting on the rock was singing to me.

She was like nothing I had ever seen before. Her skin was the color of sundrenched sands and her body curved like it was caressed by the tides. Her long flowing hair glistened and shifted from the richest blues to the deepest greens. Her eyes were iridescent pools that called me forth and the sweet sound of her voice made my body respond in eager ways.

The walking stick fell from my hand like a forgotten doll as a child enters a toy store. I hadn't known Fogg's purpose for walking out there and his now defenseless stance made me wonder if he himself still knew it. I got closer to the woman and was lost in her beauty. I ignored how precarious the footing was becoming and I crossed rock after rock trying to reach her. A few more feet and I would be able to touch her.

Then I was hit by a very different wave. I was knocked off my feet and pinned to the ground. I began to struggle, trying to get free. I wasn't going to let this stop me. I had to reach her. I had to touch her. Nothing could stop me. I railed against the hands holding my arms down and the weight pressed against my chest.

A sudden flash of light and everything was different. The rain was beating down on me again. The waves crashed over the banks and I could see that the thing holding me down was Kieran Drake. He was still younger than the man who revealed Old Town but a bit older than when Fogg met him in Ipswich.

"Damn it, Lucius. Snap out of it!"

I shook my head to force it clear. "I'm good. Where's Matheus?"

"Over there with your girlfriend."

I looked past Drake and saw what the bright light was. Matheus had begun to battle the siren. Her appearance had changed. She was now larger. Her legs combined to form a snake's tail. Had it been there before and I missed it? Her fingers ended in serrated claws and her mouth opened to show a row of razor sharp needle teeth. She snarled and hissed at the old man, while he concentrated on hurling lightning bolts at the creature.

"We have to get in there and help." Drake got off me and turned toward the fight.

I reached out and grabbed my cane, but didn't have time to secure it to the rocks before the next big wave swept both Drake and me off into the ocean. The frigid water made the winds above seem balmy and I was flipped over and over again as I sank deeper into the sea. It took all my wits to keep from losing my cane. A quick spell transformed any water that entered my mouth into oxygen. That kept me from drowning, but I was still being pulled deeper by the undertow and tossed about by the currents. I had no idea which way was up.

I reached up to my mouth and with two fingers I pulled out some of the air in the form of a bubble. Holding it away from my body, I released the bubble and watched it float past me and up toward the surface. I turned over and swam up after it.

It took all my strength to resist the undertow and to keep from flipping about again. I had gotten pulled fairly deep and it took more than a few strokes to reach the surface. Once I broke through, I could see that I had been dragged back down the jetty and was now dangerously close to the lighthouse. The rocks along the banks near the lighthouse were larger and far more jagged. The rough waters were pushing me right for them.

I suddenly felt a band tighten around my chest. I was being pulled backwards, away from the lighthouse. I looked over my shoulder and saw a very wet Drake standing on the jetty. He was pulling on the rope he had magically wrapped around me and was dragging me to shore. When close enough, he reached out his hand and pulled me out of the water.

"How many times do I need to rescue you on this trip, Lucius?"

"Hopefully that's the last." I glanced over at the ongoing fight. "Shall we end this, Kieran?"

"Yes."

I ran forward and planted my cane into the ground. It held steadfast to the rocks below it. Drake planted his feet and whipped his enchanted rope at the siren like a cowboy with a lariat. It wrapped around her midsection and held tight. Matheus continued hurling lightning bolts at her so she could not turn her attention to us. This allowed me the chance to cast another spell. This one reduced her in size by more than half. Drake secured the other end of the rope to my walking stick and then he commanded it to reel in the siren. She began to spin like a yo-yo getting more and more entangled until she was fully bound to my cane.

Matheus came forward and picked a rock up off the ground. He held it up and allowed it to float in front of him. The siren continued to sing and I could feel myself being drawn in once again. The floating rock shattered into a hundred pieces and they all flew forward, and then circled around the head of the siren. Each would find a place along her jaw line to call home. Piece after piece locked into place until a solid rock gag finally ended her song.

Within seconds, the tides began to recede, the gray clouds subsided and the sun broke through giving us a bit of warmth on our rain soaked bodies. The siren was no longer a beautiful woman, but rather a hideous creature that had been terrorizing ships in the area.

"Are you okay, Master?" Drake asked the old man.

"What? Oh, just a minute." Matheus reached in his ears and pulled out two pieces of cotton. He then smiled at the two of us. "Well done, both of you."

"I thought you were going to use magic to ward off the siren's call?" Drake seemed perplexed.

"I think cotton is magic, and so did my friend Eli." He then turned to me. "Nice job on distracting the creature. Next time though, try not to get thrown into the ocean."

"I'll keep that in mind." I took off my coat and tried to wring it out. "What do we do with her now?"

"Well, there's the thing." The old man rubbed his jaw. "We stopped it because it was hurting humans. But it really was just following its nature and how do we stop that?"

"We kill it." Drake piped in.

"Still going to violence first my boy?" Matheus shook his head. "Are there any other options?"

"What about one of the islands further off the coast? We can release it there and warn the sailors to stay away." I didn't want to see the creature killed.

"The problem with that is mankind will continue to grow. The boats we see now are small and few compared to what the future will bring. And the empty islands will not always be empty." He put his hand on my shoulder. "As much as I agree with your sentiment, all we would be doing is putting off the inevitable for another day. In this case, Kieran is correct. We will have to put her down."

Matheus sent the two of us into the lighthouse to get dry as he stayed to deal with the siren.

"I'm sorry."

Surprised, I turned to Drake. "For what?"

"I know you are against killing any creature if it can be avoided. I appreciate that." He sat and I saw a look of melancholy on his face. "You have a connection to life that I lack. I once thought my detachment allowed me to make the difficult decisions and in a way it does. But it doesn't allow me to see the other side of the argument."

"That's what you have me for."

Matheus entered the room and tossed me my cane. He was more somber than normal, which was understandable with having just done what he had. He used a quick spell to dry his clothes and then went up to say a few words to the lighthouse keeper. A moment later he returned and opened the door for us.

"Come on, my boys. Let's go home."

CHAPTER TWENTY-NINE

The third gem took me back to the brownstone and by the reflection in the office window, to a Fogg not much younger than when I met him. The office was pretty much the same except the small Sears and Roebuck desk that I called my own was missing. Fogg was reading a book about soul manipulation, which meant that I, too, was reading it. It was a passage about making contact with the dead and how they can take over someone else's body. I didn't look up when the doorbell chimed. It wasn't until I could tell someone was standing in the door to the office that I lifted my eyes. I had expected to see Ariel, but instead found an older man in a suit.

"What is it, Wilson?" I asked.

"There is a gentleman at the door asking to see you. He says his name is a Mr. Matheus."

I could feel myself grin. "Really? Well, do show him in, please."

I jumped to my feet to great the old man. He came into the office with his arms held out wide, looking no worse for wear than the last time I had seen him.

"Lucius, my boy. It's so good to see you." Matheus wrapped his arms around me in a gregarious hug.

We shook and exchanged the usual pleasantries of how long it had been, how well we both looked. I showed him to the high-back red leather chair and then returned to my own seat behind the desk.

"Have you kept in touch with Kieran?"

"I have." I pointed out the window to the east. "He lives just on the other side of town. He has himself a beautiful young companion."

"An apprentice or a lover?"

"A bit of both it seems."

The old man laughed. "Well, good for him. A woman always changes the dynamic. Not always for the good, but always a change."

"Oh, yes. Natasha has changed a lot of things."

"What about you, Lucius? Any young ladies sharing this beautiful home?"

"I'm afraid I get too wrapped up in my work to socialize much. Sometimes it's as if I'm trapped in this place."

"The work is all well and good, but the play gives us the reason to do the work. I thought I taught you better than that, my boy?"

"Seems some lessons didn't get through." I leaned back in my chair and looked directly at Fogg's mentor. "Now, you don't just pop in after a decade to chat about old times. What's going on?"

"I never could get anything past you." His face went from his normal jovial to much more reticent in the blink of an eye. "I'm going to need your help with something. An unpleasant task that I had hoped not to burden you with."

"I owe you so much. Nothing you could ask would be a burden. Whatever you need done, just ask."

"My time is coming to an end. Far more rapidly than I originally thought."

My happiness to see my mentor had colored my vision. Only after his admittance did I start to see just how drawn and pale he appeared. It was a fragility I never thought possible from him.

"Surely there is something that can be done…"

"No. I have lived an amazing life with no regrets and I accept the end of it with the same eagerness that I lived each day. It is my time and I am more than fine with that."

"Then what are your concerns?"

"I fear what will happen after I pass. I've come to believe that there are forces craving my demise so as to usurp some measure of my power. And judging by the book on your desk, I'm not the only one to come to that conclusion."

I looked down at what I had been reading. "There have been some whispers of an unnamed sorcerer looking for information on that very subject. I thought if I knew more I could better prepare myself against whatever was going to unfold. I had no idea that it involved you."

"I have no doubt that it does. Which leads me to the nature of my burden."

The old man got up and wandered over to the window and gazed out at the growing city. He had always been fascinated by man's desire to expand. How any open space was seen just as potential and not for its own beauty. New York was a prime example of that.

"Once I am gone, my spirit will leave this plane and with it a certain amount of enviable knowledge. But my corpse could be used to pull my spirit back, allowing someone to capture it and gain that information."

"Then your body should be cremated, should it not?"

"That's the trick. As long as my corpse exists, it is the only means to recapture my spirit. But if it is destroyed, then that opens up a handful of options that I'd prefer not to make available." He turned to face me. "That's the burden I must place on your shoulders. I need you to take my body and keep it hidden. Keep it safe. Can you do that?"

"Of course, I can…"

"No!" He cut me off in mid-sentence. "Don't tell me what you will do. Don't tell anyone. This is a secret you have to take to your own grave."

"I've been around you long enough to know when you're not telling me something. I also know that if you don't want to tell me, there's nothing I can do to change that. All I can do is abide by your request and hope that whatever you're keeping quiet is something I can do without knowing."

"I greatly appreciate the faith you have in me, Lucius."

I gestured to the stack of books. "As you can see, I've been reading up on the subject. Being in possession of the corpse is only one part of the process. It seems relatively easy for a willing spirit to return for short periods of time or to take over another body. But to bring a spirit back by force, even if you possess the spirit's given name, still seems almost impossible. Surely you can't be too worried about this."

"Almost impossible means that it is still possible and that can't happen. I can't control what other people do, all I can control is what happens to my remains once I am gone and to prevent the worst case scenario I'm putting them into your hands. The only person I can truly trust."

"You have my word. I shall do as you ask."

Matheus seemed relieved but also very tired.

"Would you care for something to eat or perhaps a room to rest in for a bit?"

He smiled at me once again. "I am a little weary from my travels. If you wouldn't find it too terribly rude, I would like to lie down for a short while."

"Come with me. I'll show you to a room that you can use for as long as you'd like." I lead him up the stairs to the second floor and into one of the guest rooms. The old man sat on the edge of the bed and removed his shoes. I turned to leave him, but he stopped me before I reached the door.

"Like you, I allowed the work to dominate my life. I never had time to find a wife or to have a son. That is until I took you in. When I smile at you, Lucius, it's with a father's pride and love. I hope you'll always remember that."

"I shall. Sleep well, Matheus." I left the room, quietly closing the door behind me. By the time I had reached the bottom step, I heard the doorbell chime again. I waved Wilson off and opened it myself. To my surprise I found Drake waiting on the other side.

"Hello, Lucius."

"Kieran. What a pleasant surprise. Do come in."

I lead him into my office, offering him the same seat Matheus had only recently vacated.

"This is turning out to be a very odd day indeed." I sat behind my desk once again.

"Then what I sensed was right?" Drake slid forward in his seat.

"What did you sense?"

"That Matheus was somewhere in the city. His presence is so powerful and familiar, I was certain he was nearby. Am I right?"

"He is. Very near in fact. He just laid down a moment ago."

"How is he? Did he say why he was here or where he has been for the last ten years?"

"I'm afraid we didn't talk too much as he was very tired from his trip. He made some arrangements with me and then went upstairs to rest." I closed the book on my desk and pushed it aside. "I'm sure you can ask him all of that once he's slept a little."

Drake smiled. "It will be good to see him again."

"Can I get you a drink? And where is Natasha?"

Before he could answer, Wilson spoke from the doorway. "Pardon me, sir."

"Yes. What is it?"

"I took a glass of water up to your guest, thinking he might want it when he awoke. But I fear…"

His words trailed off, but neither Drake nor I were listening. We raced up the stairs and into the room. Matheus lay on his back, arms at his sides and a sweet, innocent smile on his face. I checked for breath and then pulse but found neither. Kieran stood beside the bed silently.

"He knew he was dying, didn't he?" Drake continued to stare at the body.

"Yes. He said it would be soon. I didn't realize he meant today."

"He wouldn't have said it even if he knew for sure. It's not the way he did things."

"No, it wasn't. He wouldn't want us to sit around fussing over him, waiting for him to pass."

"That's what the arrangements he discussed with you were about. What to do with his body?"

I nodded.

"Did he say anything else?"

"He said he never had a chance to have a family until he took us in." It was a lie but Fogg was trying to make Drake feel better.

"What did he want done with his remains?" Drake looked at me finally. "Is there anything I can do to help?"

"He asked me to take charge of his body and put it someplace safe. He forbade me to tell anyone and to take the knowledge to my own death."

Drake patted me on the back. "There are no more capable hands for him to be in. You'll do the right thing."

Kieran took one last look at Matheus and then I walked him down the stairs. He stopped in the foyer by the front door.

"There are folks in the city who should hear about his passing. I'll take care of that. Perhaps tomorrow night we can meet at the pub and share a toast to our mentor."

"I'll be there." I held the door open for him.

As I closed the door, I shut my eyes for a moment and when I opened them I was back in Howard's bar.

It was still the middle of the morning as gems didn't take long to view, but I felt exhausted afterwards anyway. The easy part was out of the way. I had watched, or rather lived them as Fogg had asked. But what was I supposed to get out of them? Drake went from being a pompous ass to a decent guy yet still ended up Fogg's mortal enemy and trying to do who knew what to the city. Was it Matheus' death that split the two apart or maybe the fact he trusted Fogg with his remains and not Drake? Would it have killed Fogg to take the extra two minutes to tell me what I was supposed to be looking for in those memories?

CHAPTER THIRTY

I was jarred from my thoughts by a pounding on the front door. You would think the 'Closed' sign would've been enough to send the person away, but they continued to knock. After another minute I realized there was only one person I knew that was so persistent he'd bang for ten minutes on a door. I went over, flipped the lock and held it open for him.

"Good morning, ex-detective."

"Funny. You should give up working for Fogg and hit the comedy clubs."

"No chance. Those crowds are far more dangerous than the stuff I deal with now." I relocked the door and returned to my booth.

Sebastian slid in across from me. "They've got the majority of the NYPD in Fogg's brownstone. Half of them are too winded to move and the other half are dumbstruck by some warehouse room that's bigger than Ebbet's Field. They're never going to find him in there, are they?"

"Not unless he wants them to." I started putting the things back into the satchel. "I'm sorry you got suspended."

"That's why I'm here. I figure if I help you resolve this, I'll get my badge back faster."

"Probably true."

"Okay. So where are we and what do we do next?"

I thought about it a minute, trying to figure out how the detective could help. "This is a battle between sorcerers, but it means they're both thinking like sorcerers. I wonder just how much two detectives could do to throw the whole thing off. What we need is a way to discredit Drake. Something spectacular that will knock out his campaign and send him reeling."

"We need to find it today then, because tomorrow is the election." He looked at the satchel. "Did Fogg give you any idea where we should start looking?"

"He suggested we find Natasha, but she could be hiding in anybody."

"Wait… what?" The detective was rightfully confused by that one.

"Do you really want to know?"

He thought about it for a minute then shook his head. "No. Not really."

"It would be helpful to find some kind of connection between Drake and the dead reporter. Something definitive that shows a previous relationship. Maybe prove he was the one feeding Fiallos information about Fogg. If Fiallos was killed by an implanted spell, then showing that he was involved with more than one sorcerer will be helpful."

"That reminds me. The preliminary report should be ready from the coroner." Sebastian got up and moved over to the bar. "Maybe if we're lucky, they won't have heard that I'm suspended yet and they'll give us the information. Is there a phone behind the bar?"

"It's between the Scotch and the vodka along the back."

He found it and dialed the all too familiar number. There are very few cases where you call a coroner for good news. They get involved after the worst case scenario has already happened. So if you have the number memorized, you deal with a lot of death.

Sea Bass got someone on the phone. "Who's this? Blaine? Hello, Blaine, this is…"

I jumped up to get his attention. "Wait!"

I ran over and took the phone out of his hand. The detective was confused, so I covered the mouth piece and explained.

"Let me handle it. I know this guy." I moved my hand away. "Hey, Blaine. It's Jimmy Doyle. How are you? Good. Yeah, kind of a mess right now. That's why I'm calling. Yeah, that's right. Okay. Yeah, that's kind of what we were expecting. Wait. What? Nope, I've never heard of that either. Well, I appreciate the information and once things have calmed down, I'll come by and say thank you properly. Take care."

Sebastian looked a little suspicious. "You have a financial arrangement with one of the guys at the morgue?"

"You'd be disappointed if I didn't." I sat on one of the bar stools. "Now don't go and get him into any trouble."

"What can I do? I'm suspended, remember?"

"It's pretty much what we thought. Fiallos died of a heart attack."

The detective leaned on the bar. "Then they should call off the search for Fogg. There's no murder to question him on."

"You don't really think it'd be that easy, do you?" I gave him a disappointed look. "Drake is claiming that he can test and see if Fiallos was killed through magical means."

"Which we think he was."

"Right. So all he has to do is say so and that will be enough to keep them trying to bring in Fogg." I shook my head. "If Drake wasn't a power-hungry mad man, I'd almost be impressed."

"So we're back to square one."

We both sat quietly for a moment, trying to decide what to do next. Drake seemed to be controlling all the pieces on the board, including us. He'd gone through and systematically eliminated our friends and allies. He even managed to get Fogg on the run in his own house.

The detective spoke first. "I think we stay with what you were saying before. All the power he has right now is based on him winning the election. From the Chief on down the line all are afraid to say no to him because they think he's going to be the next mayor. We have to stop that from happening and then find a connection between him and Fiallos."

"We could try to get access to his notes. Check with his editor at the Times. The only problem is that newspapers are notoriously tight lipped about stuff like that. If you weren't suspended maybe…"

"That's the thing about taking away a cop's badge." Detective Lee pulled out his gold shield. "Sometimes they forget to ask for the actual badge."

"You were holding out on me?"

"I was not." He smiled. "I was just waiting for the right dramatic moment."

"You know, I'm starting to think that I'm a bad influence on you."

"What about the other part? The preventing him from winning the election thing."

I hopped off the stool. "I have something in mind for that. But I'm not waking her for at least another two hours. Which leaves plenty of time for you and I to go visit the newspaper. Let's go."

I grabbed the satchel from the booth, along with my coat and hat. We headed out the front door and I locked it behind us. It was going to be another very long and crazy day.

CHAPTER THIRTY-ONE

The office of the Times was down on Eighth -- a horrible place to park. We had to use a garage two blocks away and hoof it over. A quick flash of the badge at the front desk and we were told who we wanted to talk to and where to find them without a single question asked. I was sure that would change once we got upstairs.

We got into the elevator. It was the two of us and the uniformed operator.

"What floor?"

"Fifth."

He pushed the lever forward and the box began to rise.

"Are you gentlemen having a good morning?"

Both of us stared daggers at him until the floor was reached, the lever pulled back and the door opened.

The operator shifted uncomfortably. "Uhm…. Have a nice day."

When we stepped off the elevator, we were met by row after row of desks filling a room the size of a basketball court. Along with the desk, each one had a phone, a typewriter and a chair. This was what they called the 'bullpen.' It made my workspace look luxurious. At the very end of it there were two offices. One with the door open, the other with the door closed. We decided to start there.

The open door was the one we wanted. Its glass window pane read 'Mike Campbell' in a series of peeling letters. The office itself was somewhat small. A desk with two chairs in front and one behind. A coat rack, a line of bookcases on the far wall and a dying fern on the window ledge. Hanging from the rack was a set of dry cleaned shirts, three still in the plastic wrapping along with two empty hangers. All the shirts were exactly the same. They matched the one being worn by the man behind the desk.

"Can I help you?"

Sea Bass was quick with the badge once more. "I'm Detective Lee. We were told that you are, or rather were, the direct supervisor for Eric Fiallos."

"Yes. He worked for me. Please come in. Sit down."

We took the seats and I noticed the man staring at me. I tried to be nonchalant. I looked around the room. Paid particular attention to the dying fern. After a moment, the man turned back to Sebastian.

"What is this about? I was led to believe that Eric died of a heart attack."

"Before I can say too much, Mr. Campbell, I must make you aware that this is an ongoing police investigation and what we say here is not for print." He was keeping it as authentic as possible.

"Of course, Detective."

"The preliminary report from the coroner is that Mr. Fiallos died of a heart attack, and normally that wouldn't be a police matter. But he was found in the home of Lucius Fogg. I understand that Mr. Fiallos had recently been writing rather scathing articles about Fogg. Am I correct?"

"Yes. It was kind of a companion piece to the news that broke Saturday about Kieran Drake and his claims about Old Town. Eric had a source telling him that Drake's claims were real and that Fogg was intimately involved in the cover-up." Campbell turned back to me. "Have we met before? You look really familiar."

"I get that all the time. One of those faces."

Sebastian cleared his throat to get Campbell's attention back. "Were you able to verify the source of the claims?"

"Not me personally. Eric had been a respected member of our staff for a decade. He was certain the source was legit so I let him run with it."

"I'm going to need the name of his source." The detective had his notebook out ready to write down the name, like asking for it was just a formality.

It was a nice try.

"Detective, surely you know that I can't give out the name of a confidential source. It would put the reputation of the Times in jeopardy and no one would trust us again." Campbell had made that speech before. "Besides, I honestly don't know it."

Sea Bass leaned forward, confidentially. "You let him run with the story, so you at least believed it to be real. Right?"

"Well. Yeah. That Fogg guy has never seemed right to me. All those weird cases he gets involved with."

"Now, the NYPD doesn't like to look for murders where there aren't any. We see a heart attack and normally that's it. Pack it up and head to the bar. But Fogg has always rubbed me the wrong way, too. And if you ask me, your guy just happening to have his ticker go while sitting in Fogg's office seems like more than just a coincidence. I got rules to follow though. I can't keep digging if I don't have a shovel. If I can't go to my boss and show him a reason to keep suspicion on Fogg, then he might just get away with murder."

The editor thought about it a moment before responding, "Let me see what I can do. Wait here."

Campbell got up and left the room. I was impressed. Sebastian was working this guy perfectly. It's not often I sit back and let someone else do all the talking, but it was the right move in that case.

Campbell returned with a notebook and handed it to the detective. "I happened to see Eric grab a fresh one before he headed out last night. He dropped this one into his desk. I can't let you have it, but you can take a look at it."

"We just need the information. Reading it should be enough."

Campbell nodded. "I'm going to wander over to the break room for a cup of coffee. I'll see you gentlemen in a few minutes."

He was about to walk out the door, but suddenly turned back and stared at me again.

"Are you positive we haven't met before?"

"Have you ever been to Cincinnati?"

"No."

I shook my head. "Then no, we've never met."

Campbell headed out seemingly satisfied with my response. Sebastian turned in his chair so I could see the notebook as well. The whole thing was filled with tiny handwritten notes. Luckily his penmanship was legible. We scanned through some of the pages, trying to find where he was first contacted by Drake. Finally we came across an important part. A description of a night that Fiallos said changed his life.

I decided to take a chance and go to the meeting. I figured it would be some crack pot with blurry photos proving aliens or whatnot. Worse case I could get the cab fare and dinner reimbursed by the paper. Plus, we were meeting at the Remington Arms. Not many crackpots could afford that. I was told to go to room 1012. I was met at the door by a nice enough looking man with sandy blond hair. He invited me in and offered me a drink. I declined but took the seat he offered me next. I pulled out my notebook, but he said that it wouldn't be necessary. That I would remember everything I needed to know.

The man took a moment to get ready. He set up a glass orb onto a rolling cart and then pushed it directly in front of me. I made a joke about a séance which he didn't find funny at all. He told me to place my hand on the orb. I had made the trip already and had nothing else to do on Halloween, so I figured I'd play along. When I did, the entire room shifted and suddenly everything was moving at ninety miles an hour.

I saw flashes of things that would make the folks at Universal Studios jealous. I watched a vampire pull a woman into a dark alley and drain every ounce of her blood out through her neck. I saw a man transform into a werewolf before my eyes and then slaughter a fully grown bull. I then saw these creatures running around city streets. Streets I recognized as being in Old Town.

I realized I wasn't watching these things happen, I was remembering them like I had been there. I suddenly knew about a pact to keep the supernatural in Old Town made up between a vampire, a werewolf, a hunter and a sorcerer. I knew the names: Black, Shaw, Ravenstorm and Fogg.

It stopped as quickly as it had started. I lifted my hand away from the orb. I was still trying to process all of the information. The man explained to me that those were his memories and it was easier for him to share them then trying to explain everything. He gave me the memories I would need to write my story. But I wasn't to break the fact that these creatures lived in the city. He was going to do that himself the next day. I was supposed to go after Lucius Fogg.

I was hesitant to run with it. But the next morning when the man came forward and announced his candidacy for mayor, I realized I had been handed a unique take on one of the biggest stories of my career. Everyone was going to be scrambling for information and I had a head full of it. I did the stories. Even got a call from Drake saying he was pleased and he would remember me after the election.

Something doesn't feel right, though. Everyone is so focused on Old Town and Fogg that no one is looking into Drake. He's bypassing all the vetting a candidate would normally get. I started doing some digging. I tried to get to Fogg, to get the other side of the story. But I've had no luck.

And now Drake wants to see me again. Back to the Remington Arms. My gut tells me something is wrong. I guess that's why I'm writing all this down. Hopefully I'm just paranoid and I can toss all of this into the bin in the morning.

The note ended there with plenty of blank pages after it. The only reason to get a new notebook was so he could leave behind what he had written.

"That connects him to Drake, but there is no date on this. Did he go last night or the night before?" Sebastian shook his head. "And without this notebook, we can't prove a link between them."

"We could try the hotel. Check and see if anyone remembers seeing them together."

Campbell wandered back in holding his coffee mug. The detective got up and showed him the pages in question. The editor read them over. I watched as his eyes got larger and larger. I could tell when he got to the end because he suddenly scowled, thinking that his man had indeed been killed and that the source he thought of protecting could've been involved. He then started flipping through the earlier pages, looking them over. After another minute, he handed the notebook to Sea Bass.

"Take it. There is nothing else in there that needs the protection of the Times and what Eric wrote was meant to be found and used in a situation like this."

"I appreciate that, and I will get to the bottom of this personally." The detective dropped the notebook into his pocket.

Before another word could be said, a copy boy ran into the room looking frantic.

"Mr. Campbell, come quick! Someone just tried to kill Kieran Drake!"

We followed the excited boy back out into the bullpen. All of the reporters were huddled around a desk with a radio on it. Campbell's approach got everyone's attention.

"What is going on?"

One of the reporters turned to give him an update. "Drake was leaving the police station when a guy came up and fired on him six times. No one seems to know how the bullets missed him."

This was horrible news. Drake dead would solve a lot of problems, but an assassination attempt would help build Drake's popularity. He'd be in the forefront of everyone's mind when they walked into the polls the next day. And Drake would use it to his advantage. Whoever took a shot at him pretty much handed him the race.

"They just captured the shooter and have him inside." The reporter continued. "Drake is completely unharmed."

Campbell jumped into action. "Call down and get the presses stopped. Batson, see if you can find Drake and get an interview. LaRoche, find Mayor Harris and get a comment. Kirby, get over to the station and find out more about the shooter. Did we get a name on him?"

The reporter responded, "They said it was Dennick Shaw. I'm looking him up in our records."

My stomach dropped. Bad news turned worse. Shaw was the impulsive type and I could see him getting worried as the day went on, but this just played even more into Drake's hand. I pulled Sea Bass toward the elevator.

"We have to go."

He could tell something was up. "What's going on? Where are we going?"

"Police headquarters. We have to do a jailbreak."

The detective stopped cold in front of the elevator doors. "Like hell. Have you gone insane? You want to get this guy Shaw out of jail? We can't just walk in and sneak him out a back door. They call it police headquarters for a reason. It's full of cops. And why the hell would we break him out anyway?"

"Because Shaw is a lycanthrope and tonight is a full moon. So unless you think having a werewolf sitting in your holding cell is a good idea, we need to get him out and now."

CHAPTER THIRTY-TWO

"It's impossible! We can't sneak into police headquarters and break Dennick Shaw out of the holding cell!"

There are three things I can say I hate without a moment's hesitation: the taste of coffee, the sound of fingernails on a chalkboard and having to admit that something can't be done. But like finding tea to drink instead of coffee, you just have to find an alternative.

"Well, since we can't go in and get him, maybe they'll be nice enough to bring him out to us." I headed to a row of pay phones just outside the Times' office. "I think you need to call the mayor."

Detective Lee stopped and stared at me. "The mayor is not going to take my call."

"No, I expect not." I opened up one of the booth doors. "But you're going to raise hell and swear that you're going to go to the press with all the bad things you know about the city. When they transfer you to someone else, I need to know that person's name."

"And where are you going to be?"

I opened up the door to the booth next to it. "Right here, ready to make a call of my own."

Sea Bass went into the booth and started to close the door, but I stopped him.

"I need to hear the name."

"Right."

The detective dropped a nickel into the phone and dialed the number. I stood there listening to it ring a few times before it was finally answered.

"Hello. This is Detective Sebastian Lee of the New York City Police Department. I would like to speak to Mayor Harris, please." He took a deep breath and listened to the denial. "I don't care if his day is full. I just got suspended and if the mayor doesn't want to talk to me then I'm sure the folks at the Times will. I'm standing right outside their building using one of their payphones. And the mayor should be quite aware of all the things I could say to them... Yes, I'll hold."

I leaned into the booth more to make sure I could hear. Sea Bass started tapping his foot while he waited. Patience was never his strong suit.

"Yes, I'm here. Who am I speaking to? Well, Mr. Thomas Veitch, you are not Mayor Harris and that is whom..."

I ignored the rest of the conversation and moved over to the next booth. I dialed the number for police headquarters and asked for whoever was in charge of the Drake assassination attempt. I was told that it was Detective Summerfield and they put me through.

I heard two short rings and then, "Summerfield".

"Yes, Detective, this is Thomas Veitch from the mayor's office."

"Oh, Mr. Veitch, what can I do for you?"

His tone flipped quickly. Veitch was obviously a powerful player on Harris' staff as I had expected.

"The mayor is concerned about the media circus that the attempted assassination of Drake is going to bring. He wants you to process Shaw and move him to Rikers immediately."

Summerfield was hesitant. "Transferring a prisoner in a case like this takes time to set up. I can't just throw him in a squad car and hope for the best."

"I've been lead to believe that you are a detective that can get things done. I'd like to tell the mayor that very thing."

"All right." He caved in faster than I thought he would. "We have a plan we use for high profile prisoners. I should be able to get him moved within the hour."

"The mayor will be very pleased to hear that, Detective. I'm quite sure he will remember your role in this."

I hung up the phone and turned to see Sea Bass glaring at me.

"You're not getting one of my guys into trouble, are you?"

"Well, not on purpose."

"Great. Who was it?"

"Summerfield."

"Never mind then. He's an ass." The detective smiled. "So what now?"

"Do you know the plan to move high profile prisoners to Rikers Island?"

"I should, I came up with it."

"Good. Then you should know the best place for an ambush along the route." I tossed him the keys to the Studebaker. "I have one more call to make and then you can drive. I have notes to read."

The planned route was a clever and complicated one. It bypassed all residential or high traffic areas as best as it could. Which meant it zigzagged through industrial areas and warehouse districts. With all the turns it would be impossible to follow the transport without being seen. Along the path there was one alley the transport would turn down to avoid passing between an elementary and middle schools. This is where we decided to free Shaw.

The one more call was to Gregor Tsarev. Gregor was an odd type of friend to have and that's saying something for a guy who counts a golem among his closest. Gregor was completely human, but he was also the head of the Russian Mob and he felt he owed me a favor. I decided to call it in.

The detective parked the Studebaker across the street from the alley opening. I had a good line of sight for what I would need to do. I had my notebook opened up in front of me to a specific page and had a second one marked for quick access.

A trash truck came down the street and pulled into the alley. It parked about thirty yards in, near a dumpster, and lowered the front lifts. Once the dumpster was on the metal arms, the driver just sat there waiting. The truck was far enough in that someone coming up the street wouldn't see it until after they turned into the alley.

"You just happen to have a friend who owns a trash company?" Sea Bass seemed skeptical.

"Among other things, yes. It's good to have friends. You should try it."

He looked down at my notes. "You sure you can do this?"

"I've made it work before. Are you sure they'll only be one guy in the back?"

"Yes. They wouldn't have had time to come up with a new plan nor would they think they'd need to. I've only been suspended half a day."

"And here you are already breaking the law."

He was about to snap back at me when he noticed the transport coming up the street in the rear view mirror. I nodded to the trash truck driver who began lifting the bin.

"What is all that gobblygook? It doesn't look like words."

"It's a spell Fogg gave me when the front door started getting stuck. He said it would open any locked door."

"So you've used it before?"

"No."

The detective got nervous. "Why the hell not?"

"Because I don't like using magic unless it's absolutely necessary and case related. Now do you mind, I have to concentrate."

The truck turned the corner into the alley and had to stop a few feet in. I fumbled through the words on my notepad and spun my index finger in a circle as instructed. The back doors of the transport popped open. The guard in the back jumped to his feet with his gun at the ready. The two from the cab jumped out and ran around as well. When they found nothing amiss other than the doors being open, they relaxed. Sebastian on the other hand was holding his breath. He'd never seen me do magic before and if I messed up it would put us in direct conflict with his brothers on the force. I had to get it right. I flipped to the other page in my notebook, extended my hand palm down and lowered it as I read the words. This spell Fogg had given me when I needed to get past a set of security guards to help a client. The guards' eyelids fluttered, they stumbled a few times and collapsed into a pile fast asleep.

Sebastian finally exhaled as we ran across the street. He waved off the trash truck while I hopped in the back of the transport and pulled out my pick tools.

"Doyle. I'm surprised to see you." Shaw looked a bit ashamed at having to be rescued.

"Well, I'm not exactly happy about having to do this."

I started working on the cuffs. They were chained to the floor of the transport. Sebastian checked on the three cops.

"They all seem fine." He looked at me. "Why not just use that first spell again?"

"Because this isn't a door. Magic is all about the details. Fogg gave me a spell once to make Dobermans chase their tails for an hour. Turns out there was one German Shepherd in the pack. It didn't work on him."

"What did it do to the Shepherd?"

"Nothing. He bit me in the ass." I heard the start of a laugh. "And if you make one joke I'll put you to sleep as well."

I got the cuffs open and the three of us ran back for the car. Sea Bass tossed the keys back to me. Shaw slid into the back seat.

"How long will they be out?" The detective got in on the passenger side.

"About thirty minutes give or take."

"They'll be reported as no shows by Rikers in twenty. We have to get your buddy here out of sight."

Shaw piped up from the back seat. "Take me to the Dawn. I can disappear easily enough from there."

I pulled the car out and headed for the bar where we first met. It's never a good idea to take a fugitive back to his regular hangout, but Shaw wasn't a normal fugitive and the Dawn wasn't a normal hangout. It was the central hub for the werewolf clan when it wasn't a full moon. If anyone had routes back into Old Town without being noticed he did and they would all start at his bar.

"What the hell were you thinking, Shaw?" I stared at him in the rearview mirror. "You didn't really think you could gun down Drake, did you?"

"Actually I did. I got tired of waiting for you and Fogg to handle it. The full moon is tonight and I have to make sure my clan is safe. I thought maybe Drake was so focused on his duel of wits with Fogg that he wouldn't notice a good old fashioned act of violence."

"You may have just given him the election," Sea Bass added.

"He was expecting it to happen." Shaw looked out the window at the passing traffic. "When I got there, I took aim and fired. I was in point blank range. I couldn't have missed. But when the bullets should have struck him, it was like he suddenly moved three feet back and to the right."

Sebastian turned in his seat. "You think he can move that fast? I thought Drake was human."

"He is." I assured him. "If I had to guess, I'd say he used an illusion spell. Made it look like he was in a slightly different place then where he was actually standing. If that's true, then it means he was expecting someone to take a shot at him all along."

Shaw tapped the back window. "Oh, he was more than expecting. He was counting on it. Before they took me away, he leaned in and told me that he was surprised it was me and not you who resorted to a gun."

A few minutes later we dropped Shaw off at the Dawn. He thanked us then ducked inside and we headed back toward Howard's.

A minute later Sea Bass threw me a question. "You said you hadn't tried that spell before. Why?"

"Because I'm not a sorcerer and I don't want to be one."

"You don't want to use magic? I'm not a fan of the things Fogg gets involved with, but I could totally see using different spells in my everyday life."

"That's just it. Using magic isn't everyday life. It's tapping into a power that I don't understand and honestly don't think I ever will. I live in a house where time doesn't pass. I'm served food by a woman I've never seen actually cook. I deal with vampires, werewolves, demons, sirens, golems and about a dozen other things that most of the world think just exist on movie screens. And the only way I keep my sanity though all of it is to stay grounded in my humanity. Ignoring the temptation of all that I could have if I just took the short cut and cast a spell."

Sebastian shook his head. "I don't see how using a spell or two makes you less human."

"Being human means you're born, you live your life the best you can, jumping from one happy moment to the next and then you die. But all the sorcerers I know seem focused on immortality or power and it corrupts their worlds so much that when they finally get what they desire they've lost all the things that make life worth living. Fogg may be one of the most powerful men on the planet, yet he can't walk out his front door. I don't see that exchange as being worth it."

"You're probably right." Sea Bass gave me a smirk. "I couldn't see you pulling rabbits out of hats anyway. Sawing a woman in half could be fun though, depending on the woman."

We laughed and it felt good. It was a brief moment of relief in the middle of the chaos.

The detective sat back in his seat. "So what do we do now?"

"We need to find a way to reach the most people possible at once."

"My ex-girlfriend works over at one of the television stations. I could probably talk her into letting us go on air live, if I can convince her it's an emergency."

"Wait." I was stunned. "You had a girlfriend?"

"I'm going to ignore that. What do you want to do with the airtime if I can get it?"

"I'm hoping to have a very special message for all those going to the polls tomorrow."

I pulled up in front of the detective's car and let him get out. He leaned into the open window from the other side.

"What time do you want me to ask for?"

I thought for a second. "Make it seven o'clock. We'll get the most possible people then."

"A lot of kids go to bed at seven."

"And they don't vote, so let's not worry about them."

"I'll see what I can do." He started to unlock the door to his car. "Where will you be?"

"Trying to find the right person to give the message. Which means I have to start with my girlfriend." I tipped my hat to him. "I'll meet you at the station tonight."

CHAPTER THIRTY-THREE

I checked my watch. It was almost four in the afternoon. A little less than three hours until the full moon and the werewolves would head for Old Town. That wasn't my concern anymore. The supernatural secrets of New York City had to take a back seat. Whatever Kieran Drake was planning I had until morning to derail it or everyone would suffer the consequences.

I headed up to Emma's apartment. She got up at three each work day so I knew I wasn't going to wake her. I rapped my knuckles gently on the door. I could hear movement on the other side and then saw a shadow cover the peephole. She slid the chain off and opened the door. I stepped in as she closed it after. When I turned I saw the best sight of my day.

"Ten minutes sooner and you could have joined me."

Emma was wrapped in a dark blue towel and nothing else. Her wet hair laid straight down her back. Her pale skin glistened in the sunlight through the window. No matter how bad my day got, and this had been one of the worst, seeing her always made me feel better.

"You want a drink?"

"Like you wouldn't believe."

When we started dating, she began to keep a bottle of single malt in her apartment at all times. It wasn't high-end by any means, but I appreciated the thought more than the brand name. I took a seat on the couch while she poured me a drink.

"How are you holding up?"

She didn't come out and say Ernie's name, but it was obvious what she meant.

"I've been so focused on this case that I don't know how much it's soaked in yet. Maybe the distraction is a good thing for now."

She walked over to the couch and handed me the drink. She then dropped her towel and climbed into my lap, straddling my legs and putting her chest up against mine.

"I thought it was my job to distract you."

She kissed me and I kissed her back. I had things to do, problems to solve, a missing woman to find. The last thing I should've been doing was making out with Emma right then. But I needed to. I needed to get lost in the passion for at least a few minutes. To feel her lips pressed against mine. To feel her breasts rub against my shirt every time she breathed. To run my hands along her smooth silky skin. I wanted to push everything bad out and just focus on the woman in my arms.

I couldn't do it. A moment was fine, but that was all I could afford. I stopped kissing her and she quickly got the idea. She slid off and sat next to me on the couch.

"How bad is it?"

I wanted to lie, but I didn't. "Drake has been a step ahead of us on everything. He seems to know what we are going to do before we even think of doing it."

"Why does he want to be mayor?"

"I don't think he does. It's just part of his bigger game." I shook my head in frustration. "At least I think there's a bigger game."

She turned and leaned against my arm. "There's one thing that doesn't make sense to me."

"Only one?"

"Did you come over here planning on being a smart ass?"

"No. What's the one thing?"

"If he's got this thing so far planned out like you said, then why did he screw up and not register for the election on time?"

Now it was my turn to turn towards her. "What? He's registered."

"No, he's not. That's why he was stressing the write-in vote. You'd think he would have declared in time so his name would be on the ballot. It would have been a lot easier for him."

"Maybe he was just..." Then it hit me like a ton of bricks. "Of course. We couldn't believe he wanted to be mayor because there's no real power there. Well, that's because he doesn't want the job. He just wants the signatures."

"The signatures? Is he some kind of psychotic autograph collector?"

"In a way, yes." I got up and started walking as I thought. "He's going to turn the ballots into contracts. They sign for the ballot and then write in his name, they are unknowingly making a deal."

Now Emma was sitting on the edge of the couch trying to figure it out, too.

"A deal? What kind. What do they get and what does he get?"

"I'm thinking he gets their soul and they get nothing."

"It doesn't sound like a very good deal. Why would he need souls?"

I was just starting to put all the pieces together in my head. I had read something about souls, or rather spirits. I had read it when I was viewing Fogg's memories.

"He wants to forcibly call back a spirit. He's making a deal of his own with a demon from the underworld to bring back a spirit that wouldn't come back on its own. He turns over all the souls of the people that vote for him and the demon gives him the spirit he's after."

"You're making huge assumptions here. What spirit would be so valuable to Drake that he'd go through all of this? And how can you be sure you're even in the ballpark?"

"Because I think Fogg made the connection just before he threw me out of the brownstone. That's why he gave me the memories he did."

Emma got up and wrapped the towel back around her. "You seem to have figured this out, but I'm still completely lost."

I grabbed her by the arms and kissed her again.

"Thank you. You've helped me incredibly. But I need one more favor and it's a big one."

"Am I going to need to be dressed to do it?"

"Yes."

"Okay. Wait here. I'll be back in a few minutes."

She sauntered off into the bedroom and I enjoyed watching her go.

A half hour later we were back in the Studebaker and Emma was holding the erector-set locator on her lap. The notes Fogg gave me explained how it worked and how it needed someone connected to the person you are looking for to make it work. Since we were trying to find Natasha, that meant it had to be someone she had possessed. Emma seemed much more likely to say yes than the waitress at the diner and I couldn't see Mr. Whiskers being all that helpful in the search.

"So what am I supposed to do with this thing?"

"You are supposed to think about Natasha and try to pick up on her trail."

"Her trail? Seriously?"

"Yes, seriously. I'm told that spirits leave kind of a spectral trail and if you have been in contact with a spirit then you should be able to use that device to follow the trail."

She still seemed skeptical. "This looks like something a five-year old would build. Did Patches make this?"

"No, Fogg made it."

"I thought magic was all ancient artifacts and magical pendants."

I pulled the car over to the curb. "Look. This may not be the most impressive device or have some romantic history attached to it, but it is the device we need to do the job at hand."

"You're kind of sexy when you get defensive." She smiled and then sat up straight. "Okay, where is the on-switch?"

"Just hold it in both hands and think about Natasha. You should start to feel a mild vibration somewhere in the construct. Where the vibration is tells us which way to go to follow the trail."

"I can do that." She closed her eyes for a second then opened them again. "Are we just going to randomly start here and hope for the best?"

"This isn't a random location. Ethel at the diner told me that when Natasha finally left her body she was standing inside a bank. That building across the street is that bank. This is the last known location for Natasha before she jumped into someone else."

"Let's give it a shot then." Emma closed her eyes again and started to concentrate.

I sat there quietly, watching the people on the street walk by. Maybe I was looking to see if I could spot Natasha on my own. Completely impossible as she could be in anyone, but I wasn't very good at being useless and that's what I was until Emma gave me a direction to drive.

"I might be getting something, but it feels like the whole thing is vibrating."

Fogg had mentioned that. "Think of it like trying to hear one person in a room full of people. Try to focus on the specific spot where the vibration is coming from."

She nodded and continued to focus. Another few minutes passed and I was starting to think what my back-up plan might be if this failed. I wouldn't need it.

"She's that way." Emma pointed to the northeast.

"That's a diagonal line. You couldn't just say forward, left or right?"

"You want to work the magic Erector Set and I'll drive?"

"That way, got it. I'm going to drive north for a bit and you tell me when the vibration begins to move on the construct."

I drove a mile and a half north before she told me to turn right. Then about two miles east a quick left was called for. It became a bit of a serpentine pattern trying to figure out the exact building. Once we got it narrowed down to a small enough area, we circled the block a few times until Emma was certain of the location. It was a fifteen floor apartment building that you'd have to have a very fat wallet to live in.

I parked the car and we walked up to the front of the building. Two things displeased me, one that was there and one that wasn't. What was there was a large doorman who seemed keen on asking people why they wanted into the building. That meant what wasn't there was the usual list of residents and apartment buzzers. Not knowing who I was going to see, it would be difficult to con my way into the building.

"This isn't good." Emma went for the understatement. "I can't exactly walk in there holding the magical metal doohickey."

"Maybe what we need here is a weasel. Follow me."

There was a payphone about half a block down the street. I used it to call an acquaintance named Larry Loeb. Larry worked at the Hall of Records and on more than a few occasions traded information to me in exchange for vials of a mild love potion. The potion wouldn't make anyone do what they wouldn't normally do, it just evened the odds for Larry and he definitely needed that. Being that it was ten minutes to five I knew this was going to be a costly call.

"Loeb here." His familiar whine chirped through the phone.

"Larry, Jimmy Doyle here. I need some information in a hurry."

"In a hurry you say?" I could hear him rubbing his hands together. "That's going to be expensive."

"I figured as much. I need to know all the residents in an apartment building. Eight four two Monument Drive."

"Three vials."

"I can bring the vials by tomorrow, but I need the information right now."

"Four vials then."

"You realize, Larry, that I will pay you the four vials and take the information. But the next time I need something, I may just go out and find a different source. One who doesn't try to unfairly extort from me in emergencies."

There was a long pause on the line for a moment and then finally. "Three vials. Give me a minute to find the list."

I covered the phone and turned to Emma. "He's getting the list."

She leaned against me. "Remind me never to negotiate with you."

Another few minutes passed before Loeb returned.

"You're in luck, the list isn't that long. Must be some big apartments. Only about sixty-five names. There's a few vacancies as well."

Loeb started reading off the names. He got about a third of the way through when I stopped him.

"That's good right there. Does it say who the building manager is?"

He flipped through some papers. "Yeah, it's David Watkins."

"Thanks. I'll be by in the next couple of days with your vials."

I hung up the phone and started looking at the building again. The top of the building specifically. Most of the names he read off didn't mean much to me, but there was one that was too obvious for it not to be her. It had to be her.

"Come on, I know who she is possessing."

Emma was surprised. "Just by hearing the list of residents? Who is it?"

"Maria Huntley."

"Are you serious? *The* Maria Huntley?"

"It makes perfect sense, doesn't it?"

She nodded. "Yeah, I guess it does. So how do we get in there? It's not like we can just walk up and say we're there to see Ms. Huntley."

"Oh no, it seems you and I are suddenly in the market for a new apartment."

CHAPTER THIRTY-FOUR

Emma wrapped her arm around mine and we walked up to the doorman with our heads held high. The trick to getting into a place is twofold, confidence and a bit of knowledge. Drop the right name or two and act like you belong and they're more than likely to accept that you do in fact belong.

"Can I help you?"

"Yes, my good man. My fiancée and I are looking for an apartment and this building came highly recommended. I was told there were a few vacancies and I should pop by and ask for Mr. Watkins."

The guard seemed hesitant. "Let me check to see if he's available. Would you mind telling me who recommended the building to you?"

"Ms. Maria Huntley. My Emma here and Maria are very close. You could say they practically share the same space."

And the right name was dropped. The guard opened the door for us and ushered us inside. He then asked us to wait for just a moment as he ran over to the security desk and rang for Mr. Watkins. The building manager must have sprinted half the distance there as our wait was only a minute or two at the most.

"Good afternoon. My name is David Watkins. I'm told you'd like to see our vacant apartments."

"Nice to meet you, Mr. Watkins. I'm James Farber and this is my fiancée Emma."

"Farber?" The manager's eyes widened a little more. "Any relation to Jonathon Farber?"

"He's my uncle."

The Farbers were an insanely rich couple that Fogg and I helped out a year or so prior. I wouldn't normally do that to a client, but the Farbers' was an odd situation and it wasn't the first time I needed to use their name. I was pretty sure that would seal the deal and it did.

"We have a few vacancies at this time. Is there something in particular you're looking for?" This was his way of asking how much we wanted to spend.

"Emma here loves the view of the city. Perhaps you have something on an upper floor, maybe looking out over the park." That told him we had money to burn.

"I think I have just the thing. And your fiancée will be very happy with her neighbor."

It would have been indiscreet for him to say that the apartment he was going to show us was next door to Huntley, but he wanted us to know as a selling point. He led us to the elevator and took us up to the fifteenth floor. There were only four apartments on the entire floor. I knew which one was Huntley's and which one was vacant from talking to Loeb.

Watkins let us into the empty apartment and showed us around. All of Emma's place would have fit in the kitchen there. You could have had a decent football game in the living room and the master bedroom could have been cut in three and each would be considered a big room. He then took us over to the balcony to show us the view.

"One of the best views in the entire city." He slid open the door to let us out.

Emma looked uncertain. "I don't know. I read about that woman in Chicago that went out on her balcony and it collapsed. Are you sure it's secure?"

"One hundred percent. Let me show you." He walked outside and began jumping up and down. "It's as safe as if you were standing on the street below."

"Emma and I need a few moments to confer. Excuse us." I reached over and slid the door shut and locked it. I then turned to Emma. "Let's go."

We made our way of the apartment and down the hallway, ignoring Watkin's banging on the glass door. We quickly found Maria Huntley's place. Emma was about to knock on the door when I stopped her.

"Let's not give her a chance to prepare."

"What if you're wrong and it's not her?" Emma was genuinely concerned.

"It's the only lead we have. I think we have to go all in on this."

She nodded her agreement and I dug out my notebook. I used the unlock spell one more time and the door opened up. I walked in prepared for anything. Flying lightning bolts, concussion blasts. I expected the worst. It wasn't what we got. Ms Huntley sat quietly staring out the window.

"Natasha?"

She turned to look at us. "You're a pretty good detective, Jimmy. How'd you figure out I'd be here?"

"If I was recently freed after six decades and could only survive by possessing other people, I'd find the richest person I could that had no family to notice I was acting different. You left Ethel's body while you were at a bank and when we tracked you to this building it narrowed it down to just Maria Huntley."

"Wealthiest single woman in the city. You'd think I'd be having fun or something. But I can't get Drake out of my head."

Emma stepped up. "You know the truth now, don't you? He's just been using you. He did it on Halloween just as he had done it all those years ago."

"Why? Why would he do it?" A tear rolled down her cheek.

"You were a distraction." I felt bad saying it, but only the truth mattered. "Drake needs access to Fogg's house. It didn't work sixty-five years ago so he's trying it again."

"So I was just his pawn." She was crying harder now. "He never loved me. He never wanted to teach me. He just wanted to use me."

"He did more than just use you." Emma walked over and put her hands on Natasha's borrowed shoulders. "I've seen your memories. I know the hell he put you through over and over again. You gave everything you had to please him and it was never enough."

Natasha hunched over sobbing. "I've been such a fool. I let him walk all over me."

"You can change that." Emma put her arms around her. "Help us stop him. All of this has been a ploy by Drake to get power. So much power that he can treat the whole world like he's treated you. Only you can stop him now."

"I can't face him. I can't look at him again."

"You won't have to." Emma helped Natasha to her feet. "All you have to do is come with us and tell us your story. That's all. Will you help us?"

She stood quietly for a few moments, staring at Emma. I found myself staring at her, too. All that Natasha had put her through and Emma was trying to comfort the woman. Trying to convince her to stand up against Drake. It would have won me over. Luckily it worked on Natasha as well.

"All right. Tell me what I have to do."

Emma, Natasha and I headed down to the lobby. The doorman looked puzzled by our being without that building manager, but there was no way he was going to say anything in front of Ms. Huntley. Once the two ladies were outside, I turned back to the man and whispered.

"It seems Mr. Watkins is having a spot of trouble with the glass door in the apartment he was showing us. You might want to pop up there and see if you can give him a hand."

"Yes, sir."

The drive across town put us at the television studio at six forty-five. Emma took the time to catch Natasha up on all the things that had happened over the last few days. I figured I'd have to sweet talk my way past the guard, but when he noticed the passenger in the back seat we were waved through immediately. I found Sea Bass waiting for us outside of the news studio.

"Did you find the person you were looking for?" He seemed a bit panicked. "My ex hasn't promised to give us the time yet, but she's willing to hear what we have and why we need to go on the air. I hope you can make a damn convincing..."

He stopped in mid-sentence when he saw Natasha get out of the car.

"Who do I need to convince?" Natasha asked the detective.

"You're Ms. Huntley..."

"So it would appear."

"You won't have to convince anyone, ma'am. I'm sure they'll put you on right away being as you own the majority of the network." Sea Bass stepped back and pointed to the door to the studio. "Right through there, ma'am."

Natasha walked into the building like she owned it. And for the moment she did. A woman ran up to greet her. She kept looking back and shooting daggers at Sebastian while trying to kowtow to the visiting royalty.

"I'm sorry, Ms. Huntley. Detective Lee didn't say the air time was for you."

"That's fine, my dear. But I would like to go on live. Now."

"Of course. You can sit right here." The woman practically shoved the anchorman out of his seat. "We'll be coming back from commercial in thirty seconds."

A make-up man ran up with a giant powder puff.

"You put that anywhere near my face and you'll be sweeping out a television station in Omaha, Nebraska before you can blink."

The make-up man ran off and the countdown to air started. Natasha no longer looked sad, but rather determined. She had made up her mind. I hoped she could be convincing as she was our last shot.

The camera's red light went on. "Good evening, ladies and gentlemen. What I am about to say may be the most important thing you will hear in your life time. If there are any other adults around you who are not watching, please ask them to pay attention as this concerns everyone in New York City. You have been told some pretty fantastical things lately.

Things that are difficult to believe. Well, I'm going to add to that by one, but it's the one thing that you must believe.

"Some of you know me by the name Maria Huntley. And this is in fact her body. But she is not the one who is speaking to you right now. I am actually Natasha Drake, the wife of the man who is asking you to write his name in on the ballot tomorrow. But there are things about my dear Kieran you don't know. As to how I am in this body, the answer is simple. I am a spirit. One that has been trapped here for sixty-five years after I was murdered by my husband.

"Kieran is a power-crazed man who wants to ruin your city and your lives. But I'm not telling you not to vote for him because of what he might do. I want you to know what he has already done. How he married me and trained me as a sorceress not out of love, but as part of a master plan. He yelled at me, he beat me, he treated me as less than human until the time came and then he murdered me as part of his plot.

"Now you may not believe what I am saying right now. But ask yourself if it's any more farfetched than what Kieran has been saying the last few days? He has come out of nowhere and asked you to trust him. He asked me to trust him too and it cost me my life. Are you ready to trust someone you've known for two days, just because they ask you to?

"When this camera turns off, my life will be over. I will leave Maria Huntley's body and move on finally. Everything I loved and cared for is gone. The people you love and care for are still around you and deserving of your protection. Don't let them down. Good night."

The camera light switched off. Natasha turned and looked at Emma and me. She nodded once and then her body went limp followed by a sudden jerk and Maria Huntley was in control once more. I wasn't sure how much of Natasha's memories would linger. I found out quickly though.

"Did you record that?" Huntley was on her feet talking to the stage manager.

"Yes, ma'am."

"Good. I want that re-run every half hour from now until the polls close tomorrow. And call up the other stations and newspapers. Make sure that's leaked to them as well. I want everyone in this city to know what an absolute bastard Kieran Drake really is."

It was up to the media to undo the damage Drake had done. All we could do was sit back and wait for the election results. As for Natasha, I hoped where ever her spirit ended up she would find some happiness.

CHAPTER THIRTY-FIVE

We left the studio feeling like the crisis was over. I was about to say goodbye to the Detective and take Emma to dinner before she had to go to work. That all changed when a squad car screeched to a halt in front of us and a uniformed officer jumped out of the car.

"Detective, the Chief sent me to find you. He figured with what was just broadcasted you'd be somewhere around."

I looked at him feeling a bit hurt. "Did everyone know about this ex-girlfriend but me?"

"You really want to talk about this now?" He turned to the officer. "What's going on Jones?"

"First, you've been officially reinstated." The officer then looked at me and then back to Detective Lee.

"It's okay, you can say whatever it is in front of Doyle."

He nodded. "We've lost contact with the units assigned to Fogg's brownstone."

"Maybe they are catching their breath." I threw in.

"The last we heard through the radio was a scream."

"Fogg wouldn't...?" Sebastian looked at me for help.

"No, he wouldn't. But Drake would. He wants something in the house and I think we just made him desperate."

The Detective pushed past the officer and got into the driver's seat. "Get in, Jones. Jimmy?"

"I'll be right behind you."

Emma and I ran for the Studebaker. I turned the engine over and floored it, tucking in behind the squad car as it roared out of the parking lot and onto the streets. Sea Bass wasn't hitting the brakes at all as he screamed through one intersection after another. He had already lost one good man because of Drake.

Emma sat in the seat next to me, holding on tight to the door handle.

"Reach into the back seat for me. There's a small satchel."

She leaned back, got the bag and pulled it into her lap. "Got it."

"Good." I pulled my .45 from my shoulder holster and gave it to her. "At the bottom of the bag you'll find two small boxes. One is marked with the number forty-five. Load the gun with the bullets in the box."

She flipped the cylinder out, dropped the current rounds out into her free hand and dropped them into her pocket. She then grabbed six bullets from the box, slipped them in, flipped the gun closed and handed it back. Having a girlfriend who could handle a gun was really a benefit.

"Now grab my back-up piece from the glove compartment."

She pulled the gun out and looked at it. "Not like you to carry a .38?"

"It was a gift from Sea Bass when I went solo for a while."

She switched to the other box, the one marked with a thirty-eight, and loaded that one as well. She then handed it to me just as we pulled up in front of the brownstone. I dropped the two boxes of bullets into my jacket pocket.

The Detective was out of the car and looking around. Four squad cars but not one officer in sight. The four of us met by the Studebaker.

"First, I'm going to need a gun since they took mine when the suspended me."

I pulled out the .38 and handed it to him. "I've got you covered. It's filled with demon rounds."

"Seriously, demons again? I really need to stop hanging around you." He turned to Jones. "You are to take Ms. Martin over to the diner on the corner and stay with her. Don't come back here no matter what. Do you understand?"

"But what if...?"

"What did I say, Jones?"

"I understand, Detective."

Emma grabbed me by the neck and kissed me, hard. Then she turned and kissed Sebastian on the cheek. She looked at both of us and I could see the fear in her eyes.

"Be safe."

"We'll be back before you can finish a piece of their apple pie." I watched as the two of them headed off, and then turned back to Sea Bass. "Once more unto the breach."

The front door was still wide open. I positioned myself on the right side of the jamb, Sebastian on the left. I took a quick peek in and saw no one in the foyer. A nod told me he was ready. I went in high, gun aimed at the top of the stairs. He went in low covering the office and the downstairs hallway. A few feet in I caught site of an officer on the floor. I covered the detective while he checked on his man.

"He's alive but out cold. Looks like he was hit pretty hard."

"He's about as safe there as anywhere." I gestured to the door behind Sea Bass. "Let's check the office."

A quick visual sweep told me two things. The office was empty and Fogg had been keeping an eye on the situation from where he was hiding. Sitting in his chair was the Little Lucius puppet.

"You've got to be kidding me." The detective just shook his head at the sight of the dummy. He about lost it when the puppet spoke.

"Good evening, Detective Lee."

"We're flying blind here, boss." I kept my gun pointed at the office doors. "Can you fill us in?"

"Drake showed up about a half hour ago. He and his two companions took out the police rather quickly." The dummy's little wooden mouth moved with the words. "They've split up and are now searching the house."

"And we both know that he's not looking for you."

The puppet nodded. "Agreed."

"Any chance he'll find it?" I was trying to come up with a plan.

"Given enough time, maybe." The dummy looked at me. "If I come out now, he and his companions are too powerful. He'll use me to get what he wants."

"Then you stay put until Sebastian and I can take out his friends. Once the playing field is balanced, you can finish what he started sixty-five years ago."

"One's in the kitchen, the other is on the second floor. Good luck, gentlemen."

I headed back to the office door with the detective in tow.

"The companions are the demons?" he asked.

"Yup."

"Do you ever take on something simple, like a mugger with a switchblade?"

"Yeah, just last summer, when I was on vacation." I headed back out into the foyer. "We'll do the second floor first."

We headed up the stairs slowly and quietly. I was in the lead looking forward. Sebastian followed keeping an eye on our six. I got to the top of the landing and saw two more officers on the ground but no creatures. I kept aim at the hallway while Sea Bass checked on his men. Both were out cold.

The thunderous sound of glass breaking drew our attention to the last door on the left. We made our way down the hall quickly, flanking the opening on either side. I gestured for the detective to swing around first. His left foot planted and a creak roared out from the loose board below it. Before he could finish his pivot into the doorway, a black leathery wing flashed out, sending him flying back five feet and slamming him hard into the wall.

I spun around into the opening and fired. The shot buried itself in the leading edge of the demon's left wing. The creature didn't seem to notice the wound as it dove across the room and grabbed me by the throat. His wing knocked the gun from my hand. I expected to hear a snap next and then nothing else forever. Instead I heard a voice that sounded like gravel in a high-speed blender.

"Doyle. I was hoping to find you. There are a lot of demons who want your skin." He sniffed me. "You don't seem like anything special to me."

"This is only our first date. I become more charming over time." I pushed against his chest to get free, but the creature's grip was too strong.

"I heard you thought yourself to be clever." He put his face right up to mine and his breath just about knocked me out. "Clever would have been not coming back here tonight. You should've let Fogg die and moved on with your life. But then again, I've never found any human to really be clever."

I drove my knee up into his stomach with as much force as I could muster. It felt like I had just rammed it into a cement post, yet he didn't even blink.

"Any final words?"

I heard a click behind me and smiled. "How about 'ouch'?"

"What?"

I heard the tell-tale bang of the .38 and then a searing pain ripped across my left arm. The bullet then buried itself deep into the demon's right eye socket. The creature staggered and dropped me. I hit the floor hard and scrambled for my weapon. I wouldn't need it yet.

Five more times the detective fired his gun. Five more bullets slammed into the head of the black-winged monstrosity until there wasn't much of a face left. Its leathery skin began to crack across its chest and limbs. Its wings started to crumble and flake off in bits of dust and debris. Within seconds the whole thing had dissolved into a pile of dust and ash.

I found my gun and got to my feet. Sebastian was looking over his work and shaking his head.

"I'm never going to get used to things like this."

"I hope you never do." I tossed him the box of bullets for his gun. "Re-load quickly. They know we're here now."

"Sorry about shooting you."

I held my arm. It was just grazed. "You've wanted to do that for years."

He gave me a half grin. "True."

We moved back into the hallway. The detective was in the process of dropping the spent cartridges when we were both sent flying. The other demon had decided to come upstairs, through the floor. Wood and carpet blew past me so fast I had to cover my eyes. The creature stood, straddling the hole it had created. I fired off two shots, aimed at its head, but its wings folded across in front of it. The bullets hit, but did little damage to the wings.

I had four shots left and I couldn't waste them. From flat on my back I wasn't going to get a better angle. The box of bullets Sebastian was holding had scattered across the floor when we got knocked off our feet. The demon's legs coiled a bit. It was getting ready to leap. My mind was racing, trying to come up with what to do. Then I noticed the handle on the door behind it turning. The handle was black.

Fogg stepped into the hallway with his cane held in his hand like a club. He swung it in the direction of the creature and a large electric blue bolt of energy leapt from the head of the cane. It crashed into the right leg of the demon, sweeping it out and sending the creature into a spin. Its weight shifted to its other leg and the creature flipped and twisted around until it fell into the hole in the floor.

I had the top of the demon's head in my sight and I didn't hesitate. A double-tap later and the creature started cracking apart and falling to the floor below.

Sebastian and I got to our feet again. He was still loading his gun.

"Those won't be necessary, Detective." Fogg indicated the bullets. "There are no more demons in the house. There is only Drake and he is mine to deal with."

"You're not taking him on alone." I stepped over the hole in the floor. "We can help."

"This is going to be a battle of magic, not fists and guns. You have done an exemplary job on this, Jimmy. But there isn't much you can do now."

Fogg headed for the stairs. Sebastian jumped over the hole and stood next to me.

"You're not going to just accept that, are you?"

"Hell no."

"I didn't think so." He poked his head into the room Fogg had come out of. "Do you have a plan?"

"Not yet. But I'm working on it."

Sebastian pointed into the room. "That's the bathroom. Are you telling me that the whole time my guys were in here looking for him, Fogg was hiding in the bathroom?"

"Makes you wonder, doesn't it?"

I headed off after Fogg with the detective following close behind.

CHAPTER THIRTY-SIX

Fogg turned down the back hall just past the kitchen on the first floor. The one I didn't notice for the first five years I lived there. Every time I went down the hall I'd find something new. This day was going to be no different.

"Where are you going?" I had to walk quickly to keep up with Fogg's pace.

"Why, the dueling room of course."

Detective Lee was also hurrying to keep up. "You have a dueling room?"

I shrugged my shoulders. "It's news to me."

A few doors from the end on the right hand side, Fogg opened the door and went in. We scurried in behind him. Inside we found another improbably large room for the size of the actual building. It was rectangular in shape, at least a good fifty yards long or more and half as wide. The floors were wooden with a red carpet about six feet across running from one end of the room to the other dead square in the middle. The walls were also covered in wood and every few feet you'd find a different hanging sword from various time periods. A few chairs were scattered about along the walls, out of the way of the main fencing strip.

"If you're going to have a magical showdown with an arch-rival, this would be the place to do it." The room was interesting, but the gravity of the situation never left my thoughts. "How do you get him here? You're not going to wait until he just wanders in are you?"

"I was going to give him a clue to where I am."

"A clue? Like leave bread crumbs?" I shook my head. "I don't think…"

Before I could finish my thought, Fogg let out a voice that rumbled like an earthquake and I was certain that the whole city could hear it.

"KIERAN DRAKE!"

I had to shake my head to clear the ringing in my ears. By the looks of it, the detective was having the same problem.

"A little warning next time you're going to do that." My hearing was finally getting back to normal. "Where do you want us?"

"I'm assuming you are going to refuse to leave the room, so please stay along the far walls and out of the way." Fogg suddenly looked at the door. "He's here."

Drake strolled into the room like he owned it. He was wearing a white suit that was obviously more money than Sebastian and I made in a year combined. His sandy blond hair bounced just a little as he walked. His excitement at reaching his end game showed on his face. Whatever we had done to screw him up, he didn't seem to care.

"I like the choice of locations. Very fitting." Drake stepped onto the red carpet strip and faced his opponent. "I don't remember you having a flair for the dramatic."

"I chose this room because like fencing, magic takes discipline. Something you have always lacked."

"You may call it a lack of discipline, but I prefer to think of it as drive and ambition." He crossed over to the wall and started looking at one of the epees. "Now if my not wanting to help the little people out with their inconsequential problems is something you look at as a weakness, well then, it's a fault I'm happy to have."

"Your faults are greater and more numerous than that." Fogg walked over and pulled out an epee of his own. "You suffer from the greatest fault of them all, a lust for power. You would risk the lives of everyone in New York City just so you could capture what is left of our old master's abilities. It's a shame you felt that your own talents were inadequate."

Drake pulled the sword from the wall and started testing its bend. "My dear Lucius, are you trying to goad me into getting angry? Like you were supposed to anger the siren that night so many years ago now? You were to distract her and instead you got caught up in her song. Please tell me that isn't your plan for me. Because then you had Matheus and me to back you up. Now you just have the two dim-witted gunslingers that can't seem to get out of their own way half of the time."

"No, this is just between you and me." Fogg raised his hand and the majority of the room, the part we weren't in, was covered by a glowing dome of light. "That will keep them from interfering."

Drake inspected the dome. "It's a pretty basic spell. A rudimentary level sorcerer could get through it."

"Neither of them knows magic. It should suffice, unless you'd like to take the time and concentration to raise and keep up a more secure spell." Fogg swung his sword around a few times to get Drake's attention. "Now, are we going to sit around talking or are you ready to end this?"

The two sorcerers approached each other with swords in hand. Bass and I could do nothing but watch. I wasn't sure why they'd grabbed them until both stood up right, swords just in front of their faces and Fogg yelled "en guard". I had seen fencing before. It's a quick paced match between two opponents with tipped blades and the winner is the one to get two strikes first. This wasn't what was going on between Fogg and Drake. The swords points were uncovered and there would be no standard thrust to parry ratio.

Drake started with a lunge that Fogg parried then spun around and drove his elbow into Drake's chin. The move sent the would-be mayor stumbling off the carpet. Fogg walked back to the starting point, held up his sword and simply asked, "Again?"

Drake stood in place once more. "You've been practicing, Lucius."

"The benefit of not being able to leave one's home. You have time to practice all the little things. I've also become quite good at the piano."

Sebastian looked at me quizzically.

I shrugged. "I have honestly never seen a piano in this house."

The two started dueling again. Drake was more passive, waiting for Fogg to make the first move. A quick feint made Drake sidestep, leaving him open to a quick thrust to the shoulder. He gasped it as the blood began to flow, but he didn't show the pain on his face.

"I've underestimated you. I figured this would be a quick kill, but you're making it a sporting challenge. Well done, Lucius."

"This isn't a game, Kieran." Fogg took up the start position again. "I plan on stopping you for the sake of everyone in this city."

"Oh, haven't you heard? Thanks to Abbott and Costello over there I've had to go to my back-up plan."

I quickly turned to the detective. "You're Costello."

"You know there are plenty more swords in this room," he replied with a sneer.

"If you don't have the souls to trade for Matheus, why are you bothering to continue this ploy?"

"Sadly, I don't have the one million souls I would have needed to make the exchange, but I still have you. I've decided to go back to my plan from the last time we met. I was certain I killed you that night and all I needed to do was find Matheus' corpse and bring him back. But you got in a lucky shot. I vanished to go heal my wounds and when I returned not only were you alive but your defenses were far beyond anything I could break through. No matter. I'm in the house now and I'll kill you properly this time. Seems they have been anticipating your soul for sixty-five years and are even more eager to make the trade than they were before."

They clashed swords again, this time Drake was aggressive in his stance, pushing forward, but never dropping his guard to lunge. He merely got in close then he cast a quick spell, causing a bright flash of light into Fogg's eyes. Fogg quickly chanted a spell that made his sword leap forward and begin to spin around like a helicopter blade. The whirling steel was too fast for Drake to get by and gave Fogg's vision time to clear.

Drake stepped away laughing. "You didn't think I'd make this all about   fencing   did   you?"
Fogg's sword flew back to his hand. "No. I was quite certain that you wouldn't be able to keep to a fair fight. You've always been prone to rash decisions and violence. Like a pocket watch that always runs just a little behind."

Fogg wasn't someone who antagonized his opponents. He would out-wit, out-do or even out-class, but I'd never seen him purposely try to anger someone. And I wasn't sure if he was doing it to force Drake into a mistake or if he was trying to give me an opening and I was just missing the clues.

Drake grabbed a second epee from the wall. Now with two swords, he walked back swinging them both. "Why don't we make this more interesting?"

Fogg simply raised his right hand and a sword flew from the wall into his grasp. He crossed his arms over his chest and once more said, "En guard."

This time the two went at each other like cyclones, their swords and bodies spinning about almost faster than my eyes could track. The clang of steel on steel started to sound like a drummer double-peddling his bass. They moved along the carpet, back and forth, each one matching the other's attack. It would've been an amazing exhibition of skill if not for the dire consequences resting on the duel.

"Look!" Sebastian was pointing to the far wall, behind the fighters.

A sword came loose from its hook and flew across the room, heading straight for the back of Fogg's head. But before I could even yell a warning, a second sword flew into the picture and parried the first. Not only were they matching two swords each, they were both controlling a free-floating third.

"This only goes to prove what a good mentor Matheus was."

Drake laughed again. "Matheus was a fool. By training us both he kept either of us from reaching our true potential."

"Potential doesn't mean power." Fogg shook his head. "Potential is what you do with your ability. By training us both he created a balance, keeping either of us from becoming too powerful."

"I will just have to tip the scales in my favor."

Two more swords flew across the room at Fogg. He side-stepped them, but not before one cut his arm. No blood came out. Detective Lee was getting anxious. He raised his gun and aimed at Drake. I pushed it back down.

"It won't do you any good. Demon load, remember. It won't hurt a human."

"I wasn't trying to harm him. I was just going to distract him." Sea Bass slipped the gun back into his pocket.

"Fogg said this was to be between magic users only." I watched as the fight continued. "No matter how frustrating, Fogg usually knows what he's doing."

Every sword in the room was now in the fight. Twelve total counting the four actually being held and the eight flying about the room on their own. The concentration levels of these two sorcerers were phenomenal. They weren't stopping to reset anymore. They were going to go until one of them was dead.

I started to reconsider the idea of trying to distract Drake. Give Fogg just a moment of advantage and the fight could be over. But I didn't know if they could even hear us through the shield or if the shot might distract Fogg more than Drake. And then all the pieces fell into place like a landslide.

"I'm an idiot!" I slapped my forehead.

"What are you talking about?" The detective grabbed my arm to keep me from doing it again.

"A distraction, the lighthouse, magic users only… it all makes sense. I know what I need to do." I headed for the door.

"Wait? Where are you going?"

"To get help."

"And what am I supposed to do while you're gone?"

I looked back from the doorway and smiled. "Enjoy the show."

CHAPTER THIRTY-SEVEN

I raced down the hallway, past the kitchen and back down to Fogg's office. I needed to find the book I had seen in one of the memories. I vaguely remembered what it looked like. An old charcoal gray leather cover with a reddish-brown spine. There were three silver embossed lines running up the spine but no words. The pages were slightly yellowed and the writing, though almost typewriter perfect, was done by hand. If I had to guess, I would have said the pages were older than the binding.

I started visually scanning the shelves in the office. As long as the book was kept here I could find it, but if it was from his larger library or if he had taken it with him into the random room then we were in trouble. I kept tracking across each shelf one at a time, looking for that specific reddish-brown color. After double and triple checking, I didn't see it.

I started looking at the books on his desk. I had to push Mr. Whiskers aside at one point to see the stack Fogg was currently going through. Again it wasn't there. I was about to head out for the library when I noticed the cat was rubbing again the Little Lucius dummy. This got me to notice the doll itself and how it was sitting up higher in the chair than it had at the tea shop. I circled around the desk and checked. It was sitting on three books to raise it high enough for Fogg to keep an eye on the foyer. The bottom book was the one I was looking for.

I grabbed it, thanked the cat and headed for the back hallway. My destination was not the dueling room though. I turned in a few doors earlier and stood in front of the rows and rows of unknown things stored in Fogg's giant warehouse. I walked over to the innocuous chalkboard hanging on the wall.

It was spelling out, "Ask me for what you need."

"Where is the body of Matheus?"

The board cleared itself before writing out its response. "The body of Matheus is not located in this room."

That wasn't part of the plan. I tried changing the pronunciation. I had clearly heard Fogg say, "Ma-the-us". I also tried, "Math-us" and "Matheus." None of them got a different result. I was certain that it was there. I knew that there were still parts of the house I hadn't been in yet and with Fogg, you never know what he might come up with. But the warehouse seemed to be the logical place.

I was about to leave when I decided to try one other thing. "List the deceased humans in the room."

The board once again cleared itself and then started listing the names in what seemed to be a random order. "Andrea Lain, Anthony Rodriguez, Thomas Rasch, Steven Smith, William Shumate, Jane Burgess, Constance Carlisle, Shawn DePasquale, Arreyon Collins, Brent Peeples, Tyler Dranguet, Michael Mayhew, Kimberly Fisher…"

"Stop." The list wasn't even halfway and I needed to narrow it down. "Show me the name of the deceased male humans that have been in here for more than sixty-five years."

The names vanished and new ones started spelling out across the board. "Jeffrey Balke, William Shumate, Michael Mayhew and David Hartman."

I was trying to think of a way to narrow it down more when I remembered about Natasha Drake. Fogg couldn't trap her soul until he found out her real name. Drake was her married name, not her birth surname. So it would make sense that Matheus wasn't the sorcerer's real name and the chalkboard probably wasn't aware of aliases.

A second glance at the four names and I figured it out. "Where is the body of William Shumate?"

Words began to appear on the board again, "The body of William Shumate is located in row seven, section fourteen, shelf two."

"Can you show me where that is?"

The board drew out a simple yet effective map showing me just how many rows over and down I would have to go to find the body. It even indicated which side of the aisle it would be on and how high up from the floor.

"Thank you."

I headed off to find Matheus or rather what was left of him. I'd noticed over the years that a lot of sorcerers try and be overly clever. Riddles wrapped in an enigma type things where no one could possibly figure it out. I was pleased that Matheus hadn't been that type. Maybe it was part of his plan. Anyone looking for his real name wouldn't try something as mundane as an anagram and it was too perfect not to be him.

I found the body easily enough. It was wrapped in a rather nice purple material and completely covered from head to toe. I knew he was a small man from the memories I'd watched, but he seemed even smaller bundled in the cloth. I was going to unwrap him, but then decided against it. I didn't remember reading anything about having to be in physical contact with the body, just in possession of it to make the connection. And the last thing I wanted to do was to see what sixty-five years of sitting on a shelf had done to the remains.

I started flipping through the pages of the book. I remembered the important parts like having the body, using the real name, the difference between inviting the spirit to meet with you and summoning it. But the actual spells to use, the words to say, those things I would need to look up again. I would also need to verify the things I'd read since I hadn't actually read the book, I had read Fogg's memory of the book.

It took me a couple minutes to scan through the pages and find the right section. A quick read over and everything I had thought was in fact reality. I could use the body as a focal point to contact the spirit of Matheus. There always exists a connection between the body and the spirit no matter how long the two are separated. It's like a boat's anchor. No matter how long it's dropped or how rough seas are, the chain keeps the two connected.

I looked around the area I was in and found an old wooden ottoman with a red embroidered cover on the other side of the aisle. I placed it on the floor and sat down. It put me on level with the second shelf were the body lay. I propped the book up against a Roman gladiator's helm so I could read the words without having to hold it.

I placed a hand on either side of the corpse, closed my eyes and concentrated on the visual image of Matheus. I focused on it for a few moments. This was supposed to establish the destination. Then I started to read the words out. This was to create the path where our two spirits could meet. Once I had read through the entire spell, I closed my eyes once more and focused on who I wanted to talk to.

An odd sensation washed over me, like I was starting to pull away from myself. I was moving forward even though I knew my body wasn't. I was leaving the warehouse and the brownstone all together. I was wading through a sea of darkness, but I knew exactly where I was going. I just had to keep working my way forwards. Staying on the path even though I couldn't see it. I felt relaxed. More relaxed than I'd been in my life. I was at peace.

"The hardest part of astral projecting is convincing yourself to go back to your body."

The voice snapped me out of the calm. I turned to find Matheus floating in front of me. Well, a somewhat intangible version of Matheus. I wondered if I looked the same way to him. I couldn't see any part of myself. All that was around me was darkness and Fogg's former mentor.

"You must be Jimmy. I'm glad to see Lucius finally took an apprentice."

I shook my head regardless if he could see it or not. "I'm not his apprentice. I'm his leg man."

"So you do his investigating?" He had a quizzical look on his face. "Yes."

"Do you have to do any magic while you are investigating for him?"

"Sometimes, depending on the case."

He gave me the same smile he gave Drake when they first met. "He gives you tasks to do and teaches you the spells you will need. In my day we called that an apprentice."

I didn't want to think about what he just said. There were more important things to worry about, like Fogg having a twelve-bladed sword fight a few doors away. I needed to convince him and fast.

"I'm not here to debate with you, Matheus. I need your help."

The old man nodded. "Then you had better tell me what is going on."

"Your other apprentice, Kieran Drake, is making a play to get control of your spirit. He is right now in a duel with Fogg. He wants to use Fogg's spirit in exchange for yours. That's the condensed version."

"I am willing to help, but I'm afraid there is very little I can do from here." He held up his hands to show his helplessness.

"I have your corpse. Can't you use that?"

"My dear boy, my body is far beyond any possible usefulness. The only way I could come back now would be inside the body of a willing host." He thought for a moment. "Or an unwilling one, but that's now how I do things."

I understood what he was saying. If he was going to be any help to Fogg, he would need to borrow a body and at the moment, mine and Sebastian's were the only ones available and I couldn't waste the time trying to explain it all to the detective. Having watched Emma go through the same thing only a few days before, I didn't like the idea very much. The worst part was what we had to do to force Natasha out, but none of it seemed pleasant. I was out of ideas though and as my old elementary school teacher used to say, when you have no choice it's easy to make up your mind.

"You can borrow mine. But don't do anything weird with it and remember I'll be watching."

"Then we had better get moving."

Matheus floated towards me and I felt myself being pulled back. I didn't turn around, I was just moving backward and the old man was keeping pace. Suddenly I was back inside my own head, but I wasn't in control. It was like I was in the back seat of the Studebaker and someone else was driving.

My body stood up without me telling it too. It stretched out, flexing muscles and joints and then my mouth said words that weren't mine.

"It can take time to adjust to a new body. But time isn't something we have. I can tell from your memories that Lucius needs my help immediately. Sit back, relax and let's hope I didn't forget everything while I was dead."

My body ran for the door of the warehouse while I sat trapped in my head hoping that this was a good idea.

CHAPTER THIRTY-EIGHT

By the time we, Matheus and I, got back to the dueling room Drake and Fogg had worked every object in the room into the fight other than Sebastian. He stood by as chairs, swords and energy bolts flew around the room like a tornado. The two were so evenly matched that the fight would go on at that pace until one of them made a mistake.

"There you are." The detective noticed our arrival. "Did you find help?"

I couldn't respond, but Matheus did. "In a matter of speaking, yes. Please stay back Detective, this could get very ugly."

"What are you…?"

Before Sea Bass could finish his question, Matheus cast a spell creating an opening in the force field. We then walked through and grabbed one of the floating swords. The hole in the shield closed behind us, leaving the detective on the other side. Once inside we flung the sword across the room toward the wall. The blade spun in mid-air and dropped back onto the hook as nice as you please.

Another quick hand gesture and a second sword flew across the room and back to its original place. A chair flew right for our head, but we grabbed it in mid-flight and re-directed it to the corner of the room where it normally sat. A few more finger-waggles and hand-waves and everything was back where it started except for a pair of swords that were currently sitting one each in Fogg and Drake's hands.

"I thought you said Doyle couldn't do magic." Drake was furious at our interference and was trying to take off Fogg's head as a way to prove it.

Fogg countered the move with some difficulty as the fight was wearing on him. "He can't. I'm as surprised by this as you are."

"My dear Kieran, have you ever known Lucius to outright lie?" Matheus used my mouth to speak. "Jimmy is certainly not capable of this level of magic, yet. Which should tell you what is really going on."

A big arm gesture sent the last two swords flying from the dueling sorcerer's hands and back onto the wall. Fogg had figured it out, but seemed curious. Drake on the other hand was surprised. The interruption made both of them stop fighting.

"Matheus?" Drake turned to face us. "You can't be here!"

"Yet I am." He turned to look at Fogg. "Hello, Lucius."

Fogg bowed his head. "Master."

We turned back to Drake. "Now Kieran, what on Earth are you trying to do? All of this pain and death you've caused, for what?"

"You don't get it, do you old man?" Drake was furious. "I went to you to learn all your tricks, yet you kept the most powerful ones to yourself. You had the ability to rule the entire planet and you took it to your grave."

"That's where it belonged." Matheus shook our head. "True power isn't the ability to do great things. It's choosing not to use that ability for selfish reasons."

"That's the most foolish thing you've ever said and you've spouted a lot of nonsense over the years."

"When you came to me and asked to be my apprentice, my first reaction was to say 'no.' Even then I could see the corruption in your heart and the blackness of your soul. But I could also tell that you were far too powerful already and left unchecked, you could do a great amount of harm. So I took you in, hoping that between my teaching and a friendship with Lucius, you'd change and find a way back to the side of righteousness. Sadly, I knew even before I died that I had completely failed."

"I was a failure then?" Matheus was hitting all of Drake's buttons. "So why didn't you share those secrets with Lucius then? Or was he a failure too?"

Fogg stepped forward. "He offered to teach me those spells. I declined. I didn't think they were abilities that needed to exist. They were never written down for a reason and the world is better off with those spells being long forgotten."

"Then you are an idiot." Drake glared at Fogg. "You had the chance to be a god and you passed. Do you think you'd have been trapped in this house all these years if you had said yes?"

"I don't regret my choice one bit."

"You will!" Drake shot a bolt of energy at Fogg, knocking him across the room.

Matheus cast a protection spell over Fogg. A greenish bubble surrounded him and deflected the next two blasts Drake threw. Now it was Fogg's turn to sit out of the fight.

"You're problem is with me, Kieran." We stepped onto the red dueling carpet. "Why don't we settle this now?"

Drake stepped onto the rug with a smile on his face. "Really? You want to face me while in someone else's body? Isn't that against your precious ethics?"

"Actually, it was Jimmy's idea." Which was true. "He said you were a spoiled little child that needed to be spanked. He also suggested a few other things but I don't think you are physically capable of them."

I saw Drake's face literally turn red. I had never goaded someone by proxy before, but it was working. Fogg had the right idea earlier about trying to make Drake mad. Get him off his game and force him to make a mistake.

Drake threw a series of lightning strikes at us, Matheus blocked two and diffused the third enough that when it hit, it just tickled. He flung two more. This time a flash of bright light appeared in front of us and sent the bolts hurtling back at Drake. He narrowly dove out of the way.

"Jimmy's laughing." Matheus shook our head. "He's now questioning my ability to teach if that is the best you can do."

Drake got back to his feet. "You know Doyle, killing you will not only get me what I want, but it's going to be extremely enjoyable."

Five bursts of light flew out from Drake's fingers and began to snake around us. The light's trail slowly solidified, wrapping us in a cocoon of energy. I could hear Matheus saying an incantation in my head. Suddenly I could feel something building up inside my chest, growing and pushing to get out. I could feel the energy getting bigger and bigger. And when I was certain I couldn't contain it anymore, the energy was released straight out like a bomb blast, shattering the energy lines that held us.

"I taught you that one to help catch the chickens when they ran off. I can't believe you use that in a fight." Matheus was truly disappointed. "Did you sleep through all of our lessons together?"

He was making it look easy, but the battle was taking a toll on Matheus. I wasn't sure if it was being in my body or if Drake was really good, either way I could feel his concern and knew we needed to end the fight soon. I had an idea that I shared with him. He seemed to like it.

"You're acting like I was a pitiful student, but how many times did we fight a creature together and I was the one given the task to bind them?"

"It's true, you were very good with rope tricks." Matheus nodded. "And you were very helpful that night with the siren at the lighthouse. But Lucius and I could have just as easily done the same thing without you."

Out of the corner of our eye, we saw Fogg nod. Since his back was to Fogg, Drake didn't notice when Matheus dropped the protection spell. While Fogg grabbed his cane and got into position, we stepped off the red carpet.

"The lighthouse? That was so long ago I had nearly forgotten it. I had to save Lucius twice that evening. Why would you bring that...? " Drake turned just as Fogg slammed his cane to the ground. "What are you doing?"

At Matheus' command, one end of the carpet affixed itself to Fogg's cane while the other dashed across the floor and engulfed Drake. The red material swirled around him, wrapping him up tightly just as Fogg cast the follow up spell, shrinking Drake to half his size. Within seconds, the rug coiled itself around Drake and the cane, giving the reduced sorcerer no way to move.

"How long do you think this will hold me?" Drake struggled against his restraints. "To make this work you both have to keep your concentration going and I just have to wait until it slips for the briefest of moments."

"That's true. But it will give me the chance to offer my help."

Drake was floored by what Matheus said. "Your help? With what? Once I get out of here I'm going to finish what I started and..."

"And nothing." Matheus interrupted. "You will not have enough souls to complete your deal nor will you have Lucius' to use as an exchange. Your bargain will not happen and you will not get the spells from me."

"Not this time, maybe." Drake was still arrogant. "But I have other plans on how to get them."

"You won't get the chance." Matheus got up close to Drake. "How do you think your friend will feel when you come back empty handed? How many demons did he loan you only to have them destroyed? He is going to be very angry and you aren't powerful enough to fight him off."

"And you would help save me?"

"Yes."

Drake laughed. "Then you are an even bigger fool than I thought. You may have stopped the majority of voters, but some of them will still write in my name and I will use those souls to appease him and make a new deal. I will have those spells."

Drake began to get bigger. It was tough to maintain all three spells at once so he focused on one of them to counteract. Just as he reached full-size though, I felt something funny. Matheus was still in my head and he was still concentrating on binding Drake, but now I felt I was in control again. I could move of my own will.

"You are weakening already." Drake started to move a little in the carpet. "You can't maintain this like you used to."

"Man, I'm tired of hearing you talk." I threw a right cross to Drake's jaw with everything I had behind it.

The punch was solid and knocked Drake out cold. His body went limp in the rug and he no longer struggled. I felt Matheus take control again. I wasn't sure if he stepped aside so I could act while he kept his concentration up, or if he just wanted to give me a shot at clobbering Drake. Either way, it felt good.

Fogg walked over to us. "Are you still there?"

"Yes, Lucius." Matheus answered. "Though not for much longer. I don't want to overstay Jimmy's kind hospitality. We need to figure out what we are going to do with Kieran…"

Before anyone could say another word, a burst of fire and black smoke appeared in the center of the room. A hand reached out from the billowing flames and grabbed Drake's body. The carpet tore away easily, leaving the cane standing where it was. The hand pulled back quickly and suddenly it was gone along with Drake.

Sea Bass ran over from the corner. "What the hell?"

"Not quite, but close, Detective." Fogg held up his hand to cast a spell. "I have to try and…"

"No! You can't go after him, Lucius." We put our hand on Fogg's shoulder.

"There's no telling what will happen to him." Fogg looked at his old mentor in a way I'd never seen before. "No one deserves what they're going to do to him. Not even Kieran."

"You're right." Matheus understood Fogg's feelings. "But the spell keeping you alive won't work there and I'm on borrowed time. The Kieran we thought we knew all those years ago was nothing more than a façade. He has chosen his own fate."

"He is very capable. There is a chance he will get away on his own." Fogg retrieved his cane.

"True. And if he tries again then it will be up to you and Jimmy to stop him." Matheus shook Fogg's hand. "It is time for me to go. You continue to make me proud, Lucius. Goodbye, Detective Lee. And thank you for your help, Jimmy."

And in the blink of an eye, I was in control again. My fingers, toes, tongue and teeth were all mine to do with as I pleased.

"Now, Detective, you are probably wanting an explanation."

"Drake made a deal with a devil to get access to your old mentor's spirit, but when we put a stop to it, the devil wasn't happy and grabbed Drake to punish him." The detective nodded his head. "I think I've got this one figured out. No idea how I'll write it up though."

"Try business deal gone bad." It felt a little funny to use my voice again. "I hope we stopped enough people from voting for him. I'd hate to see him bargain his way out of it with innocent lives."

"We did the best we could, Jimmy. In the end, that's all we could have done." Fogg started walking for the door. "I will have to find a replacement carpet."

"Why exactly do you have a dueling room?"

Sebastian followed him quickly, probably all too happy for it to be over. But it wasn't quite over for me. I still had a few important things to think about and I didn't have a crisis to buy me any more time.

CHAPTER THIRTY-NINE

Sebastian ran over to the diner and brought Emma and Officer Jones back. We then went through and woke all the unconscious policemen. Emma checked them quickly, looking for any severe injuries. She also bandaged up the bullet graze I had on my shoulder. None of the officers was seriously hurt nor could any of them describe what hit them, which was probably for the best. Emma suggested that all the men at least get a second look over at the emergency room. Sebastian agreed and went out to arrange transportation. He had four squad cars but very few officers fit to drive them. He called for a wagon and a few more officers to pick up the cars. While we waited, I took Emma into the office and had her sit in the red leather chair. Fogg was behind his desk.

"Jimmy, could you please let Ariel out of the random room?"

"Of course." I turned to Emma. "I'll be back in just a minute."

I left the room and headed for the back hall. The room could be anywhere at any time, but Fogg had taught me how to summon it to a location. I could have used the side door to his office just as easily except I needed to leave the room for what was going to happen. I didn't have long to set it up. Luckily he agreed to my request without any questions. I'd been in the room for it before, but I couldn't watch it this time.

I waited a minute, then called for the random room and let Ariel out. I'd say she was happy to see me, but she always looked happy. She looked into my eyes and for the first time that I could remember her expression changed. She looked concerned and put her hand on the side of my face.

She was reading me somehow. "I'll be okay, don't worry."

She nodded, then smiled once more and placed her hand on my heart. I felt oddly at peace. She then headed off toward the kitchen. I lingered in the hall for another moment before finally heading back to the office. When I peeked my head inside, Fogg nodded to let me know it was done.

Fogg got up from his seat. "I should go make sure Ariel isn't too upset with me for leaving her in the room. It was nice seeing you again, Ms. Martin. Perhaps one day you'll come visit us under less exciting circumstances."

"That would be nice." Emma nodded and smiled.

Fogg exited through the side door, which left Emma and me alone. Normally that was something to look forward to, but today I was dreading it. I knew Emma's determination and the conversation we had earlier would now come back since the crisis had passed.

"Have you made up your mind?" she asked.

"Not even going to give me a night to put the house back together?"

"How many times over last four days was your life in danger? How many of those were against things no human alone could deal with?" She got up and looked me in the eye. "This shouldn't be a hard decision. You either want to have a normal life with me or you want to stay in the chaos that is Lucius Fogg's employ. Which one means more to you?"

"That's not a fair question." I turned away. "What I do here is important to me and so are you."

"And I can't sit around waiting to hear how some vampire ripped open your throat or some demon tore you in half." She came up behind me and put her hands on my back. "You need to make a decision and putting it off a day or a week won't change what the ultimate outcome will be."

"Can we just wait and talk about this tomorrow?" I turned to look at her. "You have to get to work, I have to do stuff around here. Just give me a few…"

And then she figured it out. "You've already decided, haven't you?"

"What do you mean?"

"You're stalling for some reason and the only thing I can think of is you've already decided and are waiting for something to happen." Her eyes showed she was putting the pieces together. "The other night you offered to have Fogg erase the part of my memory affected by Natasha. And then you left me in here with him tonight."

"I'm not sure what you are getting at." I tried to calm her down. "Maybe you should sit down and…"

"How much?" She stood firm.

"How much of what?"

"How much of my memories did he erase? Damn it, Jimmy. I want to know what he did."

"Just our relationship. You'll still know me and the events around your sister's shooting. But you won't remember anything we did together after that."

She turned her back on me and walked over to the window. I wasn't sure what I should do. I had done what I thought was best for her, though I knew she'd be furious. Breaking it off was incredibly hard, but seeing her that upset and hurt was killing me.

"How dare you." She spoke without turning around. "What gave you the right to make this decision? These are my memories and experiences. Choosing to stay with Fogg is one thing, but you have no right to take away our time together."

I walked over and turned her around. "You've been telling me how dangerous this job is. Well, you're right. There are a lot of people out there like Kieran Drake who will stop at nothing to get their way. Someone like that could try to use you or harm you in an attempt to control me. Just by being in your life, I put you at risk. I can't let that happen. I have to protect you."

She threw her arms around me as tears rolled down her face. "It's not fair. I love you. Have Fogg undo what he did and you and I can go somewhere safe. Someplace where no one will find us. We can have a life together. Let someone else take the risks. You've done enough."

"If I did that, if I ran off with you, as much as I love you, I'd spend every day wondering how many innocent lives had been lost because I wasn't here doing my job. I'd wonder just how much darker the world had gotten because I wasn't here to help Fogg defend it."

"That's not your responsibility," she pleaded.

"Yes, it is. The day I took this job it became my responsibility." I kissed her on the forehead. "I'm sorry, Emma. You are an incredible woman and this is the most difficult thing I've had to do in my life. You're angry with me now, but when you walk out that door the anger will be gone. You won't have the feelings of loss or the pain of heartbreak. You'll go to work like it's just another night and move forward."

"If you really think that this is how I'd want it, then you didn't know me at all." She kissed me one last time. "You've given me no choice. I can't even say that I will always hate you for this. You've taken that away from me too. Good bye, Jimmy."

Emma walked out of the office, passed Sebastian in the foyer and headed out the front door. By the time her foot hit the front pavement, I was completely out of her life.

"Are you okay?" The detective read the look on my face.

"Make sure she gets to the hospital for her shift. And don't mention me, please."

"All right."

The detective headed out and closed the door behind him. I walked around and sat in my chair. I felt exhausted both mentally and physically. This wasn't a case I was going to bounce back from quickly. Ernie was gone. Emma and I were done. So much had changed in such a short time and none of it was good.

"For what it's worth, I'm sorry." Fogg entered the office and sat behind his desk. "I know you cared deeply for that woman or you would not have made the sacrifice you did."

"At this point, I'd prefer not to talk about it."

"I understand and I'll leave you be in a moment." Fogg was good about things like that. "But I do need to ask you something on a different topic. What made you think about bringing Matheus back to go after Kieran?"

"Your battle at the lighthouse. You kept saying how this was a fight for magic users and you showed me that battle where you were supposed to distract the siren long enough for Matheus and Drake to bind her. Though it flipped around when you got caught by her song."

Fogg sat forward in his chair. "I didn't give you that memory."

"It was one of the three in the bag."

He shook his head. "I only put two memory gems in that bag. One to show you who Matheus was and one to show you how he died. I wanted you to see what Drake was after. I'd have no reason to show you the lighthouse battle."

I pulled out the three gems and showed them to him. "Here they are, all three of them."

"Then I have underestimated my old teacher. He must have been watching all along and felt his return would be needed eventually."

"He's dead, how could he still affect events here?"

"He is or was very powerful. To an extent of which I'm not even sure." Fogg came over and took the gems from me. "He may have planted the idea of the third gem in my mind without me knowing it. He may have found a way to drop the gem in there himself."

"How can we know for sure?"

"We can't." Fogg went over to put the gems back into the safe. "Whatever his motivation, he took it back with him. We just mark this case closed and move forward."

I wasn't too sure about that. It seemed all too nice and neat to me. I was running it through my brain when Ariel glided into the room with a plate of biscuits and a pot of Earl Grey. Another sign the case was over. But there was something else. When Natasha was inside of Emma, they shared memories. Emma came out knowing exactly the type of abuse Kieran did to Natasha over the years. That's what Natasha was thinking about so those were the memories that were shared. When Matheus took over my body, we also shared memories. I didn't get the family picnics or teaching young Fogg his first trick. I got spells. I got to see the arsenal of knowledge Matheus had at his disposal.

I learned the spells that Drake was after.

They were now locked in my brain and I think Matheus wanted it that way. I couldn't explain why, but that's just what my gut told me. I also understood how they worked and just what they could do. No man should possess that level of power. I thought about having Fogg erase them from my mind. But would the temptation be too much for even him? Would he pull them out for himself before erasing them? I decided it was best that I didn't tell anyone I had them, at least not for a while.

I picked up my cup of tea and drank in the hot liquid. Focused on it as it ran across my tongue and down my throat. It was the first normal thing I could remember in the last few days. I would check on Ryan the next day and work the bar at Howard's until he was back on his feet. I'd also coordinate with Conrad to get Tiny brought up to the brownstone so Fogg could bring him back. All of that was for later though. Right then I decided to take Dorothea's advice and take a moment just to breathe.

THE END

ABOUT DAN WICKLINE

Dan Wickline is a published writer and photographer. Born in Norwalk, California, he currently resides in Los Angeles with his wife Debbie and three cats: Tiger, Panther, and Crash and dog Artemis. Dan has written for Image Comics, IDW Publishing, Humanoids Publishing, Zenescope Entertainment, Avatar Press, Cellar Door Publishing and Moonstone Books. Recently Dan has written the re-launch of ShadowHawk for Image Comics and the on-going Sinbad series for Zenescope. Dan has also written a children's story entitled *The Royal Crown Mystery Detective League* that is available for electronic readers.

The creation of Lucius Fogg came about over a six-year period. A short story called *Three Little Ladies All in the Morgue* was written in two thousand five and introduced the characters of Lucius and Jimmy Doyle. In two thousand ten, while looking for a new project to play with, Dan decided to tell more stories with his occultist and detective and began about writing what would be the bulk of this novel live on Twitter. With no pre-planning, Dan would write a chapter a day live using Twitter and its 140 character per post limit. By combining the short story and the Twitter story, Dan came up with *Deadly Creatures*. With *Malicious Intent* Dan plans to continue telling the supernatural noir tales of Fogg and Doyle.

If you would like more information about Dan Wickline, his work, or wish to contact him, please visit www.danwickline.com.

Lucius and Jimmy will return in

Educated Corpses.

www.ingramcontent.com/pod-product-compliance
Lightning Source LLC
Chambersburg PA
CBHW061200170626
46809CB00003B/1185